AK-239

AK-239

The Enemy is Already Here

ROGER R. ELLIS

ISBN-13: **9780692793695**
ISBN-10: **0692793690**

This is a work of fiction.

Names, characters, places, and incidents either are the product of the author's imagination or are used fictitiously, and any resemblance to actual persons, living or dead, businesses, companies, events, or locales is entirely coincidental.

Further, nothing contained herein is intended or should be interpreted as expressing or representing the views of any person and/or persons, or any branch, department, unit, of the U.S. Armed Forces, U.S. Forest Service, U.S. Geological Survey, or any defense contractor, any private hotel or any private business.

So there!

(So there's a legal term. So there!)

WARNING: Due to some graphic language, parental discretion is advised.

AK 239
Version 1.1

Other Books by Author

Book Two:
JOHN DENNING
PROYEKT 252:
CALIFORNIUM

Christmas 2017

Thank You

F irst, to my Russian friends, all who wish to remain anonymous:
Please accept my most sincere and deepest apologies for my poor transla-
tions, incorrect numberings and spelling.

I'm sorry but you guys have a really, really weird language, alphabet and
numbering system!

But thank you for your truly valuable insights into your fascinating and
rich culture.

Without your help this book would not have been possible.

With over one million of your websites blocked, you are much more brave
than me.

Thank you!

And saying thank you to some very special people by name seems also to be
quite trite, without whose assistance this book would not have been possible.

Many people were legally not able to be named individually or were too
humble, you know who you are and thank you.

Except for my family, they are not in any particular order and I certainly
don't mean to slight anyone not higher on the list.

All of you are at the top of my list and I can't thank you enough:

My editor in chief (and wife): Mary
My children: Robert, Rebecca & Bethany

John Dunham 1957-2016

Ruth Ann Dyke Zirkle
Jeanne Petrie Lampi

Thank you, David
(You know who you are!)

Captain Jason Salata
Naval Special Warfare Command
Coronado, California

Chief Jeremy Kastner
United States Coast Guard

Robert Richter, M.D.
Don Burgess, Ph.D.
Pepper O' Shaughnessy

Captain Ken Curry
Former USAF, B-52 Aircraft Commander

Michelle Masden
Pilot/Owner Island Wings Air Service
Ketchikan, Alaska

Special thanks to: Norman Polmar

United States Navy
United States Special Operations Command
United States Naval Institute

Federal Bureau of Investigation (FBI)
United States Forest Service
United States Geological Survey

All the good people at:
Inn at Creek Street and the New York Hotel
Ketchikan, Alaska

Richard Bass 1929-2015

In Memorium

John Dunham 1957-2016
My best friend

Table of Contents

PRINCIPALS – CAST

Principal Characters in Bold
In Order of Appearance

Captain Valentin Vasili
Commanding officer, *Severstal*, *TK-20*

Admiral Victor Perchinkov
Minister of Defence, Russia

Ivan Mironovich
President of Russia

Kapitan-Leytenant Casmerov
Kapitan-Leytenant - 3rd Rank, *TK-20*

Kapitan Nikolai Alexi
Kapitan, 2nd Rank, *TK-20*

Olga Kasparov
Anchor, Russian *TV-12*

John Denning ("JD")
FBI, Special Agent, Former BMCS
SEAL Team Six

Mohammed Al-Aqsa (MAA)
Engineering student
Portland State University

Tom Watson (CPO)
Chief Petty Officer
USS *Alaska*

Jennifer Tavana (FBI)
Former Lieutenant Commander
USS *Alaska*

Tad Murphy
Seaman, Sonar Technician, ST
USS *Alaska* (And an idiot)

Fred Turner
National Security Agency
Satellite Analyst

Jerry Fredricks
National Security Agency
Data Systems Specialist

Jack Tanner
Captain of *The Black Pearl*
Fisherman

Mike Gardener
First Mate, *The Black Pearl*

Tom Watkins
FBI, Special Agent

Yusef Abdullah
Portland Restaurant Owner
Friend of JD's

Sally Abdullah
Wife of Yusef Abdullah

General Petrov Andropov
Russian General, Siloviki Clan

General Sergei Aleksandrov
Russian General, Siloviki Clan

General Aleksandr Bortnikov
Russian General, Siloviki Clan

Viktor Sokolov
Assistant to President Mironovich

Nikolai Alexi
TK-20 Kapitan, 2nd Rank

Dmitri Rostislav–
TK -20, Sonar Officer

George Ruddy, Ph.D.
Former Mathematics Professor,
Harvard University

Robert S. Stone
Police Chief, Ketchikan, Alaska

Yura Stone
Wife of Police Chief
Emergency 911 Supervisor

Tony Stone
Police Officer
Son of Robert Stone

Vladimir Peskov
Sr. Scientist, RUS
Russia Uranium Specialty Company

Bert ('P' man) Parks
Lieutenant Commander, *USS Alaska*

Al Reynolds
Mining Claim Holder
Bokan Mountain, AK

Tatiana Ivanov
Medical Doktor (MD)
Moscow, Russia

General Victor Zelin
General, Russian Ministry of Defense

Katrina (The Wolf) Volkov
Girlfriend of George Ruddy

James McMillan
Officer of the Deck,
USS Ronald Reagan, Aircraft Carrier

Captain George Murray
Captain of the *USS Ronald Reagan*

Commander Orlov
Russian GRU Special Forces

Brigadier General Bahadur,
Iranian Defense Forces

Jimmy Thomas
Pilot, Ketchikan, Alaska

Boris Babkin
Russian Fortress Designer
Bokan Mountain

General Norton
General, USAF Aerospace
Defense Command Center
Peterson AFB, Colorado

John A. (Skull) Smith
FBI Hostage Rescue Team
(HRT) Gold Team Leader

Kenneth Baker
Rear Admiral, United States Navy

Stacy Macavoy
Anchor, ABC 7, Anchorage
Alaska News Today

Wayne Christian
Reporter, ABC 7, Anchorage
Alaska News Today

Andrew Gibbs
Lieutenant Colonel, U.S. Army

John Anderson
Senior American Diplomat

Andrei Alexeev
Senior Russian Diplomat

ACRONYMS

In Alphabetical Order

AOAIA
Advanced Oceanography
Acoustic Intelligence Analysis

APKWS
Advanced Precision Kill
Weapon System

ASW
Anti-Submarine Warfare

ASWOC
Anti-Submarine Warfare
Operations Center

COMINT
Communications Intelligence
U.S. Department of Defense

CPO
Chief Petty Officer
U.S. Navy

CIA
Central Intelligence Agency
United States of America

CSS
Central Security Service
Answers to DNI

DARPA
Defense Advanced Research
Projects Agency

DNI
Director of National Intelligence
Answers to POTUS

DOJ
Department of Justice
Unites States

DRFM
Digital Radio Frequency Memory
Confuses Radar

ELT
Emergency Locating Transmitter

EMP
Electro-Magnetic Pulse

EXACTO
Extreme Accuracy Tasked Ordnance

FBC
Full Background Check

GRU
Russian Main Intelligence Directorate
Foreign Military Intelligence

GSW
Gun Shot Wound

HALO
High Altitude Low Opening

ICBM
Intercontinental Ballistic Missile

JOOD
Junior Officer of the Deck

JOOW
Junior Officer of the Watch

MBD
Men's Bathroom Door

MWC
Missile Warning Center, USAF, Colorado

MOSS
Mobile Submarine Simulator

NBC
Nuclear, Biological, Chemical

NSA
National Security Agency
U.S. Department of Defense

ONI
Office of Naval Intelligence

OOD
Officer of the Deck

POTUS
President of the United States

PTSD
Post-Traumatic Stress Disorder

RCT
Reactor Controls Technician
Maintains Nuclear Reactor Systems

Richag-AV
Russian DRFM System

SAP
Security Access Program

SEC DEF
U.S. Secretary of Defense

SERE
Survival, Evasion, Resistance, and Escape

SIGINT
Signals Intelligence
Answers to DNI

SOCOM
U.S. Special Operations Command

SoSuS
Sound Surveillance System

SSBN
Ship, Submarine, Ballistic, Nuclear

SWAT TEAM
Special Weapons and Tactics

TFS
The Fat Squad

TIM
The Invisible Men

UCMJ
Uniform Code of Military Justice

WEP
Weight Efficiency Program

TK-20 PHOTO

Nuclear Submarine
Typhoon (941 Akula)

Akula in Russian means: Shark
Photo Max V. Nimos

My Private Diary

The following events
will sound like they're
coming straight out of some novel.
I can assure you, they are not.
These events actually took place
and brought us
to the edge of World War III.
How do I know?
I was there. My name?
John Denning (JD).
I'm not some nut writing a book to
make money.
I'm writing this to warn you…

Your government is not telling you the truth.
The enemy is already here and
We are all in grave danger.

Should I meet an untimely death under
suspicious circumstances
always remember:

Follow the money. Follow the power.
Who has the most to lose?

We lived through all of this
to tell you about the nuclear detonations,
the lies, and the cover-up.

Several of us kept detailed diaries.
This is not my story.
This is our story.

<u>LONG LIVE THE TRUTH!</u>

Yes, I am shouting. Are you listening?

Very truly,

John Denning (JD),
Former BMCS,
SEAL Team Six

Undisclosed Location

PROLOGUE
Barents Sea, Russia

Captain Vasili's Diary

The next world war will be over in seconds!

Not years.

Not minutes.

Seconds!

At least, that's what our president believes.

Who am I?

Valentin Vasili, Captain, Russian Navy, Northern Fleet.

First, please forgive my written English. I thought the Russian language was bad but English is crazy. Hopefully, this is only minor inconvenience.

I had the conn (control) of the *Severstal, TK-20*, a massive Typhoon (NATO designation) class submarine that was supposed to have been scrapped.

It wasn't.

Instead, I had her underway in Barents Sea, Russia.

I'm a thirty-year veteran of the Russian Navy, and was as loyal as they come.

I'd consider myself a serious man given an impossible task.

My biggest worry: Will I ever see my wife again?

I'm married happily. Three grown children. All of them migrated West.

My wife and I live near St. Petersburg on the water, near the Finnish border. A lovely place. Nice and quiet.

I have no living family in Russia but my wife, who I deeply love.

I love to travel, especially to the West but always content to return to Mother Russia. I've been much happier. Especially when tensions with the West and my beloved Russia were far lower.

However, those days are long gone. Another Cold War is brewing between Russia and United States and it looks as if our president is, primarily, to blame.

The U.S. and Russia are expelling each other's citizens at a rapid pace and, now, both countries have leaders or former leaders that have become very wealthy off their own citizens. This wealth has nothing to do with hard work but rather only due to positions of immense power and control.

In fact, many heads of Russia and former U.S. Senators and U.S. businesses have common business interests with our siloviki clan (More on the siloviki later).

So with all of this "supposed" perestroika and glasnost since 1980 I'm confused.

What I've been ordered to do could start World War III.

My mission is clearly strange.

"Alaska? But why?" I ask.

Admiral Victor Perchinkov, is my boss and new Minister of Defence. He is a cautious, slender, grey haired man in his sixties that makes no moves without blessings of his president.

My friend, the admiral, is also a close business and government loyalist. All submarine orders would now be given directly from admiral who will now work from president's office! This is highly unusual, as all orders always come from naval command.

In addition, my old friend, the admiral, had been given as his first task to sack fifty of my friends, all naval commanders in the Northern and Baltic Fleets. These men are all very well respected commanders.

Why?

For refusing to follow the president's direct orders.

Harass NATO and Americans whenever and wherever you can!

Today, each and every one of those loyal Russians cannot find work anywhere in Russia as they've been put on a list.

I'm old enough to remember, not revisionist history, but our true history.

"Lists" were part of the old Communist way of life.

You were either on the "good" list or the "bad" list.

But you were on a list with the government who knew everything about you.

Stalin created a state security service called Ministry of State Security.

Ironically, our beloved president has resurrected that very name and looks to be putting KGB back together.

Stalin also famously purged hundreds of military leaders who weren't willing to murder anyone standing in his way to fulfill the greater glory of Rodina (Mythical Motherland)!

As a loyal Russian soldier, you were required to do anything for Rodina.

Turned out to be do anything tyrant at top demanded!

Death!

Murder!

Whatever!

You did it all in furtherance of the godhead.

Sorry, I'm on tangent, back to admiral.

If you want to keep your job, the admiral is not someone with whom you question.

So I had my orders and, as far as admiral was concerned, that was that.

However, as my admiral friend should've known by now and contrary to what many think of Russian commander, I am also deep down rebel, so I persist in my questioning.

"Strange unmarked suitcases, twenty-five scientists, twenty-two civilian women, heads covered, a *GRU Spetsnaz Team* (Russian Special Forces), and rooms on my boat are off limits to me?" I border on insubordination.

However, "my friend" the admiral, had other plans for me.

The admiral reassuringly said, "This is for your safety, Valentin."

"My safety?" I interrupt.

"If those scientists are doing dangerous something on my ship, I must know."

Admiral Perchinkov, didn't agree. "We will be in touch."

The Admiral started to leave, then stopped.

"Remember, Valentin, this ship is now our *Red October.*"

With that, my old friend, the admiral left my submarine. I didn't appreciate such vagaries but the admiral knew I loved reading Tom Clancy novels and, except for ending of *The Hunt for Red October*, so did the admiral.

So my sub, with 125 souls on board, depart from a covered port at Severodvinsk, Russia shipyard under the cover of darkness.

We are pulling the old matryoshka doll switch on the West.

Nothing in Russia is exactly as it appears on surface. Even dig deeper and things appear identical, they never really are.

Russian nesting dolls are children's toys that have large, hollow outside with several more, increasingly smaller, identical hollow dolls hidden inside. And hiding inside one of those, when everyone else had given up looking, was our Trojan horse.

My Typhoon class sub is so large it looks like two submarines sitting side by side. The original Proyekt (Project) Number was 941 and has two large separate hulls sitting side by side. With complete remodel my new sub has one huge, Top Secret, sound suppressing, skin on outside hull that covers five separate, watertight, interior hulls. All five hulls have been totally redesigned.

Trouble is one of the hulls has rooms entirely off limits to me!

Unacceptable!

Anyway, while NSA with COMINT/SIGINT (U.S. Communications intelligence/Signals intelligence) satellites were watching what they thought was *TK-20* slowly being dismantled from a satellite 25,000 miles in space, it was only fake shell of my *TK-20*, much like the matryoshka, children's toy.

My *TK-20* had spent last five years, nearby, covered in secrecy, being retrofitted. There are several Top Secrets aboard this ship, only one of which I knew.

The caterpillar drive!

The new, ultra-quiet propulsion system made famous in Tom Clancy's novel: *The Hunt for Red October*. Anyone with "real knowledge" knew this was just the work of science fiction, right?

Wrong!

Friends of mine have quietly been working this very system for thirty years. And with help of several Western scientists and Russians in Skolkovo (Russia's Silicon Valley) we made Phase I of *Proyekt* (English: *Project*) 239 a reality. How was this done?

Boatloads of cash!

With billions of rubles from President Ivan Mironovich our scientists had done the impossible. We make world's first propulsion drive without any moving parts!

Not easy task. But something about which I am excited!

Kapitan-Leytenant Casmerov, third rank, repeats his question to me, shaking me to reality.

"What should be our depth, sir?"

I curtly answer, "Hold steady. Thirty meters."

Kapitan-Leytenant Casmerov answers, "Yes, sir. Steady. Thirty meters."

"What's the depth under the keel?" I ask.

"One hundred ten meters," said Casmerov.

Today the air temperature is a warm -1 degrees C, above the icy waters around the Kola Peninsula.

Didn't matter.

We are already underwater, shadowing a new *Borei* class submarine, *Knyaz Vladimir.*

This old Russian maneuver was bait and switch tactic to hide true intentions of my *Severstal.*

My Russian Typhoon class *Severstal* (*TK-20*), the largest submarine ever built, was supposed to be pulled apart on dry dock at Severodvinsk, Russia and then shipped to Sayda Bay piece by piece.

Instead, in direct violation of New START Treaty between the U.S. and Russia, *TK-20* was secretly enhanced and heading west, just in case Western satellites or surveillance had picked up our movement.

They hadn't.

No one had.

I help come up with greatest invention since electricity. I had been promised, don't worry, Vasili, invention will be used for protection and peaceful purposes. Instead, looks to me, I'm driving my young crew right into World War III!

As I stared at navigation console, I no longer think about mission but rather think of my wife.

I hadn't told my love that my mission was open-ended. Meaning, there was no date given where I would return. This would always worry her so, instead, I left her a note that simply read,

On mission,

Love, Valentin.

This nuclear ballistic missile submarine could stay submerged for four months if needed and we are loaded with enough supplies to do just that, and far more.

Both *Severstal* and *Borei* class submarines are known as SSBNs (Ship, Submarine, Ballistic, Nuclear). While *Severstal* is nearly thirty years old, no one but myself and a very small group of Russians knew it had been upgraded and all of her ballistic missiles removed!

That's right!

I knew all ballistic missiles had been removed.

However, she was then reequipped to be much more silent and much, much more deadly.

(More on that later.)

Meanwhile I think,

Why?

I didn't wait thirty years to captain the greatest ship in the world just to murder millions, if that was the plan!

I had faced death on several prior occasions but those instances were for something in which I believed. This, start to feel like provocation.

I was not given half of it.

However, Nikolai Alexi, Kapitan, 2nd Rank, was given a full briefing but, I, the captain of my own boat, Valentin Vasili, wasn't even invited!

This kid is part of siloviki clan and more trusted than I, a loyal officer of thirty years! I snarl to myself as I look at the kid who just turned thirty!

Still, I am confused: I pretend to travel towards old NATO underwater listening stations that have long been abandoned. The Cold War G.I.U.K. Gap between Greenland, Iceland, and United Kingdom was only way Russian ships and subs could travel if we wanted to reach the oceans of earth.

I then proudly, think: Was... was only way we could travel to reach other oceans!

The West appears clueless as to my president's true intentions. The United States had pressed its famous 'reset' button and had reduced its air, naval and ground strength to unprecedented low levels in light of "our new peace."

NATO no better.

For example, Royal Norwegian Navy sold their military base at Olavsvern. The base was built into side of solid rock mountain and housed submarine hangers that could withstand direct nuclear strike.

NATO cost: Five hundred million to build.

Base tracked all our sea vessels from Russian naval bases on the Kola Peninsula, but no more.

Base sold for five million U.S. dollars.

Mere one percent of cost to build!

Now rented to a "research group" owned by Russian government!

We are finally going to see some peace dividends. This caterpillar drive, I've helped work on my whole life, could be put to some important peacetime uses, I thought.

As they say in America: Boy, was I stupid!

Just before I left I saw my president, president of Russia, Ivan Mironovich, on TV.

He made yet another bold pronouncement on, state-controlled, Russian *TV-12*.

The president said,

"Russia & China will co-operate with all of our friends and allies. We have many mutual economic and military interests around the world. We shall continue to hold regular, joint military exercises with China to show America and the West that we will not be bullied."

I also saw German banking expert, Hans Meiner, interviewed. He said, "Russia and China have become the world's leading buyers of gold to weaken the world's dependence on the almighty U.S. dollar. A new Cold War has already erupted in the financial sector."

China's President, Ji Xixping, stated, 'The world's economy is now at a critical juncture.'"

Any one of these statements alone would not have worried me but there are other worrisome events taking place in my country.

Several government ministries have now blocked over one million Russian web pages and invited Chinese experts to show them how to block even more.

At home, journalism had become a very dangerous business.

Scores of journalists: Jailed.

A worse fate has befallen six dissidents: Murder.

One was a friend.

It was safer these days to be common criminal than it was to be dissident or opposition journalist.

And siloviki had common criminals on their side.

Illegal drugs, alcohol and cigarettes, local gangs are either allowed or sometimes controlled by a local clan family.

I've also noticed dozens of hardened, underground bunkers being built in or near important government buildings and homes.

In fact, I recently rode on the underground subway that goes from President Mironovich's house outside Moscow to a leadership command center, at the Kremlin, completely underground.

These hardened sites are for one purpose and one purpose only.

Preparation for a first strike nuclear war on the West!

So there I was, on my couch, watching my favorite TV show starring: Olga Kasparov.

She is friend and very, very cautious journalist interviewing President.

More courageous journalists had openly nicknamed our president: Ivan the Terrible, Ivan the Terminator, or just Crazy Ivan.

The President, in his humility, preferred: Ivan the Great!

So I have nice tall glass of Russian Standard Platinum vodka watching president on TV say:

"The Americans try to blame Russia for everything wrong with the world. We Russians have a word for this: Russophobia."

"For example, Guccifer 2.0 has hacked U.S. Democratic Party emails and state election boards."

"Americans claim Guccifer is Russian intelligence services."

"However, our intelligence services tell me these are disgruntled people in CIA and in American intelligence agencies who don't like or trust their own corrupt bosses. Edward Snowden has proved the American government has been illegally surveilling millions of their own citizens. Russia would never interfere in the internal affairs of other countries."

Notice president didn't say he wouldn't surveil his own Russian citizens?

President continues,

"However, I will stand up to the arrogant American leadership that's not trusted by their own CIA. We love American people but I shall never allow our seas to become a pond for NATO or the American military in which they can freely play. We shall help our friends like the Syrians and the Iranians. And we shall build up our defensive forces in our territory, especially on The Crimean Peninsula." said Crazy Ivan confidently.

I practically spit my expensive Russian vodka across room!

"Our territory?"

"The Crimean Peninsula?"

I understood exactly what Crazy Ivan was saying.

First, this speech would rally ordinary Russians to an increasingly dictatorial president, claiming to stop Western aggression while he moves further and further into "our territory."

Ukraine!

Second, it was to misdirect attention away from Russia and my *Severstal*. And it worked!

While a brand new class of Borei sub, *Knyaz Vladimir*, would pretend she was on sea trials tooling around Barents Sea, for photo ops, I dove *TK-20* deep, deeper, silent and in opposite direction.

As I did, I put on pair of old iPod headphones and hit play '*A Mad Russian's Christmas*' by Trans-Siberian Orchestra[1] (Listen to the first minute).

How appropriate, just ten days 'til Christmas!

Merry Christmas, Mrs. Vasili, I thought as I commanded,

"Caterpillar drives Full speed."

"Aye, captain. Caterpillar drives full speed."
We would soon be under Arctic ice heading directly to Alaska!
And then it hit me:
Oh God no!

PALMER GLACIER - MOUNT HOOD, OREGON

My Diary

I t was clear but brisk, really brisk.
Twenty-four degrees Fahrenheit brisk.
But it was that kind of rare December night perfect for climbing the highest mountain in Oregon, Mt. Hood (11,249').

The, rare, clear moonlit night reflecting on the white snow made the night-climb easy and beautiful.

According to a cool GPS program on my iPhone 7 I was currently 8,324 feet in the air.

I'm kind of a big guy six feet four inches.

Some say handsome.

"My, my! You look like a chiseled Greek god, JD!" But that's Nadene in my office and she wears glasses.

My name is John Denning, but I prefer JD.

I've hiked to the top of Hood twice before but today would be different. Today, I would never make it.

I've never made excuses for stupid behavior, like the fools who attempted to climb this mountain in the winter without proper equipment, but I always figured,

I've got personal issues too.

Everybody's gotta fight their own demons.

If I just could corral mine, I'd be happy.

I wasn't one of those types who blamed my mother or father for all of my failings because for all of their shortcomings, with all they went through, they were pretty phenomenal people.

People tell me I love doing everything at full throttle. I guess that's true but I do it because it's just plain fun. What's wrong with simply enjoying life?

Whether it was racing motorcycles through the woods of Oregon, jumping out of planes HAHO (High Altitude High Opening) style, or helping a friend's ninety-year old mother move all of her possessions to another state, I operate at full throttle.

A friend, Doug Meyers, once told me,

"You hug your motorcycles more than you hug your parents."

I'm not married. My father passed after a long illness. So I try to treat everyone like family.

My life changed after a speeding ticket on my motorcycle.

I wound up in jail.

They claim I was doing 130 m.p.h. through Yuma, Arizona. I told the officer,

"Impossible! This thing can't do more than 120!"

So, sitting in jail, I said to myself, self, instead of causing the police so much grief, you might as well do something for your country.

What do you like to do?

Well, I liked thrilling, daring, crazy things.

So after 9/11 I joined the Navy.

After eight weeks of Navy boot camp I signed up for the toughest twenty some weeks of my life. This was Basic Underwater Demolition/SEAL (BUD/S) training, better known as SEALs. I broke my leg just three days before the end of Phase II, meaning I had to wait for the next class and take the entire nine weeks of Phase II over again, which usually means washout.

And it appeared that was exactly what was happening, although I could run on my leg after six weeks, my underwater swim times were over ten minutes behind the basic minimums for passage.

In fact, the instructors/motivators (What we called drill sergeants at boot camp) started calling me washout number one.

There were two others who washed out of Phase II and were taking the phase over again with me.

Washout number two and Washout number three.

They both quit on their first day back!

On my last possible attempt at the underwater course, I squeaked by just in time with two seconds to spare!

I went on to easily pass Phase III.

Looking back on it all, I really had come a long way.

SEAL Qualification Training (SQT), jump school, Survival, Evasion, Resistance, and Escape (SERE), now all seemed worth it as in five years I was officially a Navy SEAL!

No brag.

Just fact.

I rose to a Chief in Navy Seal Team Six (Now "affectionately" called the Naval Special Warfare Development Group, NSWDG/DEVGRU/DG) quicker than any SEAL in history, (From enlistment to DG in just under nine years!)!

But that's where the bragging ends.

Today, I really want nothing do with Navy politics (More on that later!).

Anyway, I really want to tell you about this hike.

Mt. Hood is one of the deadliest climbing mountains in the world with over 130 souls lost to date.

Of course, there are more novices who attempt this climb than many of the more difficult mountains.

Deaths average about one a year but that doesn't seem to stop anyone.

I love the outdoors.

And when things became really stressful at the Portland FBI office I would take a hike, literally!

Well, things were now especially stressful as over 800,000 terrorists are on various FBI watch lists, and that was just inside the U.S. There are only 35,664 total FBI personnel. Everyone knew it was only a matter of time before some nut or nuts would do something far worse than shoot up a nightclub and murder forty-nine people.

When I left the SEALs I applied to the FBI's counterterrorism department and became a Gold Team Instructor training FBI agents. We war-gamed chemical, biological, radiological, or nuclear (CBRN) material attacks in U.S. cities. I always thought, even if just a few true believers got hold of a nuke, God help us all!

My job was to train counterterrorism, sniper and other personnel in every terrorist situation imaginable. I met many of my current and retired friends from DEVGRU/DG here.

Routinely, the FBI would run Top Secret ops, like shut down NRG stadium in Houston, Texas a couple of months before the Super Bowl, just for practice.

Inside the stadium we would run an active sniper, or various CBRN scenarios.

On other occasions, I'd be whisked away by private jet to a major city to war game a chem weapon in a movie theater or an attack on a nuclear power plant.

More recently, however, I was doing something far less exciting and far more boring, surveillance.

Currently, I had been assigned to a potentially high-risk person of interest. But I was trying very hard to compartmentalize and not think about office work today.

"Always pay attention to your surroundings!" as I was told by my very first SEAL instructor on Coronado, just across the bay from San Diego.

Again, I had to snap myself back to reality. I know that on Mt. Hood, storms can come out of nowhere, especially in winter. You are so high that, during the day, the weather looks sunny and fine, like in an airplane. Unless you're experienced, however, you may not notice the difference between fog in the valleys below and a storm pushing quickly up the mountain. When a storm system is pushed into the side of the Cascade mountain range the sun can disappear in an instant and a zero visibility blizzard can come out of nowhere.

But city slickers in their, just purchased, state of the art, flashy clothing, and cell phones could never totally be deterred, despite all the warnings. These were the people that didn't know squat about mountaineering but, rather, were here for their latest Facebook selfie. But hey, to each his own!

During the day, the upper Palmer Chairlift would carry skiers to 8,397 feet. U.S. Olympic ski teams would train on Mt. Hood, sometimes all summer long. In fact, Hood is the only mountain in North America where you can generally ski all summer!

But this is the dead of winter. As I walked near the last tower I heard the frozen cables on the lift start. The icy cold, braded steel grumbled like an old man trying to get out of bed.

I sure hope they don't start allowing faux mountain climbers to use the chair lifts now, I sarcastically mumbled to myself.

I remember thinking, these idiots will probably get hit on the head by a rock or an icefall before they get off the chair.

Even a small rock sized chunk of ice can slice skin, brake bones or knock you unconscious. In which case, you'll be seeing Jesus before you see the top!

Most came up the south side, as it's the easiest of the fifteen ways to the top. Even in December rocks are always a major concern. The Old Chute is the last leg but the easiest way to ascend the top. But even this route is a forty-five-degree climb and nearly vertical in some places.

Rookies were always wondering up here with the latest designed, neon chartreuse parkas (Sorry I guess I am a little bitter at the novices who attempt this climb without any prep.) I always carried a good climbing helmet, crampons, ice ax, and rope. I'd spend other savings on more important things, like a nice, quiet Alaskan vacation.

My father's old friend, Richard Bass, gave me his twenty-year-old ski pants and an ugly, thirty-year-old, black drab parka. Bass was the first person to climb all seven of the world's tallest mountains. I'd always remembered Bass's comment when I was little,

"Prepared doesn't mean flashy clothing, son. It means warm clothing, proper equipment, oh, and a damn good map!"

Although times have changed, my old school philosophy remained the same, you can have MotionX GPS and Elevation Pro on your phone but if your phone breaks or your battery goes out you still need a map!

That's the advice I'd give my co-workers who wanted a hike to the top.

That, and if your phone breaks none of your hot new-fangled GPS garbage is worth your life!

If your battery goes dead,

"You're on your own, son," as Bass would say.

No sir! When your life depended on it, I wanted to pull out my old, trusty, waterproof map!

I was on point in a SEAL platoon that breached a compound in Kandahar, Afghanistan when I lost contact with my team. I wondered why, suddenly, I was the only guy in the place shooting bad guys. Our satellite feed had gone down and no one, except for me, seemed to be able to function!

After that I always thought,

Keep your stupid high tech stuff! I got my map!

Also, I didn't mind people but they were sometimes a distraction from simply enjoying nature. As I continued up the mountain I did something very dangerous. I pulled out my iPhone 7 and put in earbuds. I searched for "Sunrise" by Duran Duran.[2]

I knew this was dangerous, as I might not hear any calls for help or rocks hurling at me. But, for the moment, I wanted to be a rookie climber too and just enjoy the moment.

Sunrise!

It was beautiful.

Rays of golden light shot across the mountain and in an instant hit the fog in the valleys below like a beacon from heaven.

Whoever says there is no God clearly hasn't seen this.

As I turned my head back up the mountain my mind couldn't help but wonder to Mohammed Al-Aqsa, MAA, my new surveillance project.

My brain quickly buried that thought and I slammed that door shut.

I have to stop thinking about everything but this climb!

My mind immediately wandered again.

I found it hard to believe at age thirty-five that this sleepy little town of Portland had grown into a sprawling metropolis of over two million people. So with rising numbers of good people comes the bad.

My latest job was to track and determine whether MAA was bad or just another Muslim caught in the red tape of government surveillance. MAA had already been watched 24/7 by the Bureau in Minnesota.

MAA was only twenty-three years old and a U.S. citizen. He was born in Minneapolis to Somali parents. MAA had no friends or family in Portland and was coming only to study engineering. The FBI had given us this really stupid six-month rule from the Department of Justice (DOJ). If the guy you are surveilling doesn't do anything criminal within six months you must stop all surveillance. Court order or no court order!

Now my best friend in school was Muslim but after entire evenings discussing politics and religion I still couldn't understand how an American citizen could get on a plane and go join ISIS. But that is exactly what MAA's brother and two close friends had done! They were never to be seen or heard from again! Our best "guess" is that they were killed in Syria fighting for ISIS but no one knew for sure. After reading dozens of files at the office my team concluded something no one else at the FBI had concluded. While some of these guys were radicalized, others were just plain bored American kids looking some excitement and purpose to their meaningless life.

Suddenly, my senses transported me back to reality! The sun had completely emerged from its slumber and the snow would soon be a blistering white. I had been climbing since before 4 a.m. but this made it all worth it.

Fortunately, I was given a great pair of Ray Ban Aviator Polarized lenses and I had purchased zinc oxide at Government Camp the night before for my nose. Old school all the way!

I had spent the night with old friends from school at this beautiful twenty-five-room chalet owned by a former science teacher. We had a great night telling old stories that, now, with the passage of time, might have been just slightly exaggerated. I felt like a kid again by running on only two hours of sleep!

I smeared the oxide all over my nose. Kids would think I was some crazy old man but I didn't care. I stood out from some of the very white locals with my naturally dark skin but I could still get sunburned. You actually can get an Oregonian sunburn in December as the sun and snow will magnify and burn your skin.

As the sun brightened, I was on the Hogsback, the last stretch before the top of the mountain. I had already traversed around the Bergshrund Crevasse.

The day was perfect. Clear, except for some patchy fog in the lowlands. Just as I was admiring the stunning beauty, my crampon slipped and some ice gave away from under my foot. Okay, don't panic. Everything's fine.

While this looked like a harmless, beautiful white landscape I knew that if I fell here I wouldn't be able to stop 'til I fell another 300 hundred feet into The Devil's Kitchen.[3] It was a fumarole, a vent that releases toxic volcanic gases, such as deadly sulfur, from deep inside the earth.

Several people died on Hood just from being trapped near the gases and not being able to hike out in time. This morning I could see the deadly gases puffing like Indian smoke signals, out of what looked to be a bottomless pit. I was told, no one knew how deep that crevasse was.

I thought, and I don't wanna find out!

After regaining my footing, I looked up and couldn't believe my eyes. There were two people above me already at the top of the Old Chute, which is near the top of the mountain! As I looked closer one person had on a t-shirt and jeans!

No helmets and probably not even crampons.

Twenty-four degrees, in a t-shirt, and in December?

Morons!

With loose rocks surrounding them I actually mumbled out loud, "Crazy!"

No sooner had I finished saying that than I heard a shriek.

The guy slipped and is now shooting toward me like a bullet.

His girlfriend began screaming!

I yelled, "Dig in! Dig in! But quickly I realize the poor kid has on an old pair of tennis shoes."

I pull my ice pick but quickly realize this will likely do me no good. So, I sling the pick around my wrist and take my twenty-five-foot rope and tosses it into the path of the speeding bullet yelling,

"Grab the rope!"

As this perfect stranger hurdles toward me on his back, I wrap the rope around my waist and think,

Goodbye cruel world!

Miraculously, the guy hits my rope and the rope tangles onto his arm as he now rolls.

Unfortunately, for me, I didn't have time to calculate the inertia that would be involved in my stupidity. I'm immediately catapulted into the air on the other end of the rope, flying downhill.

Now both of us idiots are going to die today! I thought.

I struggle to get the ice pick into the ice but instead it's acting more like a ceiling fan whirling dangerously around my head, the sharp edge coming closer and closer.

Everything is now in slow motion.

Nice move, JD! I'm gonna die twice today! Once with my own icepick and then again in the crevasse!

I'm finally able to grab the handle of the ice pick but this is now the least of my worries.

In a second I'm going to hit the crevasse but first we both go flying over the smaller Bergshrund crevasse as though it's not even there!

The bloody body of this poor guy I'm attached to has been sliced like sushi over ice.

What am I thinking? In about two seconds I'm probably going to look worse than that! I snap back from feeling sorry for myself as I hear and see some jagged rocks rip off what's left of this poor guy's University of Oregon t-shirt as he hurls into the crevasse.

Dragging closely behind, I somehow manage to stop just short of going into the abyss as well. Fortunately, my old Richard Bass parka and ski pants have paid off, as they are still on me and in one piece!

"Oh God, oh God, oh God, I don't wanna die," says this bloody mass something now barely resembling a human.

Now I'm feeling just as hysterical but I take a deep breath and then flat on my stomach holding the rope and one arm I calmly say,

"What's your name?"

"Trevor," answers a quivering voice.

We're both dead.

Of course, I only thought that. I would never ever show this. Sixteen years of Navy SEAL training and one year of FBI psychology profiling comes rushing into my brain. I take another deep breath and say,

"Ok Trevor. I'm gonna get you outta here but we've gotta work together, okay?"

Trevor nods slightly.

I then begin pulling Trevor out of the crevasse.

But just as I'm about to free Trevor, I hear a girl's voice behind me yelling and screaming.

I turn my head just in time to see Trevor's hiking partner trying to run down this steep, forty-five-degree chute! I start yelling,

"Stop! Stop!"

But it's too late.

Trevor's girlfriend falls and begins sliding head first toward them.

As I turn my head again, Trevor has already heard his girlfriend falling and has pulled out a knife.

Trevor then calmly says,

"Save her! Please, save her!"

"I'm not letting go. You don't have to do this."

Her screams are getting closer and closer and now I have the decision of my life.

In that split second, Trevor made the decision for me.

Trevor cuts through the rope and falls into the blackness.

Trevor is gone and all I can hear is that blood-curdling scream. Trevor's last echo on planet earth seems to take forever to stop. I will live to the day I die with that sound haunting my head. I had been told I was brave before but in an instant I feel like a helpless child.

Standing, frozen in place, all I can think about is, my God! I just killed someone. I should've pulled harder, faster.

Seemingly, minutes go by but that's impossible. It was seconds. But in those seconds passed eternity and Trevor's screams were still echoing in my head.

Then, in an instant, I was back hearing a second set of screams hurling toward me.

She was flying like an alpine bobsled directly toward me, face first.

I stood up and ran, like an idiot, toward her and, without thinking, I dove for this poor helpless woman whose t-shirt, body and jeans are already mangled and bloody. She had no gloves and her hands, trying to grab ice and snow, are bleeding.

What am I thinking?

I thought as I flew dramatically over the top of her, grabbing her shoulder and arm for just a split second.

She sailed right passed me but in that split second I was able to grab her shoulder and arm just long enough to stop her from going into the crevasse.

This area, fortunately, is almost flat but jagged rocks still protrude through the snow.

And, unfortunately, this poor girl has hit her head on one of them.

I ran to her unconscious, lifeless, body.

I took off my parka and put it under her head.

I then quickly checked for breath and heartbeat.

Now the sulfur gases begin to engulf us and I remember starting to cough.

Some distance parallel to us I hear,

"You need help?"

I ignored them thinking,

"They'll figure it out!"

Now every Navy SEAL must pass a basic medical life-saving course but I start thinking,

That was over sixteen years ago! What do I do next?

I try to breath some life into this young woman, who could be no more than 21 years old. I now hear others yelling behind me and can hear someone talking to the 911 operator. I stopped breathing for her and again checked for a pulse.

Finally!

I was able to feel a faint heartbeat on her neck. I remember coughing again thinking,

Wouldn't it be ironic if I died and she lives?

Who said I was brave and heroic?

I suddenly realize in that split second how selfish human nature is. But it's also in our nature to help others. However, it seems too few help others today while most would walk away.

I look around for a place to move her.

A group of climbers now arrive. The first guy couldn't be more than eighteen.

"Hey man, is she dead?"

"No, did you call 911?" I answered.

Then the kid hands me his phone,

"Ya, they want to talk to you."

"My name is John Denning. I'm an FBI Special Agent. We have a female, approximately 21 years of age. She's barely breathing and unconscious. She fell a few hundred feet down ice, multiple lacerations, maybe broken bones. She looks to have hit her head and is in critical condition."

Then I look at the kid who gave me his cell phone and ask,

"Can they call back on this number?"

"Ya, Ya, sure."

I then say to the operator,

"Okay. Get them here ASAP. Were you able to pull GPS coordinates from this phone? Okay, good! We'll set up a landing zone."

I looked over to the mangled mess of a girl and said,

"Hurry. Please."

I hand the phone back to its owner while I hold the unconscious girl's head in my hands.

The teen with the phone asks, "What did they say?"

I ignored him as I try to take care of the girl.

Suddenly, the thought crosses my mind,

She might die and I don't even know her name.

A crowd of nine other looky-loos have traversed to us, just to watch this girl die.

Later I got mad thinking,

No one. Not one asked or even tried to help at first.

But what I really became worried about next were the sulfur fumes.

"We've gotta get her away from here. The chopper will be in the air in three minutes!"

Several kids finally help me pick up the unconscious girl and move her.

After she's been moved I looked into the crevasse that just took a young man's life.

I suddenly felt nothing. No worry. No sadness. Nothing. That didn't last long.

As I looked down the majestic mountain I saw what every climber on Mt. Hood fears, a huge storm is about to hit. As the storm rapidly flies up the side of the mountain the kid's cell phone rings and the kid answers.

"Ya."

The kid sounds confused.

"What? We ain't got no shovels."

The kid, looking terrified, hands me the phone.

I knew exactly what was happening as I spoke to emergency dispatch.

"You have our GPS coordinates, right? You'll never be able to land here."

We'll hunker down right where we are." Tell the chopper to stand down."

Send the CAT and a rescue team."

Hurry. No one here is prepared for this, and this girl won't live much longer!"

The dispatcher tried to tell me something positive but I just hung up the phone. We didn't have much time.

"All right everyone, start digging. We're building snow caves."

The kid, shaking, asks,

"Have you ever done that?"

I reassured him by saying,

"Oh ya, I took a wilderness survival class in high school. We did all this stuff!"

The kid seems satisfied and starts digging.

Little did he know and I wasn't about to volunteer that I about froze to death in that high school snow cave 4,000 feet lower and in much warmer weather!

Also, I wasn't about to share the following.

I nearly died when I was eighteen and fell down the mountain in this very spot!

All I could do was be a good example for some stressed out kids. I started digging with my icepick. I look around and realize I'm the only one here with an icepick.

After just about one minute at this elevation and not being acclimated I was exhausted.

I look at the kids hands next to me and they're bleeding.

As I sat back in the snow and ice, I give a deep and long sigh.

I'd be happy right now knowing we are going to make it off this cold rock, alive. It's only a week 'till Christmas. Right now I'd settle for a nice Christmas dinner at Denny's.

There are only two things I hate in this world.

Being cold and wet.

Looks like I'm gonna be both.

And, as luck would have it, on my iPhone *Dust in the Wind* by Kansas[4] starts to play.

USS ALASKA SSBN 732 - ARCTIC OCEAN

Tom Watson's Diary

It was just another ordinary day.

Ordinary, if you consider waking up at the bottom of the Arctic Ocean aboard a ballistic missile submarine.

My name is Tom Watson. I'm a Chief Petty Officer, (CPO) aboard the *USS Alaska* (SSBN 732) but this is my off time, for another hour anyway.

We are working through an All Systems Silent drill, affectionately nicknamed ASS duty, which meant no one was moving.

It's kind of funny looking at everyone wearing tennis shoes and slippers during these drills.

ASS duty is when a sonar officer hears something which sounds like a sub and about the only thing everyone is allowed to do is sit on their ass until the sound was positively identified! While humans still listen for anomalies, computers also "listen." It's our job to then determine if the anomaly is a potential threat.

Aside from ASS duty and a fool for a commander, I love my job.

Silence is a submarine's best weapon. If no one knows you're there, you can destroy the enemy before they even know what hit them!

And the Arctic is a great place to hide.

Under the ice of the North Pole it's constantly noisy. Ice creaks and groans as it calves and breaks. It's almost impossible to hear anything.

Hence, computers help with the listening.

We've programmed the computer systems to listen for specific submarine signatures so we can positively identify friend and foe.

However, if our computers have no record of a particular signature, then all bets are off and it comes down to a competent sonar technician to recognize the anomaly (More about "competent" later).

The United States and Russian subs are becoming more and more aggressive in searching for and following each other around. So, silence aboard a sub is both our first line for both offense and defense.

Effective and secure communication is a close second. Submarines have several ways to communicate. One way is ELF (Extremely Low Frequency). ELF is the only known wavelength that can penetrate deep into the earth and through sea ice. The drawbacks to ELF are:

1). It's only one-way communication and
2). The antennas and equipment are massive, hence, very expensive.

Only the U.S., Russia and, now India, have built ELF systems.

The Russian antennas are actually thirty-seven miles long!

Technically, they are not antennas at all but only feed lines as the Earth itself is the antenna! Hence, only one-way communication. Navy ops centers can talk to us but we used to not be able to talk to them.

However, we've been secretly testing a newer two-way system for some time now. The Navy laid cable and has near bottom, fixed locations under the Arctic ice for hydro-acoustic communication. A submarine communicating here could not be heard even if you're sitting next to it. You'd never know it's there!

The beauty of this system is so long as your boat is snug against the magnetic hub, and has the proper equipment, all sound is suppressed. This was critical as enemy subs are listening and, if they hear anything, they could pick up your location and potentially kill you.

ONI (Office of Naval Intelligence) now requires all Arctic communications to travel through this new encrypted system to a HAARP Station in Gakona, Alaska. The U.S. Navy re-encrypts and send communications to specialized HAARP satellites that would beam them down to ASWOC or any other military facility as needed.

Very few people are aware of the entire 'Top Secret' HAARP system. The primary reason for this exotic communications system is to find out what the Russians are doing in the Arctic without letting them know we are here and listening.

I'm one of the few who were briefed on how the entire HAARP system communicated. However, I haven't been much use to anyone these days.

My last breakup was really difficult.

I swore I'd never date someone in the Navy again.

She was the Lieutenant commander of this very submarine.

Jennifer Tavana was the love of my life.

At age thirty-two, she retired from the Navy!

She not only was the first woman to command a U.S. submarine but she also made it to that command in the shortest time of any peacetime commander.

Jennifer retired for me.

I told her not to.

But she's a very strong-headed woman.

One of us had to leave the ship and even though the discharge finished her distinguished naval career, Commander Tavana did it for me.

I'm sorry Jen. I miss you so much.

I looked at her picture that I kept hiding on the bottom of the bunk above me.

The green light goes on.

Our ASSes are cleared to move around again.

I just sat there staring at her and listening to great breakup song "So Very Hard to Go" by Tower of Power.[5]

So, I'm sitting here feeling sorry for myself and staring at this gorgeous creature and wondering what she's doing. I heard she joined the FBI and was stationed in Juneau, Alaska.

How ironic, I thought.

At least she's still "in" Alaska!

I wonder what she's doing right now?

Jen and I had a professional relationship aboard ship but off the ship things got really hot.

Wow!

I will never forget those shore leave nights.

Unfortunately, I got drunk one night and started bragging about my exploits.

When Navy brass found out about us, we were confronted.

She chose to leave the Navy rather than have me reassigned to another ship or forced out of the Navy.

In light of the way I feel about two idiots on board the Alaska, that might not have been such a bad idea.

The green all clear light had popped off for a couple of minutes now and so I put on my UGG slippers and dragged my sorry "ass" out of my Ohio class submarine bunk.

Everyone made fun of my UGGs but they were quiet and comfortable. Maybe it's the white sheep's wool that sticks out over my black slacks.

These quarters are cramped but the same size "coffin" goes for about $250,000.00 in downtown Tokyo. And I'd rather be here than in downtown Tokyo.

The USS Alaska is a SSBN Boomer, roughly equivalent to a Russian Typhoon class submarine.

As I made my way to the conn I finally stopped thinking about Jen and began thinking about our mission.

We are to monitor if Russia is going ahead with their promise of building ten airfields in the Arctic. Russia's Federal Agency for Special Construction (Spetsstroy) had promised some time ago to begin building military facilities on six islands. Then everything went dark. No subs, ships, planes, nothing for five years now.

Most people think the United States and Russia are on different sides of the world but most people are wrong.

Russia and the United States are actually less than two and one half miles apart! That's right, we may be worlds apart in culture and language but geographically, it's less than three miles. A smart Russian or Alaskan will know about the Diomede Islands.

Little Diomede is part of Alaska and, of course, "Big" Diomede is in Russia.

And even though they're only three miles apart Big Diomede is 21 hours ahead in time.

During some cold winters you can actually walk across the ice bridge that forms here.

Satellite images have shown that the Russians have been moving some of their mobile nukes, while still on Russian territory, close to Alaska. This obviously is a very serious concern, especially when you see the Russians test a weapon like their new Satan-2, which is capable of destroying everything in an area the size of France!

Meanwhile on my sub, Tad Murphy, Seaman and Sonar Technician extraordinaire, was "my" responsibility. The reason is that no one else wanted to work with or be anywhere near the guy. Usually sonar guys hang around together with other sonar guys.

Not Tad.

Even though three sonar technicians were required to be in the sonar room on each shift, people didn't hang around with Tad even while on duty.

Tad was thought of by just about everyone on board, including me, as the dumbest man on the ship.

Tad wanted to, someday, command his own ship.

This guy couldn't command a rubber ducky in a bathtub!

"Anything out there?" I asked.

"Nothin' but a whale!"

Thinking he's joking I say, "Whale?"

"Ya, it's the same one I hear every so often," Tad confidently says.

"On passive?"

"Ya, but I'd really like to go active and ping this big guy and see what he does!" says Tad enthusiastically.

There is so much wrong with that last statement I don't know where to start. First, as a sub you must listen with your passive sonar so that enemy sonar can't see you. Active sonar is that famous ping sound you've heard when you watch any submarine movie. You almost never use active as your position is immediately acquired.

It's actually a lot more complicated than that but that's the basic idea.

Then I said, "Big guy? How big is this thing you're seeing?"

"I dunno," says Dumbo.

"You do realize there's nothing but ice around us for hundreds and hundreds of miles, right?"

"Ya, so?"

"So a whale's a mammal and needs to breathe."

"So?"

So where can a whale come up for air? The ice up there is no less than five to ten feet thick in every direction!"

"I thought they could breathe under water."

So then I stare at Tad wondering if aliens took his brain?

"Where'd you study submarine warfare?"

Tad didn't answer. We all studied at the same naval school in Groton (AKA "Rotten") Connecticut. In submarine 101 you knew whales don't travel very far under ice as their own sonar tells them there is no place to come up for air. The photos you see of whales breathing surrounded by ice clearly isn't anywhere near here.

Tad then says, "The AOA didn't recognize the signature so I discarded it."

Idiot!

I thought that but didn't say it. I should've said it out loud but I didn't.

Every sound under water has a unique signature identifying itself. Several computer systems onboard then analyze and attempt to identify the object.

The "proper" acronym for one of our computer systems is AOAIA. That stands for Advanced Oceanography and Acoustic Intelligence Analysis. It's capable of identifying almost anything from underwater mountains down to a particular fish.

"I wanna see it. Pull backup," I say impatiently.

"James says there's something wrong with our backup system and he's been tryin' ta fix it."

"Where is James and where is Bob?" I ask impatiently.

Again, there are supposed to be three guys in this room on any one shift.

"I dunno. I was tellin' them a story and they left."

I'm not surprised.

I know where they are.

I head down two flights to the galley.

Sure enough! I find James and Bob laughing it up with several other guys while decorating our ship's "Christmas tree." This crazy thing was decorated with every piece of junk found on the ship. First, the tree was a faded green cheap piece of plastic Chinese crap. If there ever was a fire on board I wouldn't be surprised if it started right here.

As soon as I'm seen, everyone stops talking, as James and Bob know they are supposed to be on duty and in the sonar room.

"What's going on with Tad's whales?"

Everyone laughs. Bob, Petty Officer 3rd Class, says,

"You heard the story too? We didn't want to tell Tad."

Now I'm angry, "You know protocol. Why didn't you tell me?"

No answer from any of them.

"Was the processed signal flagged and sent to ASWOC for review?"

ASWOC is the Anti-Submarine Warfare Operations Center in San Diego, California.

No answer. Finally, Bob feels confident, "I'm sure it wasn't anything. You know how he..."

He wasn't able to finish when I interrupt,

"I want to see the fucking whale!"

Both of them look at me and realize I'm taking this very seriously.

Bob hesitantly says, "Problem was in the AOAIA software. I wouldn't worry about ..."

I'm a by the book kinda guy especially when it came to my "on the job" duties (Off the job? Please don't go there!).

"Did you tell the commander?" I interrupt.

"It's in our reports to him, ya." Says Bob.

"You know he doesn't read those things. Did you tell him?"

James and Bob just look at each other with blank stares.

So I, ignore these guys, and start to leave the galley.

On my way out I say, "Break time is over, fellas. Get back to work."

I head back to the sonar room and sit at a station.

I fervently type an encrypted message to ASWOC.

Tad is, sitting nearby, still looking stupid.

"I wouldn't worry about it. I've seen this over and over ever since we got here. I think it's just an anomaly."

I ignore him.

USS ALASKA 0922 HOURS
ASWOC URGENT
ANOMALIES AT OUR LOCATION
REPEATED ANOMALIES
AT OUR LOCATION
PLEASE REVIEW AOAIA
PLEASE ADVISE
T. WATSON

I hit send and look at Tad who shockingly asks me, "So what do you want for Christmas?"

NATIONAL SECURITY AGENCY (NSA)

One year ago

For twenty years the U.S. government didn't even acknowledge that the NSA existed. In fact, its nickname was 'No Such Agency.'

Scores of satellites were put up in space, from all sorts of sister agencies.

Naval Ocean Surveillance System (NOSS),

Defense Support Program (DSP),

National Reconnaissance Office (NRO),

Signals Intelligence (SIGINT) and,

Communications Intelligence (COMINT).

All of them had sent Fred Turner information personally.

Well not personally, but since Fred had named all of his "girls" he felt a personal connection to many key satellites sent into space by various U.S. defense agencies.

Fred Turner has been a civil servant and computer geek his whole life. He worked for the CIA in his early years at Langley looking over satellite images of ships, missiles and infantry movements of the old USSR.

Pretty boring stuff!

But the kind of job that came with a Top Secret security clearance, the highest in government. People will tell you there are all sorts of clearances above Top Secret but they don't know what they're talking about.

There are Special Access Programs (SAP) and other mission specific programs that are approved on a need to know basis. With this program the U.S. needed to know if the Russians were living up to their commitment under the New START treaty to dismantle nuclear weapons.

While the NSA doesn't have optical satellites, the optical satellites from all of the above agencies would send the NSA it's information to analyze.

So Fred moved over to the NSA in 2010 as part of a team watching Russia dismantle several nuclear ships. While they used to watch the Russians up close, a new chill in the air from Moscow forced them watch from 25,000 miles above Russia!

This created a huge blind spot where Fred couldn't see what the Russians were or weren't doing from time to time. And as good as satellites have gotten, the Russians had figured out how to fool American satellites.

The United States in its arrogance had rarely seen the need to use provisions of 'The Treaty on Open Skies', where unarmed planes are allowed to fly over an adversary's territory for surveillance. The U.S. "intelligence" community, in all its wisdom, thought: We can monitor the Russians just fine from a satellite 25,000 miles in space.

Fred's latest SAP clearance was to keep an eye on two Russian Typhoon class submarines, the Arkhangelsk (*TK-17*) and the Severstal (*TK-20*) both in dock and scheduled for dismantling ASAP. The military has acronyms for everything.

To show military absurdity, to the Nth degree, someone had put a sign on the Men's Bathroom Door (MBD):

M.B.D.
THOU SHALT NOT PASS
SAP CLEARANCE REQUIRED

A little humor at a Pretty Dull Job (PDJ).

These Typhoon class subs, the world's largest, were a fascination to Fred. They were built for the Cold War and made famous in Tom Clancy's novel, "The Hunt for Red October." But with the end of the Cold War, the Russians and Americans had warmed to each other and agreed to several START treaties. Those treaties basically reduced the numbers of nuclear weapons each side could continue to have on land, in air and at sea. The Typhoons were being dismantled as being too big and too expensive to maintain for the limited number of nuclear delivery devices each side could have.

There were six Typhoons originally built. The Typhoon SSBN division was based at Nerpichya, about six miles from the entrance to Guba Zapadnaya Litsa on the Kola Peninsula, close to the border with Finland and Norway.[6]

As far as the Americans knew, three were still in-tact but only one on active duty, the Dmitri Donskoy (*TK-208*). Aboard *TK-208* are twenty Bulava (NATO-code SS-N-30) intercontinental ballistic missiles with each missile carrying up to ten separate nuclear warheads. This gave this one sub an estimated 200 separate targets it could hit. Each missile, had a range of 10,000km or 6,200 miles. Park this off the East or West Coast and it could hit virtually any number of cities in North America.

The Russians had become more and more provocative over the past year sending submarines into the English Channel and up and down the East Coast of the United States. Fred thought it unusual the only area Russian subs had not been reported for years now, was Alaska and the West Coast of the United States.

As Fred opened his tuna fish sandwich for another boring lunch he took a second look at his screen and stopped chewing. He put his sandwich down and started manipulating two large color screens on his desk. Puzzled, he continued to search further and now only now began to chew.

He yelled out with a mouthful of food, "Jerry!"

A voice from the other side of the cubicle, rat maze, answered back, "Ya?"

Fred said, "Come here please."

Jerry Fredricks was even nerdier than Fred but knew just about everything there was to know about this now antiquated satellite system and its glitchy software. Jerry used to work in systems for the National Reconnaissance Office before coming to the NSA. Jerry rounded the corner of Fred's Fort Meade, Maryland cubicle.

Fred impatiently, says, "Look at these two pictures. See anything missing?"

Jerry looks at one dry dock screen from Severodvinsk, Russia and then the same dry dock on the next satellite pass. Jerry puzzled says, "Ya, no *TK-20* and no *TK-17*. When was this?"

Fred replies, "Last month. I was looking to archive the month and happened to see this. Now watch. Next satellite pass the sub is there again. Is it possible the image with the missing sub is another software glitch?"

"Impossible!" says Jerry with the confidence of General Patton since this would be admitting a mistake he should have caught.

Even Fred looks at the nerdy accountant type and can't believe his confidence.

"That's not *TK-20*. Whatever is sitting there is not a complete Typhoon." Fred points to the front nose cone that's missing.

"Ya, but aren't they supposed to be dismantling it?"

"But if you take a nose cone off a ship below the waterline here it would sink, right?"

"That's what I was wondering. Is it possible that's a decoy?"

You have way too much imagination, TV soldier."

"So why is it still floating?" Asks Fred.

Jerry says, "I wouldn't worry about it. They probably tore it apart early and have keel stands under the hull."

"This isn't a dry dock, Jerry. How do you get keel stands under a floating sub sitting in nineteen meters of water?

"I don't know. You're the expert," says Jerry. "They can't get half of their subs operational anyway. It's not like it disappeared into the ocean or somethin'."

"Say, you gonna eat the rest of that sandwich?"

GULF OF ALASKA

Jack Tanner's Diary
Present day

Few places in the world are darker than an overcast night on Alaskan waters, especially in late December. In the Klondike Gold Rush from 1897 to 1899 hundreds of marine accidents occurred in Southeastern Alaska and, too many mariners to count, had met their Maker in these exact conditions.

But for me, Jack Tanner, a third generation fisherman from Ketchikan, this night would give me one big frickin' fish story.

And just in time for Christmas too!

Right now, I just want to make it home for Christmas.

The alcohol has takin' a toll on me, what's left of my family and my partner, Mike Gardener.

Right now, we're in trouble.

Big trouble!

Our fifty-eight foot Northern Jaegar, I named *The Black Pearl*, is stalled and sitting dead in the water.

We're in no man's land!

We're stuck halfway between U.S Coast Guard Air Station Sitka and Station Ketchikan.

And it's all my fault!

I have no reason being out in the Gulf this far.

This is beyond stupid.

I'm going to get me and Mike killed.

And killed tonight!

Normally, I'd never be fishin' for anything this far out in December.

I'm well over forty miles from the nearest Coast Guard station.

But desperate times call for desperate...

Well, you know the word.

I owe a huge mortgage on my boat and desperately need money.

Mostly for my stupid alcohol habit!

This storm is closing in on us fast and we need to move!

I had already radioed the Coast Guard.

An MH-65 dolphin helicopter radioed back that they were at least seven minutes out, bucking gale force winds at around forty knots (But gusts were over 100!).

Hurry, I screamed into the two way!

I waited forever to make the call as we're fishing in a no fishing zone and, if we make it out of here alive, the Coast Guard will likely give me one big fine.

Mike was down in the engine room attempting to fix a fuel leak in my old Detroit Diesel.

Storm or no storm, I'm not about to ditch my only source of income into the black abyss!

You don't walk away from a $650,000.00 investment, especially when you were stupid enough to let the insurance lapse.

I'd been chasing fish all day and coming up empty. I know where the fish are supposed to be this time of year but, for some reason, they were nowhere to be found. I had three sonar systems on board but only one works. My old Veinland 3d sonar is operating but barely! I see what appears to be a large school of fish right below. Disgusted, I shake my head before yelling to Mike,

"Did you stop the leak?"

I didn't have time to hear an answer, as my boat is tossed like a toothpick clean out of the water.

When my boat returns to the water, it slams into the side of a pitch black wave.

There is such tremendous force, that Mike is thrown into the old, oily, engine and knocked unconscious.

I'm in the fully enclosed wheelhouse or, likely, would have been tossed overboard. instead, I hit the ceiling before crashing to the icy cold floor screaming in pain.

My leg has been broken, although, at this time, I'm not even aware of that.

As the ship bobs back and forth in the waves, my creaky old crate tries to right itself. I roll across the wet floor before struggling to my feet.

I wonder why it's so painful to walk.

Duh!

You have a broken leg.

To my astonishment, I see what appears to be a massive black object directly next to my ship that prevents me from capsizing.

The noise of my old ship against the side of this slick black ship is ear shattering.

In the confusion of the night I think it must be a container ship.

In disbelief, I check my instruments and see nothing!

I'd been drinking but not this much!

Totally bewildered, I panicked!

The pain is almost unbearable!

I don't understand!

How is a container ship not showing up on anything?

I must be dreaming.

I'm never drinking again.

I'm able to struggle to get off the bridge to Mike.

"Mike, Mike, you okay?"

No answer.

I feel like I have one of my benders on.

Zigzagging across the deck, suddenly feeling really drunk, I finally reach the engine compartment!

I stick my head inside.

I see Mike's bleeding forehead as he says,

"What the hell was that?"

I yell,

"Get out here, now!"

I look again and this enormous black ship appears to be submerging!

I don't know how I was able to get to my halogen work lights on that thing but I did.

To my disbelief, I see a huge, black, submarine!

Antennas all over a huge tower in the middle.

Fifty feet or more in the air!

The thing looks modern.

Slick black whale-like surface.

It slips quietly into the water and disappears into the darkness directly alongside of me!

Mike, holding his bleeding head, surfaces from the engine room, "What was it?"

I just stare at the cold, black water.

Nothing to say, I blankly look at Mike and think, who the hell will ever believe this?

PORTLAND STATE UNIVERSITY

B ored out of my mind, I sat there playing with my FBI badge and flashing it to a wall of the FBI surveillance van.

"John, John Denning, FBI."

That brought up a really painful memory.

Stop doing that, I said to myself.

I was losing my mind and getting really tired of eating fast food as I sat in a van on SW Broadway in downtown Portland.

Six months of watching Muhammad Al Aqsa, MAA, 24/7 had turned up absolutely nothing.

Nothing, unless you consider MAA's brother was still missing after going to Syria to fight with ISIS. As I said earlier, he was presumed to have been killed along with two of his friends. It appeared to the FBI that MAA had recruited his brother and friends into ISIS but there was no concrete evidence. Soon after his family had given up hope, MAA moved to Portland and started studying engineering at Portland State University and tried to get his private pilot's license. I considered these both red flags, but studying engineering in Oregon or getting a pilot's license certainly wasn't illegal.

Notes in the file from prior surveillance show MAA's mother begged Ahmed not to go and fight for ISIS. Our interview with MAA showed that he had made no comment one way or the other how he felt about his brother leaving to fight.

But as my boss once told me, "People becoming terrorists don't always understand the fine points of jihadi politics."

Our profile showed that Ahmed was always strong willed, even as a child, and that he had rarely listened to anyone.

While interesting, we needed much more evidence on MAA than his brother had been radicalized by someone. Phone and email taps, and tails, all done with a federal warrant, came up with zip.

Under our "new and improved" guidelines, if you hadn't seen a suspect doing anything illegal for six months, you "shall stop" all surveillance, period.

We had a court order allowing the surveillance to continue for another year but this would be the last day we'd be allowed to watch MAA.

Too bad because I seriously suspect this guy is planning something.

By the way, let me introduce you to my partner, Tom Watkins.

He actually had been sitting in the van this whole time but you never want to disturb Tom when he's eating and I never disturbed him as he always seemed to be eating!

So, as you might have guessed, sitting day and night and doing nothing but eat is not very healthy. Tom is a nice guy but he's about forty-five-pounds overweight and currently heading for forty-six.

He's eating a double cheeseburger and watching a video monitor of a parking enforcement officer, outside the van, write a ticket and slap it on our window.

"How much you think she makes an hour," Tom amusingly inquired.

"Not enough for the abuse she must take!" I said.

I've been meaning to ask you, have you seen your brother lately?"

"Which one?" I hesitantly asked.

You have two brothers? You never talk about your family."

"Well, they don't talk to me." I volunteered then thought to myself, "Why did I say that?"

"Why not?" Tom asks.

I definitely shouldn't have stumbled into this, I think to myself.

"I really don't want to talk about it."

Why not? Tom pushes, "What else have you got to do today?"

After a long pause I figure, "Oh what the heck."

"They don't talk to me 'cause they blame me for a lot of junk."

"Like what?" asks Tom.

Before I could stop my big mouth I say,

"My mother and my sister's suicides."

Tom stops eating and with a mouthful of hamburger he chokes out, "What?"

Well you really did it now JD. One year of FBI psychology profiling and you can't even make it work on yourself.

I pause. Take a deep breath and think about some really, really painful stuff. After a long pause,

"When I was a kid all of us, except my father, lived in this weirdo Oregon cult in the sticks. My sister got pregnant when she was sixteen to the cult leader. The cult leader who was against abortion secretly took her and, without anyone knowing, forced her to have an abortion. When she finally told my mother what happened, my mother made her feel so guilty that I think it drove her to commit suicide."

"I lived there with my mom 'til I understood better. Then one night when my mother told me I could never speak to my father again, I ran away."

"My mother, feeling guilty, I guess about all of this, committed suicide too."

"I found out he died just days before I located where he was living."

"I think he died of a broken heart."

I really am an idiot. I really didn't want to tell this story to anyone at work. It was in my personnel file but no partner ever knew this, until now. I really have a big mouth sometimes. Annoying even myself at this point, I continued, "After my sister committed suicide I tried to get my mother out but I was never allowed to see her. She died never seeing me or my father ever again."

"How awful! How old were you?"

"Ten."

"You were ten years old when your mother and sister killed themselves?"

I'm embarrassed and all that comes out is,

"Ya."

Oh my god, how many years were you in therapy?

"Sixteen."

"You were in therapy for sixteen years? With who?"

"Navy SEALs."

Tom hasn't eaten another bite of hamburger since the double suicide line but now a half chewed hamburger just hangs out of his half open mouth.

"That's disgusting. Close your mouth," I said.

Tom catches himself and swallows his burger whole with one big gulp before saying,

"So you've been kicking down doors ever since trying to save people?"

"Ya. I never looked at it quite like that before but ya, I guess so."

Just then MAA appears on another monitor and we hear him speak with someone.

All our attention is suddenly directed to this conversation.

It turns out to be just brief chit-chat.

MAA walks off campus and down the street.

Tom says, "Okay, JD you're on. Bring me back a piece of huckleberry pie."

"If you put on any more weight sitting in here eating all day the FBI's gonna put you on the 'TFS' list."

The name was not politically correct but most agents were annoyed with all of the stupid politically correct rules that put more emphasis on file names than on catching criminals.

Official name: Weight Efficiency Program (WEP).

Unofficial name: "The Fat Squad (TFS!)!"

No agent wants to be "weight" listed as you are pulled out of the field and put behind a desk, sent to a doctor and told to eat better.

Tom says, "Maybe I'll get my lawyer and sue them for my "glandular problem."

I jump out of the van, look back at Tom and say,

"And good luck with that!"

I slam the van door on Tom before he has a chance to answer.

For some reason I hadn't noticed, this city is beautiful.

Garland, lights and wreaths are everywhere.

I high tail it across the street in hot pursuit of MAA. We walk a few blocks to, Jamil's, a five-star Middle East restaurant.

No wonder my partner's huge: Portland's a great city for food!

I suspect part of that reason is that, with so much rain, ambitious people want to do something with their time. So, many people who love food spend that time working on their cooking skills.

There are more five-star food carts with Indian and Thai food here than probably anywhere in America.

I walked across the street and into a little dive that will, likely, soon be out of business. I knew Tom preferred the Pacific Pie Company, Petunia's, or Divine Pie but if they baked anything today that would just have to do, Mr. TFS.

Inside this place are only four tables. It was empty, as always. I sat down by the only window seat in this dreary, damp, dark, little hole in the wall so I could watch my target.

Sally, the sweet looking, waiter-owner comes over to me saying, "So JD what can I get you?"

"How 'bout a cup of coffee, Sally?"

She answers with a nod and disappears behind an old, greasy Indian beaded curtain.

I look across the street and can see MAA busing tables. I pull out my iPhone 7 and scroll through the video feeds we'd set up at Jamil's crowded restaurant.

This really is a waste of time. A kid is probably just trying to get an engineering degree, bussing tables. What have we become?

I also felt bad for Sally who is dying financially and no wonder, she's probably back there making her first fresh pot of coffee and it's 5 p.m.

But the slow service and little chit-chat was perfect for surveillance.

I felt like someone was watching me but when I looked in that direction, no one was there. I returned to my texting.

In the reflection of my black glass iPhone, I can see a man with a plain white keffiyeh (Muslim headdress) walking up behind me.

He walks right behind my line of sight.

The man slowly reaches in his vest pocket as if to go for a gun.

I wheel around and grab the guy's right trigger finger when I realize it's Yusef Abdullah.

Yusef quickly pulls out a piece of paper and throws it at me.

I reach down to the floor and pick up the paper.

Yusuf is upset and slow to respond, "I can't help you any longer, John."

"You're not helping me, Yusef, you're helping your country!"

"I've been your friend since school but this isn't right," chides Yusuf.

"Yusuf, please sit down. Let's discuss this."

A very long pause cuts through the strained relationship between us.

Yusuf finally pulls a chair and sits.

Sally, Yusuf's wife, who is watching us from afar, now brings some coffee and two cups. She nervously pours the coffee for us as we stare down each other.

Sally quickly leaves, as it is forbidden in their particular religious sect to linger while the men discuss business.

I then boldly ask, "How much are you losing here?"

Without hesitating, Yusuf answers, "Too much. But that doesn't mean you can take advantage of our relationship and think you can buy me off!"

"Wow! You think I'm buying you off? We don't know if this guy's dangerous or not!" I return to looking across the street in MAA's direction.

"He came to my mosque. I volunteered to get him work. Then you show up. Are you my friend or an FBI agent?"

Without hesitation I answer, "Both!"

Yusuf says. "I can no longer be seen with you! People at the Islamic Center already think I'm with the government."

"So are you against the government?"

"Of course not but…"

"So, whose side are you on?" I ask.

Yusuf quickly answers, "Mine!"

Now there's another long pause and, as we stare out the window, it begins to rain.

My phone buzzes. I check it and Tom sent the following text: Don't forget the huckleberry pie!!!

I think to myself sarcastically, that's all Huckleberry needs, another pie!

I then return my attention to what's important saying,

"How would you feel if this guy shoots up a bunch of people or sets off a bomb?"

Yusuf stands, "I can't help you any longer."

As Yusuf starts to leave I then hesitantly ask, "Did Sally make huckleberry pie today?"

Yusuf stops, and then without turning around, leaves.

Great! Did I really just really lose a twenty-year friendship over this?

What if this guy's really just someone who we're profiling for no reason?

Sometimes I hate my job.

I stand, pull a hundred-dollar bill and lay it on the table.

As I exit the restaurant, rain is pouring.

I can see Tom's very disappointed face.

Per standard procedure, I purposely walk down the street, away from the restaurant and van.

I look back over my shoulder and see Sally running out to Tom's van with a big bag.

Tom purposely pulls the van near the restaurant so Sally doesn't get too wet.

Sally hands Tom the big bag and runs back into the restaurant.

I continue walking in the opposite direction, shaking my head.

I walk around the corner as Tom quickly pulls to the curb alongside me. I casually look behind the van before stepping inside.

Tom is already tearing into an entire huckleberry pie.

"Fat squad here you come!"

Tom ignores the insult, "Let me introduce you to my psychiatrist. Wanna a piece?"

"You know what we call that? A Man Caused Disaster!"

Tom casually looks up and with a mouthful of food says, "MCD?"

MOSCOW, RUSSIA - LUBYANKA SQUARE

While Portland, Oregon today is raining and a dreary forty-five degrees Fahrenheit, Moscow's high is a brisk twenty-six degrees with six inches of snow!

At night the streets are absolutely beautiful!

Lights, lights and more lights!

It's definitely Christmas season in Moscow.

There are over 3,000 trees with Christmas lights. A giant red ball is in Red Square with a map of the world on it, the center, of course, is Moscow!

Today, a very secret meeting has been called for Russia's top military leaders at Lubyanka Square, inside the old KGB building, 900 meters from Red Square.

General Petrov Andropov, General Sergei Aleksandrov, General Aleksandr Bortnikov and Admiral Victor Perchinkov sit in General Andropov's office. It might be below freezing outside but inside it was exactly seventy-six degrees. The general's office is decorated in beautiful Italian White Carrara marble and African black woods. General Andropov loved his caviar, vodka and women. Andropov was an old friend and longtime business associate of President Ivan Mironovich and was, in fact, appointed to office personally by the president.

Generals Aleksandrov and Bortnikov were from the SVR and GRU military wings, respectively. Based on all of the most recent consolidation of power toward one man, we might as well call all of these old agencies the KGB.

Admiral Perchinkov is clearly the brightest of the bunch. The admiral is also a close, personal friend and business partner of the president.

Fact is, all of these guys are close and have many business dealings with each other.

One prominent example of their business dealings in which they've entangled some of the largest American companies, is the Skolkovo Innovation Center, Russia's Silicone Valley.

It is built on the old Russian Potemkin Village model: Beautiful and perfect on the outside with all sorts of devious rot on the inside.

It is located just outside of Moscow with 30,000 workers all under the strict control of the "president's counsel." It is a secret organization with an even more secret board of directors. About 100 major American corporations have business dealings here. This entanglement was considered so dangerous that the Boston FBI warned American corporations in 2014:

"The [Skolkovo] foundation may be a means for the **Russian government to access our nation's sensitive or classified research development facilities** and dual-use technologies with military and commercial application. [Emphasis added]."

With the end of Communism, as Russia was attempting to transition to a market economy, only a handful of oligarchs fully understood what was happening and profited immensely. They were known as the siloviki clan. They were mostly former Communists from the KGB and other military agencies. They were in the right place when this Russian form of capitalism took root.

There is nothing exactly like them in the West. The closest explanation would be to combine billionaires, mobsters and generals.

It's a lethal combination when you combine crony capitalists with nuclear weapons!

Around these cronies grew a few but very wealthy crime syndicates who would intimidate and, if necessary, kill to further their business interests, generally with the quiet blessing of the Russian government. If you were one of them you could get away with murder: literally.

Although many Russians are living far better than they were under Communism, by Western standards, many people are still far behind.

The employed were just happy they weren't forced to drive the Communist East German car, the Trabant, voted the world's worst automobile ever created!

The Trabant had a smoke-induced, ear-splitting 18 horsepower engine, and you were lucky if you could find one that ran.

Basically, the Trabant had a very large lawnmower for an engine.

In fact, the West had lawnmowers that could probably beat a Trabant in a drag race.

It cost, at the time, about five years' worth of the average East German's salary, and you were told never to buy one made on a Friday. That was because most of the "people's workers" would get their free bottle of vodka that day and would likely knock off early. There was no telling what would be missing on your beautiful new Trabant.

Today, amazingly, the official unemployment rate of Russia tracked very close to that of the United States except, of course, it was always slightly better!

Coincidence?

Maybe, but since the government now controls most everything in Russia, probably not.

As Winston Churchill once said, "Russia is a riddle wrapped in a mystery inside an enigma."

Kind of like a matryoshka doll, also known as a Russian nesting doll. The doll is a set of increasingly smaller dolls placed one inside another.

A perfect description of Russia. Things are usually not exactly as they appear on the outside.

With the end of the Cold War and the fall of Communist USSR, Russia was made to feel inferior and less than the West. President Ivan Mironovich came to power vowing to stop this slide. Ivan vowed to return Russia to its former glory.

But Russia was so far behind militarily, it could not have any hope of catching the West either in sheer military numbers or in military aerospace technology.

Admiral Perchinkov knew Russia could not beat America in a naval battle head to head. However, with sixty-five submarines (twenty-four more in the works), the Russian submarine fleet (now under the personal direction of President Mironovich) looks like Russia is trying to beat America under the great oceans of the world.

For a while President Mironovich really did try to better relations with the U.S. His FSB warned the FBI about the Boston bomber, Tamerlan Tsarnaev, but the FBI didn't catch a misspelling of the terrorist's name until it was too late. The FSB had stopped several terror attacks on Russian soil but the FSB had, in some ways, become a very sophisticated terror group itself as it now moved, seemingly, against anyone hostile to the president.

Several courageous Russian journalists had written articles on the massive amounts of money being poured into Skolkovo and submarine technology but now those voices had mysteriously gone silent. This wasn't mysterious to the average Russian over the age of forty. They could see what was happening. Russia was transitioning into this weird form of an oligarchy, run by communist KGB, oil and gas billionaires.

Six reporters had turned up dead and several others were jailed for investigating the Russian military. Opposition leaders and journalists had been trashed, imprisoned or ended up murdered as well.

A political consultant commented, "This is a now a Weimar atmosphere where there are no longer any limits."

Weimar is obviously a reference to the regime just prior to the Nazi takeover of Germany.

This is the greatest insult you can tell a Russian as the Nazis attacked Russia and killed many millions of Russians in World War II.

But there is some truth to the Weimar insult. Russia is now the third deadliest country in the world for journalists only behind Algeria and post war Iraq!

With President Ivan Mironovich graduating more pilots, taunting American warships, making new ICBMs and running massive war games, the military has boosted his popularity in Russia to over eighty percent.

Crazy Ivan was even more emboldened in his plan to restore Russia, knowing he had a far higher approval rating in the U.S. and Great Britain than their own president and prime minister!

Mironovich, through his friends, have let it be known that he does not want a repeat of the 100,000 people who marched in Moscow in 2011 against him. The President, a former KGB officer in the old Soviet Union, is so paranoid that he still believes the CIA was behind that protest. So President Mironovich is doing all he can to insure his own reelection would proceed without any disturbances.

So why are all of these generals assembled in the same room at the old KGB headquarters near Red Square?

All these Russians have seen much weakness in the U.S. and, now, believe they have a way to "help" the world.

Just in case anything went wrong, and nuclear war broke out, they could always retreat to the Metro-2 running under the Kremlin to their hardened command posts some 275 meters below ground! This Top Secret Metro-2 line is rumored to travel to several hardened military sites and directly under the president's house. Metro-2 travels all the way to Vnukovo airport, just in case they start a war and someone fights back, they can make a quick get a way.

Admiral Perchinkov presided over an aging fleet of outdated ships, mostly relics of the old Cold War. He knew what most every expert in the world had concluded. Irreversible collapse of the Navy was imminent. Instead, he managed the impossible. He modernized his 271-ship Navy at an incredibly rapid pace.

The problem was many commanders now were refusing orders to be more aggressive against Western and especially American planes, ships and subs.

The situation had become so bad that Admiral Perchinkov was promoted to Minister of Defence.

That meant the only person he would now answer to would be President Mironovich.

This quiet little move made Admiral Perchinkov the second most powerful man in all of Russia.

All submarine orders would now be given directly from the president's office to Admiral Perchinkov and not go first to naval command.

In addition, the new admiral had been given the task of sacking over fifty naval commanders in his Baltic Fleet for refusing to follow presidential orders.

Many considered this similar to some of Stalin's famous military purges.

It is clear to any reasonable observer what's going on. The president was consolidating power with his siloviki clan loyalists. Any dissenting opinion and you were, at best, not trusted, at worst you could end up missing and nobody wanted to end up missing.

Jane's Fighting Ships, the Bible of military assessments, felt the emphasis the Russians were putting on their submarines for fighting old Cold War scenarios was misplaced, but even Jane's had no idea what the Russians were really up to. In fact, no one in the West had a clue as to what had been transpiring for five years on American soil.

It's not good to keep such powerful men waiting. Not good unless you're the right hand man to the most powerful man in Russia, President Ivan Mironovich.

Viktor Sokolov was a serious man with immense power. The president trusted this child prodigy with his life. So everyone waited patiently.

Russian history is full of great drama and a great drama is once again about to unfold.

Finally, Viktor Sokolov, enters with a leather briefcase, dressed in a $2,000.00 Italian suit.

An eerie hush falls over the room. Sokolov is not happy that he is leading this meeting and that he had to walk over here from his office in the Kremlin. Sokolov was a man of business and didn't believe in chitchat.

Viktor pulls exactly four sealed envelopes from his black Italian briefcase. He passes them out as he speaks.

"Good morning. The President sends you his warmest greetings. He is sorry he could not be here personally but he assures you he is working hard to make this project successful."

"In front of you are sealed orders directly from the president."

"Your president has attempted friendship with America."

"We invited business leaders and U.S. Senators here."

"We paid them over five billion Rubles for a few speeches."

"We have wined and dined and come up empty handed."

"Those days are now past."

"The United States is pushing Russia into what we know will be disaster."

"The U.S. is waging proxy wars in Eastern Ukraine and Syria and forcing confrontations in the South China Sea. There is an increasing likelihood that one of these will flare into an all-out military conflict with the United

States. Should this occur, *Proyekt 239* would be necessary for us to have leverage against the United States and their military superiority in terms of sheer numbers. But we Russians like to play chess and we want to stay a few moves ahead of the Americans."

"Last time the Americans and their President Reagan forced us into an arms race, the result was the bankruptcy of Russia."

"This time it is us that shall force the United States into bankruptcy."

"The Americans have unsustainable debt, just as we had in 1990."

"The difference is the United States dollar is the reserve currency of the world and will take the rest of the world into bankruptcy."

"We will not let that happen, will we?"

All the generals present mumble, "Nyet."

"When the dominos fall this time we want to be the last ones standing. While America is talking about turning aircraft carriers like the, *USS Peleliu*, into homeless shelters we're building bomb shelters for millions capable of withstanding a nuclear attack."

Sokolov continues, "U.S. and NATO are now conducting war games on our borders regularly. US destroyers are in our Black Sea to 'promote peace.' Their planes and submarines are coming closer and closer to our homeland."

"It is time to increase our military operations in the United States of America."

"The Americans have noticed we have increased our submarine operations by fifty percent in retaliation to their aggression. It is only a matter of time until one of our submarines are found and sunk just like during the days of our fathers and grandfathers."

"The Americans have been trying to flood the world with cheap oil and gas to bankrupt us again. They have allowed ISIS and Iran to sell oil to undercut their own allies like Saudi Arabia, all for one sole purpose: To once again drive our Russian oil and gas companies out of business."

"Now we move quickly."

"We have President Mironovich's full authorization to proceed."

"You will see his signature and instructions in your orders."

"Phase I of *Projekt 239* is now complete."

"The President has given the order to proceed to Phase II, the AK Phase."

"Any questions?"

"I have a journalist asking questions about *239*," says General Aleksandrov.

Sokolov looks long and hard at this seasoned general before choosing his words carefully. "Journalism can be a very dangerous business. Handle it!"

TK-20, JUNEAU, ALASKA

Captain Vasili's Diary

O ne reason I love submarine is that I travel anywhere without visa.

That was little Russian joke.

On other hand, you have a much greater chance of winding up dead, especially if you are on a Russian ballistic missile submarine 139 miles off the coast of Alaska.

Our very first caterpillar sub, TK-17 disabled the U.S. Navy's underwater listening system in the Aleutian Islands. Specialists placed mock recordings of normal ocean sounds near their hydrophones to disguise our submarine sounds as we passed by.

I'm writing in my diary as there is little else I do now.

Morale of men: Good.

Good considering that we are thousands of miles from home and looks like will not be back in time for a traditional Russian Christmas on January 7th.

My last diary entry was: Oh God, no!

I think I had just realized part of my mission.

Now I had it confirmed in writing. Russians generally have hard time conveying their inner feelings. We protect these like you'd protect your own child.

I'd like to review a bit.

First, I'm told there are rooms on my sub off limits to my own crew and me.

Only after underway was I allowed to open 'Top Secret' orders given directly to me by my old friend Admiral Victor Perchinkov. Orders state that the kid, my second in command, Kapitan Nikolai Alexi, would be in charge of Phase II of mission.

I knew it!

I no longer am trusted by my "old friend."

My thirty years of command has been taken over by an arrogant kid.

I joined the Navy before this kid was born!

And then, to add insult to injury, I don't find this out until in American Waters!

This was what old Soviet Union did, not healthy democracy.

I really wished he sacked me before I left Russia!

I would be home now enjoying life with my wife.

No!

Admiral Perchinkov waited to tell me this until after I safely snuck past the *USS Alaska* sitting at the bottom of the Arctic Ocean.

I engaged our Top Secret caterpillar drive and flew through American waters which alone is an act of war!

I helped design that drive for peaceful purposes not to create next World War!

Admiral Perchinkov used my skills and now has relieved me of command.

In old USSR days, nearly all Soviet ships had aboard a political officer or commissar. These people held the same rank as commander of ship and could order an attack or force a stand-down order. The commissar's order was to be followed just as if they commanded the ship. In some key ships and army units there would be two commissars. These two could overrule any commander and take any action in furtherance of Rodina, or the Motherland.

While Rodina is only political party and banned today, some of its mythical ideas live on in hearts and minds of siloviki clan, especially with President Ivan Mironovich.

Only one more reason I didn't like or trust the president or anyone from this idol worshipping, billionaire, nut bag club.

I put kid in nut bag category.

I don't trust him at all.

I thought the horrid days of Motherland worship were gone but come to find out, Motherland has simply been replaced by new god, Crazy Ivan.

This kid is going to get us all killed.

First, the idiot surfaced underneath an Alaskan fishing boat!

I'm shocked entire American Navy hasn't already blown us out of water and put us on eternal patrol!

Suicide mission, I thought, although I would never, ever utter these words aloud.

I knew every one of these kids, under my "former" command are loyal as if they were Soviet soldiers fighting Hitler.

I've figured out what Admiral Perchinkov is up to.

And I'm not about to kill a bunch of Americans for our new Fuehrer.

Little brat was at top of his class in every school he attended and he acted like it. The brat had orders from Moscow that were as if the President had spoken them himself.

In other words, my boat had been taken over by modern day political officer!

Kapitan Nikolai came from billionaire silokivi clan parents. His father was CEO of several oil and gas companies owned by the state, including GazProm, the world's largest gas producer. So this kid would be set for life no matter what he chose to do.

But Nikolai's file also showed he had a very high level of ambition. He had risen to ranks of a commander in a GRU Spetsnaz Team very quickly.

Nikolai was also a true believer in "the glory days" of old USSR.

Nikolai indicated in his file that he would do anything, anything to return Russia to those days. Trouble was those days never existed anywhere except in books and in minds of true believers, like Nikolai's father.

Young in Russia today have been brought up in government schools and owe their entire careers to their "beloved" President.

A new twisted, modern day, version of Rodina has been resurrected from the ashes with Crazy Ivan as its godhead.

So Nikolai was in control room and it was buzzing. Several large color screens were searching the seabed in Gulf of Alaska. I was sitting at back of room in "observers seat."

I can't tell you the insult that this was being conveyed to me by the kid.

Sonar officer, Dmitri Rostislav, yells over the subs speaker system, "Conn, sonar, ten meters."

"Aye, all stop," Nikolai Alexi commands.

He then looks carefully at monitors.

They are looking at a murky seabed at the bottom of Gulf of Alaska.

A black cable no bigger than twelve inches around is seen. This cable goes into a large box that is called an Undersea Branching Unit.

"We're here. Tell divers to prepare," says Alexi.

This fiber optic line, AKORN, Alaska-Oregon Network is fastest system connecting Alaska with Internet and world. The cable is nerve center of communication between Homer, Alaska and Florence, Oregon. This branching station is intended to eventually connect Juneau and Southeast Alaska with fastest fiber optic system in world.

In meantime, my *TK-20* would be speeding up that by completing Phase II of *Proyekt* 239, not exactly in the way intended by AKORN designers.

"Divers are in hatch and sealed," I hear.

"Flood hatch and release," commands Alexi.

Soon after I hear, "Sdelannyy. Zakonchennyy." (English: "Done. Finished").

At this point I stood up to leave room and no one even noticed. I left the conn thinking,

I might as well go read a good book and finish decorating my tiny Christmas tree.

In fact, I'd rather be home reading a good book.

But I never let those worries reflect on my face. I certainly didn't want to let the green eyed twenty something's in conn room see my concerns.

My crew was ready and willing to change world or die trying.

I wasn't.

NEW YORK HOTEL

Ketchikan, Alaska

t's early morning on Christmas Eve.

As is usual for Ketchikan, it's raining outside.

The rain had followed me from Portland to my hotel last night. I hadn't seen the sun for a month, except on Mt. Hood last week. The sun also peaked out on the flight to Ketchikan when we flew above a thick layer of rain clouds.

Snow was on the mountains but an unusual warm spell, 45 degrees today, had washed away all the snow in town.

The rain was so gentle on my window that it couldn't even be heard over the TV.

An anchor from a local news show, Alaska Today, says:

"Concern has been raised that this deal will raise Russian control of the U.S. uranium market to about twenty percent. Due to low prices on the world market most uranium mines in the United States have been shuttered. Currently, the U.S. imports about half of its uranium from Russia for use in its nuclear power plants..."

I was not paying any attention.

Guess I should have been.

My flight in was unremarkable. I always loved this quirky little airport. The airport is, in fact, on a separate island across The Tongass Narrows from the quaint little town. To get to town you must be ferried across The Narrows.

Ah, Alaska, what an adventuresome place!

My room at the 'New York Hotel' was built at the turn of the last century. The room had authentic wood doors, beamed ceilings and hand quilted bedspreads!

The street wasn't really noisy but the room did come equipped with ear plugs, just in case.

I'm a night owl and generally go to sleep around 2am. However, four or five hours of sleep was all I needed so it wasn't a big deal.

The café downstairs would have great local musicians and comedians perform on weekends.

Ketchikan was a small town, filled in spring and summer with mostly cruise ship tourists wandering up and down Creek Street. Creek Street is a fun place, built entirely over a creek filled with thousands of salmon during spawning season. I overheard a tourist there once say, "Why are we taking a boat fishing, I could just fish here!"

I thought, "What's the fun in that?"

In season, thousands of tourists, dodging the rain, would buy all sorts of crazy, worthless, Chinese made trinkets, from a variety of brightly painted little shops, pretty much all owned by the cruise lines!

At a glance, about all there was to see in Ketchikan were tourist traps, rain and totem poles!

When I get back I'll probably walk downstairs to the New York Cafe and celebrate Christmas with all the other lonely drunks. The guy I met last night worked at about the only jewelry shop left open in town. The jeweler was in bright, ruby red shoes. He was very depressed that he hadn't convinced anyone "in days" to purchase a "top quality diamond" from him.

I wish the Great Alaskan Lumberjack Show was playing down by the dock.

Log rolling!

Those were the days.

The Willamette River in Portland, Oregon in July. Doug Meyers! What a jerk! He would cut a log lose from a pack then would dare me to knock him off the log. He and I would run on the floating logs to see who'd hit the river first. I think I held the neighborhood record.

Of course, Doug might have a very different version of that story.

Nothing much floats in the Willamette River today other than house boats, dead fish or dead bodies.

Anyway, my hotel room was upstairs just across Stedman Street where I could see the docks and the cruise ships. But since this is winter, no cruise ship is in port. I was so close to the water that I could literally walk across the street and fall into the Gulf of Alaska.

Technically, it's the Thomas Basin but hey, it's the same body of water.

I'd gone to Ketchikan on fishing trips in the past but this was business.

I'd volunteer for any dangerous job but this one was "supposed to be" boring and routine.

Ya, it was Christmas Eve.

Ya, I'd be spending another one on the road but I didn't have anything better to do.

I had no family in Oregon but there would be no better Christmas present to innocent citizens than to put a murderer behind bars.

I had no plans for tonight anyway.

However, this night I would never make it back to Ketchikan.

Little did I know that the next two days would change my life forever.

I was to rendezvous with another FBI Special Agent out of the Juneau office and arrest a felon by the name of George Ruddy. Now George had managed to convince the local Sheriff's office in Clackamas County, Oregon that he was dead, not a small feat.

The Oregonian ran his obituary and his, girlfriend, "beneficiary" was just about to cash a two-million-dollar life insurance policy on George.

However, my forensic team looked into the case and found good old George had fooled just about everyone. Just about everyone but us. I sent what was left of "George" for biometric DNA analysis to our FBI lab in rural Virginia.

George was burned in a house fire so badly that very little of him was "allegedly" left. Since he lived in a rural community no one noticed the fire for hours and hours. But for a body to be this decomposed the Oregon forensic specialist said he'd have had to have been soaked in heating oil, and set on fire for hours. His beneficiary said that's exactly what happened.

The beneficiary was conveniently away for the weekend and there was a leak in the 200-gallon heating oil tank in the basement.

As the story went, he was trying to plug a hole in the tank when, talking on his cell phone to his girlfriend he dropped it, causing a spark and catching him on fire.

It all sounded very "fishy" to me from the get go.

All that was recovered were teeth and bone fragments, that were, in fact, George's. But the huge mistake the couple made was to incinerate the body of another person. The second DNA sample that my team personally took turned out to be partially George's "friend," Albert Tuck.

Pseudocide is not very common, except maybe in novels but my team found out George, while looking common and uneducated, was anything but.

George received his undergraduate degree in mathematics from Harvard and his Ph.D. from the University of Michigan. He then taught upper division mathematics at Harvard University.

George was, clearly, no dummy. He had managed to fool the Clackamas County Medical Examiner and a forensic pathologist of the Oregon State Police. Had it not been for my team, this case would have been closed months ago.

But George's Oregon Trail had grown cold. A local journalist with a big mouth and a penchant for making a name for himself spilled the beans about the FBI test results and the beneficiary vanished.

No one could positively identify her and no picture of her even existed, which was highly unusual. No fingerprints in the burned house or car turned up any woman at all!

The only thing everyone said about her was she had fair skin, bright red hair and was drop dead gorgeous.

No offense to Oregon but there just aren't that many unidentified, drop dead gorgeous women living in the woods!

An avid reader of the Oregonian saw George's picture while on vacation fishing in Ketchikan. The witness swore he had spotted George on these docks getting on a boat!

The owner of that boat told the Ketchikan police that a man, fitting George's description, paid cash and asked to be taken to Prince of Wales Island.

It seemed very suspicious. There are fishing lodges over on the west side of the island in Craig but George was dropped to very specific GPS coordinates on the uninhabited south east side.

Now Alaska is made up of over 3,000 islands with only about 1,500 of them named.

Prince of Wales Island is huge.

It's the size of the country of Ireland and slightly larger than the state of Delaware!

The island is the fourth largest in the United States, with a coastline of approximately 1,000 miles!

That's right 1,000 miles of coastline.

Roughly the distance from Los Angeles, California to Portland, Oregon! The sheer vastness of this one rugged island alone would be the perfect place for someone to disappear.

Standing in my hotel room, the show, Alaska Today, is discussing President Obama's nuclear speech in Japan from 2016:

"We've all become more enlightened since President Obama's Hiroshima speech earlier this year that called on the world to ban nuclear weapons. At that time, the Prime Minister of Japan, Shinzō Abe, agreed. However, since then, Japan has become concerned that the United States would be the only major power in the world to commit to "No First Use." Meaning the United States would not be the first to use nuclear weapons in the event of a crisis. Many countries such as Japan rely on the United States as an umbrella to help protect them against aggression from their neighbors. Without that umbrella, Japan and others, are threatening to develop their own nuclear weapons. Russian President Ivan Mironovich has stated that Russia would not sign an agreement pledging no first use."

I just didn't really pay much attention to global politics.

Again, looking back, I should have.

The phone rings, so I turn off the TV and answer the phone, "Denning."

For agents that didn't know me, I used only my last name, as sometimes that was the only name on my reports.

"Ya, okay, I'll be right down." I hung up, grabbed my trusty, black drab, parka, and handcuffs, holstered my Glock 23, .40 Cal, and headed out the door.

Outside the rain had stopped but looked like it could pour at any time, typical of Ketchikan and Portland.

Feels like home.

Sitting at the dock across the street from the New York Hotel was a fifty-eight foot Northern Jaegar.

His "boat" had barely squeezed into the Thomas Basin, boat moorings and docks. Our ride had managed to back his fishing boat right up to the Stenson Bayside Float which I could see from my hotel window.

The crazy guy has red and green Christmas lights all over his boat.

It seemed there were more Christmas lights on the boats than on the businesses and homes!

But I did see a Totem Pole with Christmas lights.

So I walk across the street to the docks. As I walk toward the boat the captain is standing on the dock, which had the smell of creosote. The captain had the smell of diesel and alcohol.

The captain was talking with who, I hope, is my partner for the day. She looks much better in person than her mug shot in the FBI database.

Her black hair looks to be tucked in a tight bun and well hidden.

She stood out like a sore thumb. A beautiful woman, all dressed up and talking with this crusty old fisherman with a cane.

I sure hope she isn't a tourist but instead is my Profile Softening Partner (PSP) for the day.

The PSP was an acronym I made up that spread throughout the FBI like wildfire. In my Navy SEAL days with Black Squadron, several operators, both men and women, had been paired so as to not stand out in surveillance and espionage. In Afghanistan, the military had an acronym for this too: CEU (Cultural Engagement Unit). Women, especially in the Middle East, could look less threatening walking into a dangerous situation.

I quickly slap myself back to reality as I introduce myself.

"John Denning, Special Agent, Portland FBI."

Jennifer shook my hand and replied, "Jennifer Tavana, Special Agent, Juneau FBI and this is Jack Tanner and his partner, Mike Gardener, is on the boat somewhere."

I then say, "So you guys didn't have anything better to do on Christmas Eve either?"

Jack ignores my insult saying, "Three hours out. Three hours back. Assuming the weather holds."

I'm a bit concerned, "And if it doesn't?"

"The weather across the Clarence Strait can turn on a dime. If I see the line of death, I'm not crossing. The swells can go from nothing to 25 feet or more in no time."

"I've looked at a map. Isn't that side of the island protected from the Gulf of Alaska?" I ask.

Jack smiles, "That strait acts like a funnel. When the tide is going out and a storm is coming in, wave frequency is amplified. On the other hand, I looked at the weather, we'll be back before dark, right Lieutenant-Commander?"

Jack is looking at Jennifer and I now realize who this woman is.

She's the first woman to command a U.S. submarine!

Girls shouldn't be doing "men" things (As you'll see, this philosophy will come back to bite, torture and nearly kill me!)

For now, I pretend not to know. The Navy Times said, Lieutenant-Commander Jennifer Tavana wasn't just the first woman to command a U.S. submarine, she also made it to commander in the shortest amount of time.

Great, I thought, now I'm seeing the face of political correctness.

The girl probably slept her way to the top.

I realize everyone is staring at me.

Jennifer and I both notice the strong stench of alcohol from the crusty captain, creosote from the wood on the docks and his diesel exhaust.

We both back away from the eye-watering fumes primarily emanating from him as it engulfed us.

I try making a joke of it all,

"Ah, nothing like the smell of creosote and diesel on the open waters!"

Nobody reacts to my bad joke so I shut up.

Jennifer Tavana's Diary

Great! These boys probably think I'm too girly and have no idea who I am or what I've done. Toughen up soldier girl!

I'm getting to the bottom of this story.

This drunken idiot thought he saw a "sub!"

Probably only after a 5th of Jack Daniels too!

The only reason I'm taking this drunk's boat is to get to the bottom of this fish story that's been going all over Southeast Alaska.

These sub sightings have gone on for the past five years. And the fish stories are only growing. "Captain Jack" isn't the only moron that claims to have seen a sub. Seven Alaskans now swear they've seen a sub too. What makes me think they might have some credibility is they all describe the exact same type of boat without any pictures or diagrams and none have any naval experience or know each other.

A RUSSIAN S.S.B.N.
TYPHOON BOOMER!

Impossible!

I'm the only one, on my own time, who's gone out and interviewed all seven people. If I told the FBI what I was doing, I'd probably no longer be an agent.

While most people are wonderful here in Alaska, there are also a few crazy people that give us all a bad name.

Now everyone is staring at me, the girly girl!

My Diary

After the awkward moment the captain welcomes us aboard.

I'm thinking, well, that was just weird!

We all stood and stared at each other.

Maybe they all have PTSD!

Jennifer tosses her bug-out bag to Mike before stepping aboard.

Mike looks in the bag and starts taking inventory, "Four aluminum space blankets, four lighters, freeze dried food, reindeer jerky, a first aid kit, gauze, bandages, tape, scissors, a personal ELT and Celox."

Mike looks at Jen, "What the hell is Celox."

I'm already impressed with this "girl." She's definitely Ex-Navy. Anyone with a little military experience knows that Celox is an over-the-counter coagulant used to quickly stop bleeding.

Jen looks at me and I smile, probably the only other one on the dock, who gets it!

Mike continues in his ignorance, "Oh and a big frickin bottle of hydrogen peroxide."

I smile again thinking, Cheapest sterilization and disinfectant around!

Jennifer's Diary

My dad was a stickler for hydrogen peroxide.

I never want to hear my dad's voice going off in the middle of nowhere.

Could have used a bottle of peroxide now, couldn't you?

My mom fled Iran when I was just five. We had to leave dad behind. He was a doctor there and the government wouldn't let him leave because he was considered "necessary personnel."

My dad helped her and me flee the oppressive, totalitarian government to give her and me a better life. My mom found out my dad was jailed, tortured and killed by the Iranian government in 1990.

My mother enlisted in the Navy and studied nursing and was transferred to a Navy hospital ship. Women weren't allowed on any other types of ships in those days.

When my mother got out she went to the University of Alaska and got an engineering degree. She met a nice Aleut native on campus and before she left school they married and had their first child, my sister.

Again, this Denning guy looks handsome but he probably thinks I'm all beauty and no brains, which is exactly what he looks like.

I'm embarrassed with all of these gross men staring at me.

Mike tosses the ropes onto the ship and hops aboard.

I notice "Captain Jack" is trying to cover a very distinct limp.

As our crusty old fishing boat creeps away from the dock I make my way to the bridge.

I know I might not have another chance to talk with the captain alone about the sub.

"I know there's been a lot of talk around town about your tall tale, wanna tell me?"

Jack deflected, "Which one?"

I smile, "The one about the sub."

Jack shrugs, "Oh, I was drunk. Don't believe every story you hear."

I pause before asking, "So you made the whole thing up?"

Jack ignores me saying, "I gotta get us out of the Basin."

"Fair enough," I respond.

With that, Jack shows off his talents, by maneuvering slowly out of the Basin.

As we sputter down the Tongass Narrows, Jack is outside the bridge. I notice an old book casually sitting on the captain's chair.

I open it and realize this is the captain's own personal diary. As I thumb through the pages I see Jack, outside, is busy yelling at Mike.

I rifle through 'til I come to this page:

Tuesday
23:12 hours.
The water was black
The wind was howling at forty knots
(Gusts at over 100!)
I hadn't been drinking for hours
We're dead in the water. Engine out
Coast Guard called but still
nowhere in sight
I think we might die
But I won't let Mike know that

God please help me stop this vile habit
I will do anything
Anything
I would die tonight if I never,
Never could ever touch another
Drop of that vile thing called liquor.

I'm thinking, this is definitely the rantings of an alcoholic who likely saw something!

Jack is heading back to the bridge and, I don't know why, but I put his diary in my pocket and leave the bridge.

◆ ◆ ◆

My Diary

Mike and I join Jack and Jennifer on the bridge.

"Where we headed?" I ask looking at Jennifer.

Jennifer pulls out her cell phone,

"Our witness dropped the suspect alone at Kendrick Bay. Here are the coordinates."

Jack pulls out of his pocket an old Garmin hiking device and proceeds to put the coordinates into something that looks like it was purchased at Radio Shack in the late '90s.

So I ask Jennifer, "This is now what we're tracking criminals with?"

"Hey, it's my trusty satellite device. It will pinpoint right where you want to go," says Jack.

I then say, "Isn't that for hiking?"

"Ya, but isn't that what you might be doin'?" says Jack.

I say, "I have a better program on my phone."

"But there's no cell service in that area," says Jack. Then after a long pause, "Just as soon as it finds the satellites we'll be in business."

Jennifer reacts to me as if we may be a bit ill prepared.

I return the feeling but cover my thought by saying,

"This is why I volunteered. A nice Christmas Eve hike in the Alaskan wilderness."

Jack, clueless to all of this, reacts excited,

"Okay, I know right where we're going. Your man was let off on the east side of Prince of Wales Island."

Mike chimes in, "Looks like the south side of Kendrick Bay?"

"Ya, looks like it. The entire southern tip of the island is uninhabited." says Jack.

I volunteer, "Sounds like the perfect place for a guy who wants to stay dead."

Jennifer, "So three hours, right?"

Jack, "About."

At this point I'm very concerned saying, "Shouldn't we go back now and get some proper equipment?"

Jack says, "Like what?"

I say, "Oh I don't know, like maybe a good map!"

Jennifer, ignoring the sarcasm, "I've flown over this area. There's a barge on the south end that's occupied by only one person, an older man. The SAT images look like our suspect but I can't positively identify."

Jack says, "Kendrick Bay can be over 900 feet deep! Out in Clarence Strait the water can be as much as 1,600 feet deep. Glaciers carved out deep water around many of these islands. The Navy used to test sonar and submarines around here 'cause the water's so deep."

I'm clueless as to all of the red flags that should've been going off in all our heads.

Jennifer now whips out a detailed map,

"Okay, so this is where we're going. A Russian mining company holds claims to all these parts of Bokan Mountain and has built a dock here. We can walk right onto the beach from that dock."

I now have slightly more respect, "So we're just lost fishermen?"

Jennifer looks to Jack, "Did you bring them?"

Jack looks at Mike who's not paying attention.

Mike, "What? Oh ya."

Mike opens a drawer and pulls out some neon red overalls and some cheap things that look more like all you can eat bibs from Red Lobster!

I volunteer, "I'm not wearing target rich, school crossing jackets."

I then think, I've seen this disaster before on the slopes of Mt. Hood.

Jennifer enthusiastically throws a jacket to me saying,

"Today, we're fishermen."

"You mean, fisher people!" I disgustingly add.

Jack then tries to help, "Or fishers."

Jennifer now disgusted too,

"Whatever!"

Jack then breaks the tension, "If you need to use your phones, you have about ten minutes before you won't have a signal."

So I walk to the back of the boat and pull out my phone.

Ketchikan can now only be seen from the back of the boat in the distance. Ahead there is nothing but water and islands of rocks and trees.

It's peaceful and beautiful. On the other-hand I thought,

Maybe I should've updated my will.

◆ ◆ ◆

About two hours later I am looking at another, beautiful, Alaskan picture perfect shot. I snap a couple of shots on my phone of waterfalls gently gliding off of tall rocks and into the Narrows. The sun began to peek from between the clouds in a rare December appearance.

All four of us idiots now look like fisher "men" as we all have on neon gear, including the biggest target on the ship:

Me!

Jennifer has been talking up a storm on the bridge with Jack.

Mike walks toward me and jokingly says, "There! Now, you look like a fisherman!"

"I feel like Ken in a Barbie commercial! What's so important on the bridge?"

"Oh they're talkin' 'bout that stupid submarine thing," says Mike.

I think Mike is kidding, "What stupid submarine thing?"

Mike, "My boss thinks he saw a submarine out here. We're lucky this boat didn't sink and the Coast Guard didn't fine us or take Jack's boat for fishing where we weren't supposed to be fishing. Personally, I think my boss is crazy. I'm sure you'll be 'briefed' by your partner."

Jennifer motions us to the bridge.

As I walk inside the bridge I see they're looking at another map and sarcastically say,

"So, you found a real map?"

Jennifer ignores my sarcasm.

As I walk to the table I see a very detailed, military grade, satellite picture of Kendrick Bay and think: Okay, so she had another map all along and was just toying with me.

Jennifer says, "Ok, we'll be entering the bay from here. Kendrick islands are here, here and here. We're going into the West Arm of the bay toward Bokan Mountain. I've had a satellite pass over multiple times and there is only one person on this barge at the end of this dock.

This latest picture was taken yesterday afternoon.

"As you can see the barge is sheltered here on the south side of the arm by the dock. Jack will take us here alongside the barge. Any questions?"

"Are you sure they're no other people on that barge?" I ask.

Jennifer says, "I've had this barge watched for days. Only one man gets on and off."

I'm not convinced as I pull my firearm, "You better be right, 'cause I only got a Glock."

Jack, opens a drawer and pulls a shotgun saying, "I got your back."

I sarcastically answer, "Just don't shoot me in the back."

I notice Jack has been limping around, favoring one leg.

I think, great backup if we get in trouble: A guy that can barely walk.

I point to the radio above the window saying, "I hope that thing works."

Jack grabs the microphone, "Just push this and you'll be talking to Coast Guard Ketchikan on VHF."

Mike now disgustedly stands to leave,

"Ya, they all know who he is: Captain Jack and *The Black Pearl*."

As we draw near to Kendrick Bay my phone vibrates.

I check.

It's a text from FBI Portland that Mohammad Al Aqsa (MAA) is flying to Ketchikan!

I can't believe this. I jokingly think, maybe MAA is now tailing me.

Another text arrives from Robert Stone, Police Chief, Ketchikan:

FBI, Portland just notified us of MAA.

I can pick up your suspect and hold him for you. What charge?

I type a text back saying, No charge. You must tail him until I return tonight. This is already against the FBI's new six-month rule but I'll create a new file.

The police chief answers: This isn't Portland. NO resources.

So I text, where is he now?

He texts: His plane lands in one hour.

I text back: I'll call you as soon as I get back. In Kendrick Bay. No service.

Thank you, he responds.

I guess I was very lucky to get any texts as my iPhone 7 suddenly shows: No Service.

◆ ◆ ◆

KENDRICK BAY, ALASKA

As we enter Kendrick Bay silence runs across the boat.

Actually there are two things running: The low hum of a Detroit Diesel and our adrenaline. The sun has actually broken free and the weather, although a brisk thirty-four degrees, it's actually pretty nice.

Snow is covering Bokan Mountain in the distance and a fresh blanket of snow is on the trees and the ground.

We pass a large buoy in the water that shows the international radiation symbol in red with bold red words: ***DANGER RADIATION***.

Jennifer says, "That's weird. I was told by research geologists that there's no dangerous radiation on the surface."

I look at Jennifer saying, "What is this place?"

"Bokan Mountain used to be an old uranium mine but it was closed down in the 1970s after the price of uranium was deregulated by the federal government and the price crashed."

I notice the huge sign again and say, "That sign looks brand new."

Jennifer looks at the brightly red painted buoy and now looks through binoculars and sees there are several more of these signs leading to the old barge by the dock on the far shoreline.

"This place is supposed to be a historic site. That means no one can move anything in or out."

Much later Jennifer told me she thought right then and there, "I should've called for backup but what good would it have done except get more people killed.

Jennifer said, what bothered me at this point was: These rugged guys are going to think I'm a wuss. It's one old man on a barge. I can handle this.

Jennifer was so wrong!

The barge is really a piece of junk. Paint is peeling and the plywood frame looks ready to fall apart.

I started scanning the shoreline and entire area with binoculars looking for any sign of life. There is none. It fact, it's unbelievably quiet as we quietly glide toward our own deaths.

As we near, Jennifer is at the rear of the boat trying to look like a fisherman.

I see Mike nearby trying to help. "Here's a bucket."

Jennifer takes the empty five-gallon bucket used to separate fish. She smells it, reacts, pulls her gun and carefully places it at the bottom of the bucket.

Jack's boat slowly pulls up alongside the barge.

The windows on this rusty old boat are all boarded up with plywood.

I couldn't see any movement, anywhere.

Jennifer remarks, "It's unusually quiet. Usually, birds are making noise. That is unless people are nearby."

Jennifer later told me, practically everybody in Alaska owns a dog for warning but there is nothing but absolute silence.

I felt something was wrong too.

Jennifer already said that she would run point as she walks to the bow. We didn't need to do this as I have a no-knock warrant issued by a federal judge in Portland for the arrest of George Ruddy.

Jennifer calls out to disarm anyone inside,

"Hello? Anybody on board?"

Her voice echoes across the calm waters of the bay but returns empty. After another attempt also yields no result, I exit the bridge. It's as quiet as a mouse on the barge, as I see Jennifer motion Jack to pull closer.

As we touch the barge, Jennifer walks from the bow of her boat directly onto the barge.

She is holding a tie rope and looking like a giant target in those huge red overalls and that neon yellow jacket.

Meanwhile, at the back of the boat, even though it's December, I notice hundreds of salmon swimming around and think,

I love Alaska.

Those thoughts would soon be gone as I jumped onto the back of the barge.

Jennifer and I pull our guns as we head for the doors.

I motion for Jennifer to stand back as I'm about to kick in the door.

Jennifer stops me and checks the handle.

The door easily opens.

Jennifer just looks at me in disgust.

So much for trying to impress my partner.

I shrug my shoulders.

Inside is a dreary mess. If the outside looks to be in shambles the inside is filled mostly with trash. This is one giant room. Toilet, kitchen, bed and trash are all together. The first thing I see are stacks and stacks of sockeye salmon tins.

I walk to them and pick up a can saying, "The salmon capital of the world and this guy is eating it out of a can?"

Jennifer is not paying any attention. She's looking at some rocks on a table. They look to have a shiny silvery center. Another rock looks to be goldish in tone.

I begin going through the drawers on a desk. Nothing seems significant.

Jennifer spots a map that says, Bokan Mountain Road in large red letters.

"These look to be mine entrances," Jennifer says.

I casually walk to a stack of identical black suitcases. Curious, I pull the top one off the stack and open it.

My mouth drops open!

Stacks of fresh $100 bills. There must be a million or more in just this one briefcase. I start opening other briefcases.

It appears there are fresh $100 bills in every one!

There are twenty-two briefcases.

"Uhh, we might have stumbled into something else here," I said.

I don't realize that Jennifer has already gone outside.

I pop the last suitcase and on top of a million dollars in cash is this picture:

Kendrick Bay, Alaska – Russian *TK-20* and her Typhoon
sister, *TK-17*, in a rare daylight appearance
Photo: Kolokolov Igor

The eyewitnesses were right!

And that's a steel reinforced dock!

What the hell is going on here?

I walk out and show Jennifer this picture saying,

"Here are your Typhoons!"

She says, "Holy shit!"

"Well, now we know. There are at least two of them!"

"I know a mining company was testing up here."

Jennifer looks at the heavy machinery in front of the subs.

"That's no mining operation. That machinery looks specifically designed for these subs. It looks like they can offload something from the front of the subs, doesn't it?" asks Jennifer.

"I guess." I answer, carefully looking at all of this heavy equipment.

Jack is on the bow of his boat with binoculars toward Bokan Mountain.

I then say, "This isn't the half of it. Inside there are twenty-two suit-cases filled with…" I don't have time to finish as Jack sounds worried saying, "There's movement at the tree line."

Jennifer and I stop to look.

An older man with a white beard appears in a small, beat up Honda 4-wheel ATV. He waves to us as he approaches. I can't see well from my angle looking through binoculars.

"Is it Ruddy?" I ask.

"No," Jennifer quickly answers.

As the man rides onto the long steel dock, he is dressed in a big parka and a pair of blue jeans. He looks harmless enough as he is about 60 years old.

As he drives out to the edge of the dock where we are, Jennifer and I both pull our Glocks and have them in our ridiculous yellow rain gear.

"Hello," he says with a thick Russian accent.

Jennifer answers, "Hello. We're with the FBI and would like to ask you a few questions."

The man, a little too eagerly, says,

"All right."

The man walks to the barge from the dock. Looking closely now, I realize Jennifer is right, this dock is designed to move heavy machinery as it's defi-nitely made of heavy reinforced steel!

As the man approaches the boat he puts out his hand and I help him aboard.

"I am Doctor Vladimir Peskov, senior scientist, Russia Uranium Specialty Company. How can I help you?"

"I am Jennifer Tavana and this is John Denning, Special Agents, FBI. Have you seen this man?"

Jennifer shows the doctor a picture of George Ruddy.

"Nyet. No, no, can't say that I have," answers Doctor Peskov. "We've pur-chased mining claims all over this mountain. Looks like it's a big waste of money as all of the uranium is under water and not economically feasible to get out. We'll be packing up soon and leaving."

Jennifer later told me this too was suspicious as recent news articles on Bokan Mountain have valued the rare earth deposits alone at six and one half billion dollars, and that doesn't even include the uranium!

Jennifer asks, "Are you here alone?"

The doctor pauses before answering, "I have several associates around here somewhere."

"How many?" I ask.

Once again, after a long pause the Russian answers,

"Three."

Jennifer asks, "Mind if we look around?"

The scientist is acting a little too helpful, "No, no. Not at all."

Jennifer then says, "Could we talk to your partners?"

"Sure but they are deep in the mine and I can't contact them. They won't be back 'til late," says the Russian scientist.

This is suspicious to me as Jennifer said her satellite passes only indicate one person.

Jennifer looks at me, then hands the doctor a picture of George Ruddy,

"Please call me if you see this man. Don't approach him, he's to be considered armed and dangerous."

"Absolutely," says the Russian.

"Okay then, thank you. We'll be going now."

Jennifer and I know we're likely in way over our heads and we begin to leave.

The scientist stops me saying,

"By the way, did you look in my suitcases?"

Apparently, I hesitated just a tiny bit too long before I said,

"No, no I did not."

The Russian scientist puts his left arm in the air and makes a fist.

I was looking at this, puzzled, when the utter silence of the woods was shattered by the thumping of silenced rounds tearing into the wood around us.

Jennifer and I immediately dive for protection as we both instinctively know that a thump with no crack means:

Damn!

Those are suppressed rounds!

And they're close!

Then silence again.

Several more suppressed shots and then silence once again.

It's funny, no matter where you are, you instinctively dive and always remember the smell of dirt, wood, or whatever is near your face.

I look around the corner of the heavy wood frame.

Nothing.

I'm looking for Jack and Mike but see nothing.

No answer.

I look around and cannot see the doctor or anyone.

I look at Jennifer and only now realize:

Fuck!

She's hit!

And unconscious.

Only now do I realize my fall was instinctive.

Jennifer's is possibly lead induced.

Fearing the worst I grab her, unzip her jacket, and now notice a buckle on her overalls has been shattered.

I continue to look around, worried that the doctor and his accomplices can't be far away.

I pull off her shirt and see she is wearing a bulletproof vest but it appears to have done little good. Her Glock is nearby teetering on the edge of the deck. When I reach for it another shot goes off knocking the Glock into the water.

I'm dealing with expert marksmen.

I turn Jennifer on her right side and see blood coming out her upper back. The bullet has gone through her body and has exited near her left shoulder.

It's so near her carotid artery, she'll bleed out in seconds.

I look to Jack's boat to see if I can somehow get to that first aid kit when a sniper round flies about an inch from my head.

Okay, I'm not doing that again!

I hustle back inside the barge and can see the old Russian scientist taking off on his ATV down the dock.

I find a role of duct tape, grab it, and tear a piece off, slapping it on the entrance and exit wounds.

This appears to stop the blood so I do it again.

I peek through a hole in the wooden barge and now, for the first time, get scared.

Ya, even Navy SEALs feel fear!

I see five operators with high-powered rifles in full military tac gear only about 100 yards away and closing fast.

There is likely at least one other sharpshooter looking at us from a covered position.

In any event, my Glock is worthless at that range.

My Navy SEAL training comes flooding back.

My first thought:

We're outta here!

But I cannot leave Jennifer.

First, I take three very slow and very deep breaths as I continue to work on Jennifer.

You can do this, JD!

I begin dragging Jennifer to the back of the barge away from the sniper's line of fire. I check her neck again and finally feel a faint pulse.

I peer around the corner of our boat and can see through the deck railing onto *The Black Pearl*. Both Jack and Mike are lying in their own pools of blood, dead.

I look at the water then back to the boats.

I then peer around the barge and, for the first time, identify what appears to be an unmarked Russian GRU Special Forces team closing fast.

Little green men?

I hated that Ukrainian term!

Ukrainians coined the term when Russian Special Forces Teams in unmarked military uniforms quietly began taking over the Crimean Peninsula in 2014. From airports to military bases previously owned by Ukraine, these units sowed confusion and put down anyone who resisted. God help us if this is who they are. They are the best of the best.

Later came the marked units but the little green men had done their job. Cause confusion, diversion and paved the way for armored units.

These guys are all dressed in black.

I shake Jennifer,

"Jennifer!"

She's still unconscious.

I now realize I still have on my ridiculous yellow jacket and bright red fishing pants thinking,

We might as well have been wearing bull's eyes!

I look at the water and realize this is our only escape route.

Just my luck.

Again, with the cold and the wet.

And I'm the slowest swimmer in the U.S. Navy!

I take a deep breath, breathe into her mouth and then close it, holding her nose. I turn Jennifer around so her back is directly against my chest.

Then I fall on my back, protecting her as much as I can.

My first thought as I hit the water:

Damn!

This's cold!

I take another breath and give it to Jennifer. I then immediately place her on my side and begin a sidestroke, pulling Jennifer, so I can see around the back of the barge.

The Special Forces team is half way down the dock heading right for me.

I notice the water is deeper at the back of the barge right up to the coastline.

A tiny cove is there.

I decide this is our only chance.

I give another breath to Jennifer before disappearing into the icy black waters under Jack's boat.

The water temperature must be under forty degrees.

Hypothermia occurs when the human body cannot generate enough heat to compensate for the warmth it loses. You have maybe ten minutes, if you can breathe, before all the blood rushes to the core of your body as your extremities go numb. But I'm underwater pulling another body and every second feels like eternity.

I'm right back in SEAL training.

Miles and miles and miles of swimming.

Pain, pain and more pain.

I rolled out with a broken leg and then I couldn't pass Phase II. I had to repeat Phase II with a completely new class.

Your underwater times are the slowest the Navy has ever seen, son! was all I could now hear. That instructor was the meanest, cruelest son of a b…

I stopped myself because I then remembered graduation day when that same instructor walked up to me and said, I'm proud of you, son. I have never, ever in twenty-five years, seen a more determined guy than you!

That helped.

That helped right now.

I could use one of those other SEALs arms and legs right about now. What I wouldn't give for a breath of air. I can do it. Only a little further. It's only fifty meters underwater! I had to do twice that for Hell week!

And thanks for bringing up that painful memory, JD.

When I retired from the Navy I swore I would never do anything ever again that involved cold and wet.

And now look at me!

In addition, looks like I'm up against a full blown team of operators. It was like another reoccurring bad dream I had in BUD/S training. I dreamt I was being drown by someone I couldn't see. By someone I couldn't reach. All I remember is that I'd wake up in a cold sweat trying to catch my breath.

These operators are big, mean and decked for warfare.

I'm outta here!

If they are Russian Special Forces I am in trouble as they train in just about every form of combat the same as SEALs: HALO, SCUBA, demolitions and all have specialized training.

There's no way I can go on.

These guys are just going to track us down and shoot us where we wash up.

I pop Jennifer's head out of the water first.

We're about 100 feet away from Jack's fishing boat.

It's at least another 100 feet to land but I needed air.

The Russians are still on the dock, nearing the barge, and don't appear to notice us, yet.

Jennifer's lips are blue and so, probably, are mine. I breathe another breath into her lifeless mouth while holding her nose. I continue my sidestrokes on my way into a tiny cove, somewhat hidden from the boats.

I think to myself: I can't quit. I'm so close to the beach. With every breath it seemed as if my heart was growing fainter and fainter. Again, I thought back to my Navy SEAL training.

One instructor said,

Mind over matter. If I don't mind, nothing else matters!

Pain is just weakness leaving the body!

That was what another instructor yelled at me one day when I almost quit.

Everybody has something that makes them push way beyond where they thought they could go.

In SEAL training, you were taught one thought repeatedly.

Never put your faith in a friend or the toughest guy in the group. If they quit, you'll likely walk out right behind them.

The instructors taught you to put your faith in something deep inside you, preferably something eternal, bigger than you.

At Coronado, I'd look back to the 32nd Street Naval Base, see some ugly ship and say,

Hey, I'm in the sun! I sure don't want to be stuck in the bowels of that ugly tug in some God-awful part of the world!

Some of the smallest guys in my SEAL class had the biggest hearts and the fight and strength of guys much, much, bigger. In combat classes most everyone would root for an underdog. It's like watching a sporting event. Fans will root for the team that plays the hardest.

Suddenly, the rain pours!

Thank God!

The rain will make it harder for them to see any trace of us.

I took another deep breath and continued to swim, if you can call it that.

It was a chore to push my legs at all. The strain of holding a hundred-pound woman's head now above water would have been tough enough at these temperatures and with only one arm pushing through the water, it's too much.

I'm standing still!

It was like the reoccurring dream I had as a child.

With a high fever, I was running down my grade school hall.

The harder and faster I ran, the further and further the door seemed to get.

The harder I paddled, the further away the beach seemed.

I'm giving up.

On the other hand, this is much easier than that five-and-a-half-mile ocean swim!

The cult I lived in with my mother banned all electronic devices but I found this old cassette tape recorder left at a rest stop picnic table on Interstate 5 and after asking everyone, no one seemed to own it, so I took it!

It had one cassette tape with one song.

When all else failed, that one song got me through Phase II of underwater SEAL training.

I started singing what little I could remember:

Every man has a place
In his heart there's a space
And the world can't erase his fantasies
Take a ride in the sky
On our ship, fantasize
All your dreams will come true right away

And we will live together
Until the twelfth of never
Our voices will ring forever, as one…
Every thought is a dream
Rushing by in a stream

Bringing life to the kingdom of doing
Take a ride in the sky
On our ship, fantasize
All your dreams will come true miles away

Our voices will ring together
Until the twelfth of never
We all will live love forever, as one...[7]

I couldn't remember any other verses so I just kept singing the ones I knew over and over and over.

Strange as it sounds, it worked!

After what couldn't have been more than a few minutes,

I touched land!

As I try to stand the sheer weight of my wet clothes and Jennifer drop me back into the water. I make one more lunge at the shoreline and fall into some shallow water like a ton of bricks.

Jennifer isn't breathing. I pull her all the way out of the water to give her a few more breaths.

All SEALs were given basic medical lifesaving training but this situation was clearly beyond "basic."

I notice the duct tape on her wound is peeling and starting to bleed. Jennifer is still unconscious and doesn't look like she'll make it.

I look around knowing we can't stay here, exposed on the beach. If that is a Special Forces platoon, they will search this beach first.

I would.

So I pick her up and sling her over my back and head for some trees.

I find a sheltered area inside a huge dead tree. I am deep in a lush green forest. What am I thinking? Are you sightseeing? Or trying to stay alive?

Fortunately, this whole area doesn't have much snow.

I knew from wilderness survival training this meant this area is warmer than surrounding areas covered in fresh snow.

Also, it's fortunate that this area has no snow.

Tracks in the snow would lead those operators right to us.

Again, the whole area is beautiful.

"Maybe you should take out your phone and get a picture," I sarcastically thought to myself.

Idiot!

We're gonna die here and I want a selfie!

I take off my waterlogged trusty, old, Richard Bass, black parka.

My cell phone falls out of a pocket and I quickly check to see if there's service.

The phone seems to be working but it still says:

No Service.

I now find myself angrily shaking my cell phone trying to deny physics and common sense.

I place my parka under Jennifer's head and again shake her.

Nothing.

I check for a pulse on her neck and, getting nothing, I put my ear over her mouth.

Once again, nothing!

So, I begin chest compressions.

Nothing.

Now I remember, I am supposed to clear the mouth. I pull out a piece of green slimy something from her mouth, hopefully that's from the water.

I extend her neck and elevate her chin and start mouth to mouth. I can't believe it. I think I've remembered most of my medical training!

After several attempts, Jennifer half opens her eyes and mumbles something I can't quite make out. I put my ear to her mouth to hear what she's trying to say,

"If this is your idea of a first date, it may be your last."

I see her trying to reach for her gun. I knew then and there,

This was my kind of girl!

Suddenly we hear voices and we both freeze.

I cover her mouth.

I'm afraid she's in so much pain that she might scream.

I now see it's two operators walking the beach nearby.

As soon as they walk away I take my hand off her mouth.

She lays lifeless again in my hands.

My first thought is,

Oh my God, I've killed her!

Again!

My heart races back to Mt. Hood, Oregon just days ago when I was holding the life of Trevor in my hands.

My mind then went flashing to Trevor's girlfriend as I began to wonder if I'm cursed!

Then I remember the EMTs and the Portland Rescue Unit that rescued us on Hood said, by the time we found you in that blizzard, if you hadn't built those snow caves you would have frozen to death.

Then I wondered how Trevor's girlfriend was doing.

Last I saw her they upgraded her condition to stable.

The City of Portland wanted to thank me at a press conference.

I told myself, I don't need no stinkin' press conference.

And that's when I left town.

Now I'm thinking,

What the hell? I should've been doing compressions.

I snap back to reality as Jennifer's eyes struggle to open and she tries to speak.

"Don't try to talk."

Jennifer stubbornly shoves my hand aside saying,

"Russian! I know why they're here."

Jennifer pulls out a phone from her jacket and looks at it,

"Damn! They're jamming the SAT signal."

"You have a satellite phone?" I grab it trying to see if it'll work.

Jennifer struggles but gets out the following,

"We've gotta find their jamming device."

I joke,

"We?"

This is maybe the first time I've seen her smile.

I ask coyly, "So your Ex-Navy too?"

"Ya. Lieutenant Commander, *USS Alaska*."

At this point she's probably going to die, so I might as well compliment her.

"Weren't you the first woman to command a submarine?"

"Thanks for bringing up such a painful subject."

"You don't want to discuss it?"

"Uh, no."

"Okay. John Denning, SEAL Team Six. Nice to meet you."

"So you guys killed Bin Laden?" asks Jennifer.

"My guys, ya."

Where were you?

"Fishing in Alaska."

"I don't understand…"

"Ya, now that's something I don't want to talk about."

"Fair enough."

With that, Jennifer winces in pain and lays back.

"Easy." I grab her head and adjust my jacket under her.

"Keep going, it takes my mind off the pain," says Jennifer.

I have never revealed these facts to anyone. I think,

How did she get me to say that?

I stare off into the woods, suddenly a million miles from Alaska.

Jennifer, told me later, she'd seen that thousand-yard stare before and wisely says nothing.

All she did was sit up and grab my hand.

After an eternity and a deep sigh, I began,

"Our orders were to breach a compound in Kandahar province, five clicks from the Pakistan border."

She later told me,

I thought you couldn't look any paler but this did it.

I looked like a dead body, she said.

This is more painful than the swim. I said, "By the time we got there he was shot and on the ground. He was tryin' ta say something. I brought my ear to his lips but I couldn't hear him. I said, Buddy, I can't hear you. He kept tryin' ta speak as our medic worked on him. I just kept tryin' to hear what he wanted to say."

"He died in my arms. Bravest man I ever knew."

I lose it as the painful memory comes rushing back,

"It was my fault. He was on point. I made him announce to the terrorists that we were there and that killed him."

"Why did you announce you were there?" Jennifer quietly asks.

"The ROEs," I mumble.

"Rules of engagement!" Jennifer says.

"I hate 'em," I say with anger.

"I hate all of 'em!"

Jennifer is clearly talking about the brass and not the ROEs.

"Make the fucking armchair generals in Washington come over here and follow their own fucked up orders!"

That snapped me back to reality. Other than my team, I'd never heard anyone talk about Navy command like this.

Jennifer is probably seconds from death and yet she seems like she could care less about her life.

I've met some brave people in my time but she just might be the bravest!

She's listening, so I go on.

"My other buddy, Big John, was on the raid and we were both really close with Bull. When a review board blamed us, Big John committed suicide. I resigned from the SEALs the same day. Brought up too many unresolved issues I had with suicide. I blamed myself."

I feel like I'd just as soon die right here and now.

"I foolishly followed stupid orders and got two of my men killed."

Jennifer slowly puts her weak hand over my shaking mouth. She sits up and hugs me as my mind was a million miles away.

When I pull away from her, I realize that she has passed out. I shake her saying,

"Jennifer!"

As she comes to, her first words are, "They probably heard you, Mr. PTSD. Have you ever talked to someone about all this?"

"Ya, you."

I look around, "We gotta move."

Jennifer tries to sit up but almost passes out again.

"You've lost too much blood. I gotta get you help."

Jennifer looks over to the boats saying, "Are they off the boats?"

I peer through a large gaping hole on the side of the hollowed out log.

"Looks like it. All right, I'll swim back to the boat and try to use the radio."

Jennifer says, "Too bad we don't have on our blueberries."

She's referring to the most hated uniforms in the U.S. military. Fortunately, I heard they're permanently retiring those dogs.

"We could a used those uniforms. They'd have been the perfect camouflage in the water."

No sooner had I said that then both boats explode. Demolitions appear to have been placed on both hulls. They sink right where they sit.

I say sarcastically, "Well there goes Captain Jack and *The Black Pearl*!

Jennifer wasn't laughing so I continue,

"I got texts coming into the bay. If I could swim there, I could text help."

Jennifer says, "How far out were you when you had service?"

"About two miles."

And how far did you swim with me?"

I then had to stupidly act macho, "Hey, we had to do five and a half miles in SEAL training."

"Coronado?" she sarcastically asks.

"Ya!" I confidently answer.

"Ya, that water was probably thirty degrees warmer!" she points out.

I grind my teeth and force out, "I'm sure it was."

I pull my iPhone 7 out again and say,

"It's working but no service."

"They can't jam the entire mountain. If we can get up higher on Bokan you might find a signal," says Jennifer. "And see if you can find a first aid kit." Jennifer looks to the sunken boats.

"They sunk mine!"

Not showing any sign of worry I say,

"Stay here. I'll see if I can find you a nice big bottle of hydrogen peroxide."

Jennifer, "Okay, but I have dinner plans tonight."

I say in my worst Russian accent, "Of course you do, darlink, as soon as I take care of Boris and Boris, I'm takin' you out!"

I then go running into the woods like a chicken with my head cut off thinking,

I can't let this woman die!

Oh God, please don't let her die!

MOSCOW, TV-12

Olga Kasparov's Diary

I adjusted my blouse as I sat in front of the most powerful man in my country, President Ivan Mironovich. Several people from makeup to wardrobe were very attentive to the President while no one paid any attention to me.

"Thirty sekund!" yelled the floor director. Makeup and wardrobe went scrambling off camera.

During our darkest days under the iron fisted rule of the old Soviet Union I worked for state controlled newspaper, "Pravda," which is Russian for "The Truth."

Joke among dissidents was: There is no Pravda in Pravda!

It was probably twenty years before I was finally able to laugh at that joke.

We, in "the older generation" can remember days when bread, cigarettes and Vodka were 'free' but you'd stand in long lines, sometimes for hours and hours, for "free" stuff.

I was loyal party member in those days and was glad when those days came to screeching halt in 1991. Being a die-hard Communist, I was upset, at first, but eventually came around to see the fall of Communism in Russia was best for almost everyone.

However, some of the very well connected lost some of their power and they didn't like it.

But even well-connected today are far wealthier than they ever were prior to 1991.

In those days, communism worked but only for the party faithful, everyone else was in line.

In old Soviet there was another joke. Boy asks: Mama, where is papa? Answer: He's in line for a coupon… to get some coupons.

At least with some capitalism there are many more jobs and no food lines.

The press was much more free. Free until the man I'm sitting with became president.

Young are now romanticizing the good old days, which were never really that good.

The reason, in part, for romanticization is because of our government run school system. It makes USSR sound so much better in a colorful book.

Also, there are many, many government agencies that have been created to "inform" and "educate" our people on all of the wonders of those "glorious days."

This used to be called propaganda but now it's called "communication."

My favorite government agency: "The Ministry of Communications and Mass Media."

Older folks never closely connected to old Communist Party knew better than to believe in most government "communication."

"Five sekunds," floor director yelled. "Four, three…"

I pause, focus and take a deep breath, while waiting for little red light,

"Good evening and welcome to Russia Tonight. I'm Olga Kasparov and first I wish each and every person a very happy Christmas season. With me tonight is very special guest, President, Ivan Mironovich. Thank you so much for taking time to speak with fellow countrymen."

"No problem. Glad to be here, Ms. Kasparov," replied the very well dressed president.

I tried flirting a little.

"Please call me Olga!"

That did not go over as well as I hoped.

Ivan stares at me as if: Read questions I gave your boss!

I uncomfortably look to teleprompter understanding exactly Ivan's unspoken words.

We Russians are used to an entire subtext of thought and communication that is far more important than any spoken or written word.

Subtext.

It's all subtext.

"So do you believe NATO or the Americans are in any way a threat to Russia?" I read word for word.

The smooth talking president goes right into his dance,

"Not militarily, of course, Olga. We could wipe out NATO's military in Eastern Europe in ten minutes. We are increasing our patrols around any U.S. vessel or aircraft near our shores. We don't want confrontation but we are fully prepared to defend our lands!"

But President Mironovich, aren't the Americans and NATO just reacting to our placing of ships and planes very close to their forces? This was the question I desperately want to ask but I didn't want to end up like some of my colleagues: Jailed or murdered!

So I didn't ask the question.

The heavy hand of government had returned to Russia. But a few friends, more courageous than I, still question the absolute authoritarianism of crazy Ivan's new Russia.

However, today, I wasn't about to be one of them.

He reminds me of old American song, "Meet the new boss. Same as old boss."

I quickly return to my script provided by my boss,

"Mr. President, are we doing all we can to counter these maneuvers by NATO and America?"

"Of course our brave boys will counter any aggressive moves by the West. I fear it's only a matter of time before someone, either intentionally or accidentally, fires something at us in which case we will have no choice but to defend ourselves. And then there's no telling where that could lead, Olga."

I've become a puppet of the state. *TV-12* is owned by the Russian government, which means President Mironovich was asking and answering his own preplanned script.

I was nothing more than window dressing.

Nothing would be broadcast over the air that now wasn't directly approved by the crazy little man himself. A modern day Stalin or Lenin seems to be where we're heading with this man. Except with all the technology and weaponry at his disposal he is far, far more dangerous.

The president continued, "We want to be friends with NATO and America and find it puzzling that they would provocatively place military assets so close to our lands. We are the largest country in the world and want peace but if someone attacks us, like they did in World War II, then we will defend ourselves and prevail!"

I pretend to be pleased, "Listeners will be happy to know you have spent so much time working to protect the people of Russia from NATO and American aggression."

The President continues, "The people of our great civilization must now prepare for the worst. Stock extra food and water and prepare for maybe not having electricity or heat. Follow all of our regular nuclear drills so you know where to go in an emergency. I shall meet with NATO and the Americans to head off any possible conflict. But I assure you, if America provokes an attack, we all must be prepared."

Chills went up and then back down my spine.

Is this madman trying to start a war?

BOKAN MOUNTAIN, ALASKA

t was dusk and it was only 4:00 p.m.! The days are short and the nights are long and cold in an Alaskan winter.

I ran back to Jennifer with the only thing I could quickly find, ferns.

I hope she's still alive.

As I peek into the log, I'm met face to face with her Glock.

Yep, she's alive.

"Probably won't fire anyway," I joke.

"Let's play Russian roulette and find out?" says Jennifer.

"Russian roulette with a Glock? That, I want to see."

I now realize she's covered herself with moss and all of her clothes are neatly folded nearby.

"Me Tarzan, you Jennifer?" I joke.

She's not amused.

"No? Doesn't work for you?" I say.

What the hell was I thinking?

I reach into my pocket and pull out my Glock.

"I give the Glocks about a ninety percent chance of firing."

Jennifer playfully points her gun in my general direction and says, "Let's find out."

I push the gun aside and get serious,

How's the wound?"

"I think it stopped bleeding," says Jennifer as she looks at my ferns.

"Plan on making a call with those?"

I ignore her, "There's nothing around here. They must have a jamming device on the mountain."

Jennifer confidently says, "No. No way. How would they get it up there? Unless..."

"Unless what? I ask.

"Unless that Russian sub is closer than we think." Jennifer continues, "I blame myself. I should've turned our boat around as soon as Jack Tanner told me the story. Thanks to me, Jack and Mike are dead."

"Don't blame yourself."

"You're the one ta talk," she says accusingly.

"Those are definitely Russian Special Forces. I overheard them speaking Russian. I didn't show you but there were twenty-two suitcases on that barge filled with at least one million dollars each."

Jennifer is truly shocked,

"What?" Why didn't you tell me?"

"I was trying to when we unwittingly played: Shoot the giant, yellow targets!"

Jennifer is thinking but all that comes out is, "I'm sorry. I'm sorry for all of this."

"Your office will know you're missing, right?"

Jennifer sighs, "Probably not. I was supposed to go to the Arctic National Wildlife Refuge for a month. They might think I left early."

"Aren't you suppose to check in after field work?" I ask.

"Ya, but this is Alaska. Things are a bit more casual up here. People go away for weeks. Our best chance is with that SAT phone."

I think for a minute, "You told the harbor master where we are, right?"

"This is Ketchikan and we're the FBI. I didn't tell anyone anything," says Jennifer.

"Well only three things can happen here."

"One, we die."

"Two, we're captured."

"Three, we escape!"

"I prefer option number three!"

Jennifer, "Oh you might escape. I'll be dead by morning."

I look at her body that is now partially uncovered by moss. Jennifer realizes I'm "looking" at her. She covers herself saying,

"Don't touch the moss. Find your own moss."

I take off my shirt and pull a big chunk of moss off the inside of the tree.

I am really cold.

I start to shiver.

"All right, come over here but you try anything, I'll put a bullet in you."

I sarcastically say, "What do I gotta lose? We'll be dead by morning."

NATIONAL SECURITY AGENCY (NSA)

Fred is comfortably eating his tuna fish sandwich, again, as he carefully reviews his screen at NSA headquarters in Fort Meade, Maryland.

"Jerry come here."

Jerry walks over.

"What is it now?"

"*TK-20* looks half apart with its nuclear reactor missing."

"I thought we decided that wasn't *TK-20,*" says Jerry.

"No, I think it is. They had just dismantled so much then pulled it into that new covered dry dock to take out the reactor. By the time they pulled it back here we thought it was another sub."

"So what d'ya want from me?"

"I enlarged the SAT images as much as possible. COMINT gave me the an old *KH-11* satellite and I can't make the image resolution clearer but does that look like a Typhoon class sub tail sticking out of that covered port to you?"

Jerry can clearly see something that looks to be TK-20's tailfin sticking out of a covered port but they can't see anything else.

"Ya, looks like it. But see here the tail on the sub is missing, so it's right there."

"Does that make sense to you? How is just the tail in the water floating?"

"You're the expert. I'm just the tech guy," says Jerry as he eyes Fred's half eaten tuna fish sandwich. Without another thought and while not looking at Jerry, Fred simply hands Jerry his sandwich as they both continue to gaze at the blurry images.

Jerry finally stands up saying, "Oh well, it's Christmas Eve. What ya say we go home?"

Fred checks his government issued plastic watch he got at his twenty-year anniversary, "Jeez, I didn't realize it was that late. I probably should pull from some other SATS."

"Have fun," says Jerry as he stands to leave.

"I'm going home. Merry Christmas, Fred!"

Jerry leaves.

Not wanting to be the only idiot in the office on Christmas Eve, Fred collects his things, pauses one more time to take a long look at his computer, then leaves his tiny little cubicle.

USS ALASKA – ARCTIC OCEAN

Tom Watson's Diary

I t's Christmas morning at exactly 08:00 and what I'm about to do I really, really do not want to do.

As I walk down the hall of the *USS Alaska*, the commander's door seemed fifty feet tall.

I didn't want to knock.

Maybe I'll just go back to my bunk.

Let someone else worry about this.

I turned around and started to walk away and then stopped again.

Nope! This will bother me until I do it.

I'm already in trouble.

I alerted the highest ranked person I know, Rear Admiral Baker.

Even though I haven't heard back, I knew it was only a matter of time before my commander got wind of this and he wouldn't be happy.

I knock on the commander's door.

I knew this would be an awkward conversation at best.

This idiot, the second dumbest man on the boat, replaced my old girl-friend, Commander Jennifer Tavana.

"Come in," answers Lieutenant Commander Bert Parks.

His name always reminded me of a game show host!

He's a bald, short, stupid looking little wisp of a man that had waited forever to get his own sub.

He always tried to sabotage Jennifer and me when he was second in command. "Little Bert" was vindictive and cattier than any woman I had ever met. His nickname, that he made for himself: Bert, 'P' man, Parks.

(Don't ask how he devised that nickname.)

That gives you the idea of the brains on this guy.

Ever since Jennifer was made commander of the sub, we avoided each other like the plague.

Bert is sitting, working at his desk. He sees me standing in his door and cannot look me in the eye. Bert continues to pretend he's doing paperwork.

"What is it?" Bert asks.

"Sorry to bother you, sir, but have you seen the AOAIA report from Bob outlining all the sonar anomalies?"

Bert is barely paying attention and answers in the affirmative a faint,

"Uh huh."

"And what were your conclusions?"

Bert looks up clearly not knowing he what he's talking about but pretending so as to get rid of me.

"Don't worry about it. We're taking a look."

I don't believe him.

"Have you heard from ASWOC in San Diego about this?" I ask.

"Why would I bother them?" asks Bert.

I don't want to let him know that I've already alerted Fleet Admiral Baker and ASWOC as this will likely tick off Bert for going above him. So I say,

"Because, sir, I believe that AOAIA has never seen this signature before and so it's possible another class of sub or subs are out there."

"Ok 'chief' thank you for that. I'll look into it," says an annoyed Burt.

I pause as Bert continues to ignore me, knowing this idiot won't do a thing.

"Dismissed," says Bert.

"Yes, sir."

Again I pause, staring at this stubborn idiot before leaving the room.

"I'm sending all these anomalies to ONI, DNI and Rear Admiral Baker," before shutting his door.

I then open the door again saying as sincerely as I can,

"Merry Christmas, sir!"

BOKAN MOUNTAIN

Jennifer and I are huddled asleep together. My arms are wrapped around her bare chest. It sounds sexy but it wasn't. I had dried blood stuck to me, which was stuck to her.

So, much for sexy, I thought.

She acts very comfortable snuggled, asleep, under my chin.

Feels pretty good too.

My God, I hope she's alive!

I could feel her heartbeat all night long and knew she made it but I checked her neck again just to make sure.

"Thank God!"

Although it was cold, the tree covered area and the log-covered moss kept us from freezing to death.

I woke up a few minutes ago with a spider crawling across my face. Without opening my eyes, I calmly picked it up and placed it outside a hole in our log.

Luckily, I didn't look at it until I put it outside the log. It was large and black, with ominous bright yellow zigzags on its underside.

That didn't look good.

All we need now is to have a lethal spider bite.

FBI Hostage Rescue will find us dead, naked and huddled together months from now.

Those pictures won't look good in our performance review file!

I've gotta stop thinking like this.

I carefully lift off the moss and check her duct-taped wounds. Being satisfied she's not bleeding, I gently place the moss over her naked body. I try to wake her and realize she's trying to open her eyes but is clearly struggling.

I know that if I don't clean out this GSW (gunshot wound) soon, she will die.

I peer outside the log and see the sun once again peek out of the rain clouds.

Thank God it didn't rain last night!

I check her SAT phone and see it's still being actively jammed. I then check my iPhone and it's working but still showing: No Service.

"Funny, it's working but I didn't charge my phone and only got two percent battery left. Any last requests?" I say as she opens her eyes.

"Ya, *Funeral for a Friend*,"[8] Jennifer says without wasting a moment.

I get all excited as I search through my playlist saying,

"Elton John? I think I've got it, but the song's ten minutes long. That'll wipe out the battery for sure."

She's so far gone she doesn't react at all.

I hit play.

I see fresh blood oozing out of the peeling duct tape as I hear Elton singing,

"Love lies bleeding in my hands."

I have to get her help and fast. I reach to grab my clothes and see a book sticking out from under Jennifer's neatly folded clothes.

It's Jack Tanner's captain's log!

I open a page Jennifer has folded over.

This sad alcoholic really had a tough life.

It's not right that someone "just following orders" ended his life.

He really did see that sub.

Well, that would have been helpful to know about before we started on this little disaster, I thought as I quickly put on my clothes.

I set the diary down as my mind races through of all our options, none are good.

As I crawl out of the log I'm immediately met with a revolver.

My first reaction is to fight.

But what I see is a kindly looking old man in a long white beard that goes to his waist. He also has crazy white hair and blue eyes that pierced through to my soul. He looks different.

Different is good.

I decide to slowly put my hands in the air.

"Who are you?" the crazy old man asks.

"Who are you?" I reply.

We stare down each other forever before I think: This is ridiculous!

"My name is John Denning. I'm with…"

"Are you one of them?" Al asks with a gun pointed squarely now into the middle of my forehead.

"No. No. We're FBI."

"Do FBI agents generally sleep together naked?" asks our Santa look alike.

"No. No. It's not like that. She's shot. Needs medical help. You have a two-way radio?" I ask.

"Ain't got no radio."

My hopes are instantly crushed.

"But I know where one is," he says.

"How far?"

"In the mine."

"Can you take me there?"

"Ya, but you better take her."

"Why?"

"There's a doctor up there."

"Really?"

I study the old man to see if he's nuts or believable.

I'm not sure.

But since I really didn't have another choice, I decide to follow him.

I pick up Jennifer, again unconscious, and follow him into the woods.

"By the way, what's your name?" I ask.

"Al Reynolds," the old man answers.

◆ ◆ ◆

I'm carrying Jennifer over my shoulder as we slowly ascend Bokan Mountain. This is still a wooded area but I'm worried as we come to a clearing. There is some snow in the trees and on the ground but not on the trail.

ROGER R. ELLIS

As we near a mine entrance, I have to stop as I'm not in as good of shape as I was sixteen years ago.

There are no boards or doors or anything. Just a black hole that somehow reminds me of the crevasse into which Trevor fell at the top of Mt. Hood days ago.

Al encouragingly says, "It'll be OK. The Russians are on the other side of the mountain right now. They don't have cameras here."

Cameras? I'm confused but more I'm suspicious. I look around but without any other real choice I head into the mine with Al.

Inside the mine it's actually much warmer than in the snow. This would have been helpful to know about last night! Al turns on an old flashlight he picks up from behind some rocks. I continue to follow him deeper and deeper into the mine.

Jennifer mumbles something.

I stop.

"You okay?"

Jennifer is too weak to speak but moves her good arm up to her wound. It's bleeding again.

"Oh hell!" I exclaim as I stop and put her down.

I rip off my shirt, tear it and put it around her wound and chest. Suddenly everything goes black.

I look down the vein and see Al has travelled so far that there is nothing between him and me except blackness.

"Hey! She's bleeding!"

Al responds, "Then c'mon!"

I have no choice but to trust this crazy old man. I lift Jennifer and now carry her in my arms. I have to run in pitch black toward Al's light.

Al finally shines his flashlight toward me. It is a good thing as there is a rock that I would've hit. The fall could've killed us as we would've likely fallen onto some larger boulders.

Again, I feel like I'm in my elementary school hall with a fever and running forever.

I finally catch up to Al and just keep running. Al now starts walking fast behind me and shining the dim flashlight on my path.

We finally come to a three way split in the mountain. Two tunnels are pitch black. The other way an iron gate with thick bars block their way. Several signs are hanging on the steel bars that say,

DANGER HIGH RADIATION AREA
NO TRESPASSING
PERSONAL MONITORING EQUIPMENT REQUIRED

Without pausing, Al pulls a bunch of keys from his belt and puts one into the lock. Al quickly opens the gate. Al starts down the tunnel then realizes I'm still standing at the gates. Al flashes the light back to me, I'm still frozen, staring at the signs.

"C'mon."

Again, I figure I really have no choice and follow Al.

I notice, in the dim light, the cave walls have turned into a reddish brown.

I'm probably getting poisoned and will end up like Madame Curie.

Now I see Jennifer is bleeding again and I set her down.

I try to stop the bleeding but can't.

"Al, how much farther?" I look up and Al has vanished.

"AL!"

Al is nowhere to be seen or heard.

Now I'm screaming, "AL!"

Nothing.

I try to feel for a pulse on Jennifer's wrist.

Nothing. I try to feel for a pulse on her neck.

Nothing.

I'm walking in absolute blackness when someone grabs my arm. It's Al.

He takes me in another direction, just a few yards.

We now stop at a solid steel wall with a solid steel door.

"I hope you have the key?"

"Nope." Al says with confidence.

Al wanders down the side of this shaft until he finds another shaft, which is hard to see as a giant boulder sits in the way.

"C'mon. We're almost there!" says Al.

Again with hesitation, I follow.

This vein in the mountain is much smaller and I can barely fit. My six foot four-inch frame has to bend down to keep going. Al has now crawled into a tiny space about four feet off the ground.

"What are you doing?"

Al says, "You have to hand her to me."

I say, "What?"

I can't believe Al is able to into this space. I set Jennifer down and use my phone's flashlight to look at her face.

I open Jennifer's eyelids, one at a time, and her pupils are rolled upwards and are dilated. This signifies brain death.

I have no choice but to push her lifeless body into the tiny space.

Al pulls her out of sight.

I can barely crawl into this tiny hole.

I flash my light down the hole and Al has disappeared with Jennifer's body around a corner.

This crawlspace looks no larger than a ventilation duct in a large office building.

In fact, that's exactly what this is as suddenly a blast of air comes rushing through the vent.

We continue to crawl on our stomachs.

I'm pushing Jennifer and Al is pulling.

We finally reach a large opening. Al fumbles through a bunch of keys and can't find the right one.

Finally, he says, "Duh!"

He grabs a key from around his neck and sticks it into the lock.

Al opens the ventilation door near the ground and we push and pull a lifeless Jennifer onto a stockroom floor filled with supplies. This room is probably twenty feet high and maybe fifty feet by fifty feet on its sides. I can't believe the amount of supplies in here. I pick Jennifer up and we run through this room and exit out another door.

We are in a very modern facility hall. Bright lighting, smooth floor, and a camera system are all part of the hallway.

I can't believe that we're inside a mountain in Alaska!

It could be any modern office building!

Al waits 'til the camera pans away from us before taking me down to a door.

He pulls out an electronic card and swipes it. The door opens and we go inside.

We're standing in darkness 'til Al flips a light.

To my amazement this is a full surgical room!

It's filled with everything from heart monitors to IV fluids.

Al locks the door and I immediately place Jennifer on an operating table in the middle of the room.

I grab an oxygen mask and put it on her.

I have to look where to turn on the oxygen.

Eventually, I find it and open the valve.

Do I know what I'm doing?

No!

But I do notice a camera in the corner.

I grab a surgical mask and hang it over the camera, so the camera can't see.

"Find me something to take bullet fragments out. And get me lots of gauze!"

Al starts looking around while I take off my shirt that I had wrapped around her.

The duct tape has almost completely fallen off and she's bleeding again. Al hands me some gauze and a mean looking scalpel. It's not for taking out a bullet but this will have to do.

I probe around with this thing not knowing, at all, what I'm doing.

Finally, I see what looks to be gold in color and move it.

Jennifer winces in pain.

Al has found a pair of needle nose pliers and hands them to me. I grab the unsterilized and most inappropriate nonsurgical device and pull a large bullet fragment from her left upper chest wall. Al helps me push gauze on her wound to close it.

The door tries to open but Al locked it from the inside so it won't open.

Someone unlocks the door.

Al runs and turns off the light just before the door opens.

In walks a young Russian woman in a white doctor's coat.

Al grabs her mouth and slams the door shut. He flips the light on and she clearly is terrified. I'm standing over Jennifer holding the gauze on her wound and ask,

"Do you speak English?"

The Russian doctor nods in the affirmative.

"This woman was shot by you people. Are you a doctor?"

Again, the Russian doctor nods in the affirmative.

"Can you look at her?"

The Russian doctor now sees it's Al who's holding his hand over her mouth.

Al slowly removes his hand and she quickly walks over to Jennifer.

"Why didn't you tell me it was you, Al?" says the doctor.

Al and her clearly know each other.

"Tatiana Ivanov! The best doctor in Alaska!" says Al.

The doctor puts on a pair of gloves before touching Jennifer.

She takes the gauze away and sees Jennifer is in pain so she grabs a bottle of something, opens it and starts to pour it into the wound when I stop her.

The doctor says, "It's a one percent solution of lidocaine. This will ease her pain."

I let her do this.

The doctor actually pushes pretty hard and with a syringe, forcing more lidocaine into the wound area. Jennifer winces, at first, but soon looks to be more comfortable.

The doctor then takes a sterile scalpel out of a surgical case and holds it up for us to see and then debrides the area around the wound. She then irrigates the wound and area with an IV bag of saline. She then uses a small medical probe to search around further.

The doctor picks up the pliers we were using, shakes her head and puts them to the side.

After that, she grabs a pair of forceps and penetrates the wound deeply. Soon she pulls out a much larger bullet fragment and drops it like a big piece of lead in a metal pan nearby.

Jennifer looks relieved as her eyes fully open for just a second. She glances at the doctor and me before going unconscious again.

She again irrigates the wound then wheels around and grabs some suture equipment. She quickly returns and prepares the damaged tissues for a suture. She then uses a running suture deep inside Jennifer's upper chest. That means she is weaving it in an out continuously closing the area damaged by the bullet. She begins another running suture to close Jennifer's dark skin. The nylon suture fits snugly to Jennifer's skin.

Worried, she reacts and starts speaking in Russian before catching herself.

The doctor turns to me, "In a few more minutes this woman would have bled to death."

The doctor then turns her attention to Al,

"You can put the gun down, Al. Open that refrigerator and get me two pints of 'O' blood."

Al opens a door and this unit is stacked with blood.

"What is this place?" comes out of my mouth realizing this would have taken some time to put just this room together in the middle of a mountain!

And in the middle of Alaska!

The doctor does not answer me as she is working feverishly on Jennifer.

"I still don't know if she'll make it," says the doctor.

I panic saying, "We gotta go."

"Impossible. They will kill you and now me too. No one comes in here but me. You're safe right here," says the doctor.

Al pipes up, "She's treated me before. She's the only person I trust."

I still don't trust her; I think to myself. The doctor appears to read my mind as she says,

"You don't have to trust me but she needs rest."

"Where are your communication systems?" I ask.

"On the other side of the complex but you'd never make it. They're looking for you." The doctor then looks at Al,

"And you, they've been hunting you for weeks."

"Haven't caught crazy Al Reynolds yet!" says Al, followed by a crazy little laugh.

"They're tryin' ta poison us all with aluminum, ya know. Big shiny aluminum. It's in all their suitcases. We have ta stop 'em. The only place they can't poison us in the mine. They've stolen my mine."

They've stolen his mind all right! I think to myself.

The Russian doctor reacts to me as if: He's nuts but I'll handle it.

"What is this place?" I ask again.

Tatiana says, "Russia wanted a place in North America that was remote, had uranium, dysprosium, thorium and easy access to deep water. Bokan is the only place on earth with all of the above."

Just then a beeping sound goes off on a machine in the corner of the room.

"Can we turn this off?" I ask.

"You can but it's telling you there is excess radiation in here." The doctor walks to an air conditioning panel by the door and opens it.

I run over and shove a gun into her neck.

The doctor says, "I can either suck the radiation out of this room or you can absorb ionizing radiation into your body which will kill you, eventually."

Al says, "It's okay. You can trust her."

After considering my options, I put the gun down.

Al is in the corner peeling paint off the wall and acting totally insane.

The doctor says,

"He's a leftover from the old days when uranium was originally found. For a while in the 1950's this place was booming. He came here to find gold but instead found uranium. He purchased a couple of these mine claims long after they were abandoned then got everyone in his family to purchase claims too. When the price of uranium dropped in the '70s they all left."

The doctor and I look at Al trying to lick paint, "Al never did," she says.

"I'd say he's been here 'bout long enough," I say with sarcasm.

She smiles than asks me,

"So what's your plan?"

Al stops peeling and chewing paint.

We look at each other with nothing but blank stares.

◆ ◆ ◆

I have fallen asleep next to the table where Jennifer is resting in the surgery room.

Jennifer moves a bit which wakes me. I look around. Al and the doctor are gone!

I jump to my feet and run to the door.

Peering out I see no one in the hall.

Knowing I must move her, I close the door and go to Jennifer.

She has on a shoulder arm sling and a new shirt.

I nudge her, "Jennifer."

Jennifer struggles to open her eyes.

"Jennifer, we have to move."

"Where are we?"

"Inside the mountain."

"Bokan?"

"Yes."

"How can that be?"

"I dunno but we have to leave. Now."

Jennifer tries to lift her head but she is too weak.

I pick her up and head for the door.

Peeking out the open door, I see nothing and exit the surgical room. I pull the door shut with my little finger as the other nine are holding a nearly unconscious Jennifer.

Stopping at the same door I came through on our way in, I try the handle. It opens!

Inside the room I run and try to get into the vent we entered.

It's locked and now we're trapped. I look around and see a tall stack of fifty-five gallon drums of something in the corner. I set Jennifer down behind the drums. A large red light in the ceiling goes on and starts spinning like an old police car light.

"Great!"

Just then the steel door opens and I produce my water logged Glock, which I'm pretty confident will fire.

Crazy Al steps through the door.

"We've gotta get outta here." I say.

"No. Wait." Al looks up.

I think he's nuts.

Then the air system turns on.

"It's just the ventilation system. The radiation is everywhere in this place."

"Great! So we were just exposed to radiation in that air blast on the way in?" I ask.

Al looks like he has no idea what I'm talking about. So then I ask him,

"Can't we go out the way we came in?"

"No. It's guarded now. They know we're down here."

I walk over to Jennifer seeing she is really weak but trying to speak.

Al walks over. "How's she doing?"

Jennifer rolls her eyes as if: Not too good.

Al says, "I was in the big one. WWII. Navy. Only three things I fear in this world:

"God, electricity and German subs. You know why?"

"You can't see any of 'em but cha know they'll all kill ya!"

Al has a crazy laugh and I realize this guy isn't playing with a full deck but he saved our lives so I strike up a conversation.

"So what'd ya do after the Navy?"

"Went to L.A. and worked for the Department of Water and Power."

"What'd ya do there?"

"Repaired power lines."

Great! This guy spent his whole life with things he's afraid of."

"I came up here to get lucky and strike it rich. Wasn't so lucky, I guess." says Al.

"So the Russians are after the uranium?" I ask.

"Uranium and rare earths, I guess. We're sittin' on five million tons of rare earths. In those rare earths is thorium."

"What's thorium," I ask.

Al says, "Scientists tell me the toxicity of this thing called thorium is 10,000 times less than that of uranium."

Jennifer mumbles, "It's a good fuel to safely run nuclear power in close quarters."

I add, "Like a submarine or a mine?"

"Exactly," mumbles Jennifer. She is groggy but says, "So if the Russians aren't already mining thorium when the uranium runs out, I'll bet they go after the thorium and the largest deposit of <u>dysprosium</u> in the United States."

"Dysprosium? What's that?"

"It's used in the control rods of nuclear reactors and in bombs," says Jennifer. "I was a reactor controls tech on two ships. What I don't understand is, why wouldn't the Russians just let some front company mine here openly?"

I'm now looking at the labels on the barrels, "This is a whole lot more than some mining operation."

Al's mind has wondered off somewhere and is no longer paying any attention.

Looks like he's been in this mine just a little too long, I think to myself.

The thought now hits me, "Ruddy! He's a math professor. That's why Ruddy's here. He's working for the Russians!"

"The sub comes in here every week with supplies," says crazy Al.

"Every week?" JD wonders, "How many subs are there?"

No one answers him.

"It's all a conspiracy. They're tryin' ta poison us with their aluminum they keep bringin' in."

"It's everywhere. They're gonna take over the world."

I'm ignoring Mr. Crazy's rants when suddenly the steel door opens.

Two Russian Special Forces guys appear. They are all in black with weapons in hand. They walk through the storage room without saying a word.

I say to Jennifer and Al, "Stay here."

I watch the Russians exit and decide to follow.

Jennifer, delirious, calls out, "Is it Christmas yet?"

USS RONALD REAGAN (CVN-76)

Gulf of Alaska

E veryone on the bridge of this massive aircraft carrier is in a celebrative mood, after all, it's Christmas!

The Helmsmen, a Petty Officer and Quartermaster of the watch all have on Christmas Santa hats as they go about their duties on this dull, cloudy Christmas morning steaming through the Gulf of Alaska.

Suddenly, bursting onto the bridge is Santa in a full red and white costume. Santa is carrying a big bag of goodies.

"Ho, ho, ho! Merry Christmas!" says Santa as all on the bridge smile and clap.

Santa proceeds to hand out beautifully wrapped presents to all on duty.

Santa is Rear Admiral Robert Baker and this is his last official deployment before retirement. He is in charge of all U.S. Naval Fleets and, only by chance, happens to be on this ship.

On this day a cruiser, two destroyers, a frigate and a supply ship surround the carrier as they steam through the Gulf.

The OOD (Officer of the Deck), James McMillan, exclaims, "Santa, you've wrapped the presents so nicely."

The admiral replies, "Oh trust me, Santa had to have a little help from some of his elves."

Two "elves" now enter the bridge. One is a very pretty young female elf. The other a not so pretty male elf, who looks embarrassed to be there.

James says, "Wow! Eye Candy and Godzilla."

Admiral Baker, "Ya, it's a bigger horror show in the officers' mess. Garland, ribbons and colored paper are everywhere! Looks like Santa stepped on an IED!"

On any day, only eleven officers in the entire U.S. Navy have the honor of commanding a 5,000-sailor aircraft carrier and Admiral Baker is in charge of those eleven officers, at least for a few more weeks.

Admiral Baker says, "So where's your captain?"

James Norton and the other officers become very quiet and look at each other.

Norton nervously says, "He's in the war room, sir."

Admiral Baker is stunned, "On Christmas Day?"

The admiral heads for the door when he meets the captain of the ship, George Murray. Admiral Baker exclaims, "George, where ya been?"

It's clear George is not into the festivities as he is the only person on the bridge without a speck of holiday clothing! George is a serious man who takes his job very seriously.

"Could I speak with you privately, admiral?"

Admiral Baker jokingly looks around at all the others, "All right, Christmas is over. Scrooge is on deck!" The admiral then warmly puts his arm on the captain's shoulder and shows him the way off the bridge saying, "After you, captain."

As the two step off the bridge they are alone. Captain Murray then pulls up the AOAIA charts from the USS Alaska saying, "I think this is a new class of Russian sub. Look, this signature is clearly not one of ours and looks to have been regularly going under Arctic ice to Southeast Alaska for as far back as I have pulled data."

Admiral Baker is taking this very seriously as he looks over the AOAIA data.

"Well, this is why we're steaming to Alaska on Christmas Day, George. I just hope your wrong." Just then an off duty officer rounds the corner looking like he's had something to drink. He exclaims,

"Merry Christmas!"

The officer sees his two bosses do not react as they are overtaken by the possible severity of this situation.

The officer quickly wipes the stupid grin off his face and attempts an inebriated salute.

BOKAN MOUNTAIN, AK

somehow manage to find my way down this mountainous vein into a room with a nuclear reactor humming quietly.

The room has been hued out of solid rock. A jagged roof and walls give an ominous look to the place.

I'm standing here when it dawns on me, "Oh my God, this is a bomb factory!"

I'm a little slow but that seemed so obvious that I can't believe it took me this long to see. I'm about thirty feet above the floor of the modern looking room. I'm standing on a metal grate. It looks just like a small power plant that you'd see in any electric generating facility.

Large tubes look to be pumping cold water in and out of a nuclear reactor in the center of the room.

Many scientists hustle around checking equipment.

I see that scientist we met on the dock scurrying around.

His lies got my partner shot. Oh, he's on the list, I said to myself.

But I've got more important things to do first as a more immediate problem has just arisen.

Two guards walk out of a room overlooking the reactor room dragging the Russian doctor, Tatiana, who looks to have been beaten and tortured.

They haul her to another vein in the mountain that has not been remodeled.

They drag her limp body and I'm not sure she's alive.

I look back to the floor and see a scientist with one arm as the other arm is totally missing!

"Ruddy! I knew that son of a bitch was alive!" I mumble out loud.

I notice the guards aren't looking and I try to creep toward the area where the doctor was taken. I'm forced to duck into a room so as not to be seen.

As I close the door behind myself, it looks as if I just walked in to a Miss Universe pageant.

I think I've gone to another planet.

Five of the most beautiful women I've ever seen are playing in a game room.

The room is filled with sofas, Ping-Pong tables, chessboards, and flat screen video games.

All the women stop what they're doing and stare at me.

A woman closest to me sexily walks over saying, "Can we help you?"

I stand confused as to where I am.

The woman walks up to me and, gazing into my eyes, asks,

"My name is Katrina, what's yours?"

"John." Before I could stop myself I'd already told her my name.

No sooner had I said that than two Russian Special Forces guys burst into the room. I punch the first guy in the face, who falls into the second guy.

I escape the room as gunfire erupts from behind me.

I run down the second story platform looking for any means of escape. The entire room of scientists scrambles in all directions as the gunfire thumps get closer and closer.

As I'm running I'm thinking,

This is what we call ineffective fire. Trouble is, a few inches closer and it will be very effective, 'cause I'll be dead!

As I come to a vein in the mountain, I pull my Glock.

Good thing, as I have to shoot a Spetsnaz soldier running toward me who fires his machine gun. The soldier immediately falls.

I stop and grab the lifeless soldier's PP-2000 sub-machine gun.

I then make my way down this jagged rock tube, looking for the doctor who saved my partner's life.

Another soldier opens a door and I take him down with a quick burst of my newly acquired machine gun. It's a little heavy and not very accurate, I think as I continue down the vein.

I look into a room with bars on a door and there she is!

Tatiana, the Russian doctor is tied to a chair and beat to a pulp.

Ducking inside the room I untie the poor doctor. I lift up her head as she sees it's me.

"I don't think I properly introduced myself, I'm John Denning."

Now I realize she's too weak and her mouth so swollen that she can't speak.

"Never mind. How do we get outta here?"

She motions to the door and to the left.

I pick her up and as we run out of the room to the left. Gunfire erupts at my '6' (Directly behind me). Running away from it, I turn a corner and suddenly there are three veins in which I could go.

I take the one on the right and am immediately hit in the arm by Tatiana's fist. She motions to go back.

After I figure out what she means, I then take the middle vein.

She hits me again and I finally figure out she means to take the vein on the left.

This is the only one of the three that is not lit. I have to stop and turn on the flashlight on my iPhone.

"Are you sure?"

"Da!" she barely slurs.

"Okay." I hand the doctor my phone. "Here, hold this."

As I carry her, she holds the iPhone flashlight toward my feet.

As I carry her through this vein, I'm thinking,

Hell of a week! Hell of a week!

We finally near another gated door with bars across our path. I now realize, we are in another one of those air vents as a large fan begins blowing air.

Problem is the gate is locked.

"Great! Now what?"

The doctor reaches for her shoe and takes it off. Confused, I pick it up and out falls a key.

With it, I open the steel bars that look like a jail cell door and then have to run with her around a bend in the vein. Light rushes in to the cave entrance just ahead.

We act like vampires who haven't seen daylight for months as we shield our eyes from the brightness. It's not sunny but it's clearly far brighter than the light I've seen in almost twenty-four hours.

The sun has already set long ago behind the 2,302-foot mountain.

Snow covers this entire area and there are not many trees up this high.

I'm confused as we are clearly higher than where Al took me into the mountain.

I check my pockets and pull out my iPhone: No Service.

"Damn!"

I figure, what do I have to lose? I try to send a text to the Ketchikan Police Chief.

The text read...

AMBUSHED
BOKAN MT.
PARTNER SHOT...

I accidentally hit send but the phone says: Not Delivered.

"Damn it!"

"I have ta go back, Tatiana."

She tries to speak but is having difficulty. I lean over to try to hear what she's saying.

The doctor says,

"Go."

"Leave your phone."

"I'll keep texting."

"Lock the gate."

I hesitate but realize she's right. I hand her my phone and say,

"I'll be back for you."

I stand, unlock the steel door and step back into the mine.

I look back at the poor, beat up doctor who risked her life for us and I think to myself,

"Well, I've already lived a week longer than I thought I would!"

KETCHIKAN, AK

Diary of Police Chief - Robert Stone

The sun had already set.

I'm the Chief of Police, Ketchikan, Alaska.

The name is Robert Stone, and up until today I was a by the book kind of cop.

I'm really tired of never seeing my family for any of the holidays. We all have to work, I guess, I shouldn't complain, as my biggest case was usually a missing dog or pulling a police cruiser out of Thomas Basin.

There isn't much crime in Ketchikan. Where you going to run? You're on an island!

Anyway, our department owns this 2000 Ford Escape that can barely make it up and down the hills in town.

I hate this car!

The engine really never ran properly again after my deputy "accidentally" ran the SUV into the basin. I suspected my deputy had been drinking on the job but never did a breathalyzer, blood, or any other test as he's my son and I desperately needed the help.

It also helped that his mother had a twenty-year career as an emergency dispatcher for the entire region and, is my wife!

So, my deputy son, in plain clothes, is following this MAA character after he arrived from Portland, Oregon. I left several text messages with that FBI, Denning, guy.

"We don't know where the hell he is!"

I'm pulling into the lot when my deputy calls over the radio, "Dad, I think I just lost our suspect. He was in the bar and went to the bathroom. I just checked the bathroom. He's gone."

"I'm on my way over."

I shook my head, thinking, I better not find out my kid has been drinking again on the job. I call Tony's mother on the two-way radio, "Yura?"

She answers, "Yes?"

"Make sure everyone knows we lost our suspect. Put out that picture of him and say: If anyone sees him don't do anything but call me immediately."

I don't want any trouble.

I like my town just the way it is. Nice and quiet!

Too bad I never saw my phone, which was upside down on the seat, of the squad car.

I didn't want trouble but trouble was not far away.

BOKAN MOUNTAIN

Russian Command and Control Center

Two GRU soldiers walk up to a very large and very sophisticated door. It looks much like the large, steel door of NORAD inside the Cheyenne Mountain Complex in Colorado before the facility was pretty much shuttered.

This door has multiple biometric scans.

They put all five fingers of their right hand on a scanner.

Then they place their entire face in front of another scanner.

Finally, something right out of a Star Trek movie.

A laser shoots thousands of tiny grid patterns across their entire body.

You still cannot get in unless a security team visually sees you and then opens the door from the inside.

The first Russian does the dance and the door opens.

Inside this room is the military nerve center for the new Russian Alaska Command.

An entire wall, the size of three movie screens, take up the front wall. All of them are currently dark.

Twenty monitors with GRU operators sit busily working.

General Victor Zelin, a grey haired man who is as mean as they come, stands overlooking his creation. He is proud that he has accomplished something no one in history has done. The general has managed to place a Russian military command center on U.S. soil.

He was given military strength briefings on the Americans for years. He knew the Americans were weak. When the American economy crumbles he believed it would be his duty to make sure any military threat was communicated back to Moscow and to communicate Moscow's orders to his *Proyekt-239* team and execute them.

A lieutenant looks over to the general.

"We're ready, sir."

The general says, "Do it."

The three giant screens light up with the shape of Alaska and all North America thanks to the work of *TK-20* and their underwater team.

Soon after, the room has work lights turned on as exactly twenty-two beautiful Russian women enter the room.

The women are dressed not for combat but rather what, confusingly, looks to be more similar to evening gowns.

All the GRU operators stand at military attention. The women line up in front of the general as in some sort of bizarre fashion show, slash military drill.

The general slowly walks looking over all of them.

He is clearly pleased.

"Today you will embark on very special mission. You have been trained your whole lives for this moment. The suitcases, the money are for you. Follow your training and do your duty. You are most important to Mother Russia and me. At any moment you may be called upon to complete your mission. It may not come for years. The moment may come tomorrow. When moment comes, know you shall do this to make this world safer for all. President Mironovich and I thank you."

The general salutes them,

"Za vas!"

As all of the "beauty pageant" women march out of the room, General Zelin has one of his top lieutenants approach him.

"We still haven't found him, sir."

"Keep looking."

"Yes sir!"

◆ ◆ ◆

Inside a seemingly endless hallway of Bokan Mountain, Katrina and George Ruddy open a door to their room and close it behind them.

As they enter the dark room she flips on a light. George and Katrina begin to passionately kiss each other.

"Look!" She exclaims, placing a suitcase on a nearby table. She opens the suitcase and it's one of the twenty-two that JD found on the barge. It's loaded with one million U.S. dollars. The room is small but has a kitchen area. There is also a couch.

One-armed George grabs her and kisses her again.

"Where are we going?"

"Washington D.C." she answers.

He begins to unbutton her blouse with his one hand. She smiles and wants to take this further. She lets him slowly take off her blouse as he continues to kiss her. He walks her to the bedroom door, continuing to kiss her. George Ruddy steps into the darkness first and suddenly stops. He then slowly keeps moving into the darkness along with his redheaded beauty.

They are now in their bedroom as the door closes behind them.

I flip on a light with my Glock pointed at George's head.

"Hello, George. Special Agent John Denning, FBI." I say with just a little bit of sarcasm.

I look at the redhead and say,

"And you must be the girlfriend."

"You guys are way past pseudocide."

"We know his name is George. We've been calling you Jane Doe. And your name is?"

She looks at George who encourages her to talk.

"Katrina Volkov."

George chimes in, "They call her, the wolf."

"Lovely. Oh right, the girl from the game room. You've changed your hair. I like it."

"Nice place you have here."

"So, I have just a few questions for you. Why don't you both have a seat."

They nervously sit on the bed.

"Do you think you could give me some answers?" I ask.

Both hesitate then slightly nod.

"Good. Good. Things will move a lot faster if you don't hesitate, okay?"

Now, "How do you communicate from here?"

"From the Ops Center but you'll never get in there."

"And your plan is?"

They look at each other and I realize I'll probably not get much out of either of them but they see I'm not in any mood for story time, especially with a PP-2000 submachine gun trained on them.

"We're not doing anything unless provoked by your President and Congress," says George.

"My President? My Congress? George, I didn't get the memo, did you renounce your citizenship?"

George doesn't want to talk any more.

So I have to prod him a bit,

"And then?"

"Then we do want our instructions tell us."

"And what would that be?"

Neither answers. I look at them for a long time.

"So you would do anything including setting off nuclear devises?"

Again no answer.

"So how many bombs have you built?"

I realize I may not be getting much more info from these two so I get really sarcastic and say,

"I assume since the FBI forensic lab found your DNA on teeth fragments that you have dentures?"

George doesn't want to say anything until I walk closer with my submachine gun.

He then pulls out his dentures and shows me.

"Thanks George.

"So which one of you murdered your neighbor, Albert Tuck in Oregon and tried to make us think it was George."

Again nothing from either of them.

"Okay, do either of you have anything further you'd like to volunteer?"

George clearly doesn't want to speak, with or without dentures.

So, I stand, pick up a roll of duct tape and toss it to Katrina.

"You can put your teeth back in now, George."

I look to Katrina and say,

"He's not quit as nice looking without his teeth, now, is he? Ya know, we haven't executed an American traitor since the 1950s. But we just might make an exception for you, George!"

George interrupts,

"You're making a big mistake. These people will kill you and anyone that…"

I interrupt, "Start with his mouth."

Katrina tears off a piece of duct tape and, after hesitating, places it over George's mouth. Then the devil, in human form, decides to try her wiles on me again.

She looks at me sexily and starts to walk in my direction as if she was on the Miss Universe runway.

I train the PP 2000 right at her big Russians breasts.

That stops her.

"I'm not falling for that act again."

I grab one of George's shirts nearby and toss it to her.

"And put something on. You're embarrassing yourself."

Katrina, not happy, puts on the shirt.

"Now, please tape his one good arm to his chest. Go on. Do it."

Katrina takes the duct tape and starts winding it around George.

"Tighter. Much, much tighter."

Katrina does so grudgingly.

"Now his feet."

Katrina wraps George's feet too.

"And now yours."

Katrina starts to wrap her feet then stops.

"You will not be allowed to leave here," says Katrina.

"Guess I'm just gonna have ta change the rules then, aren't I?"

Katrina has stopped taping herself.

"Keep going."

Katrina is furious but, like a good Russian soldier, is dutifully finishing.

I grab the duct tape saying,

"Hold your hands out."

She eventually does and I duct tape her hands together.

Katrina makes the mistake of trying to speak so I duct tape her mouth too.

"Okay, now if you both would be so kind to stay right here, okay?"

"Okay."

I start to leave, stop, then come back. I decide these two need more duct tape. So I place George in a chair and duct tape him to it. Then I tape him to a wall.

Next I tape Katrina, standing, to another wall on the other side of the room.

"There."

I pick up my gun and duct tape and, as I'm about to leave the room, I look back at the suitcase loaded with a million dollars.

"Oh, I almost forgot this!"

George goes nuts when he sees I'm taking his million in cash.

I walk back over to him and sarcastically say,

"George, George calm down. You're liable to kill yourself."

I don't even think this Harvard "genius" got the joke.

I glance over at the entire roll of duct tape now on the two murderers taped to the wall.

"You know, there's just nothing you can't do with a nice, big, roll of duct tape!"

MOSCOW

Even though this is December 25th, Russians celebrate Christmas on January 7th so this is a workday like any other.

Well, not exactly.

President Ivan Mironovich and his right hand man, Viktor Sokolov, are huddled in the President's office in the Kremlin. It looks just as you might imagine. The deep, dark rich, wood from Siberia surround the walls. The crystal chandelier hanging above them alone is worth millions.

Viktor Sokolov is waiting for instructions as the president looks to be in intense thought. Finally, he answers.

"I've spent years cultivating republicans and democrats in the U.S. From U.S. Senators to American business people, we've tried to convince America we want to be in business together."

"We brought that one lecherous U.S. Senator to Moscow, gave him millions and millions of Rubles for his boring twenty minute speeches and then let him have his way with as many of our beautiful Russian women as he wanted and you're telling me one FBI agent is about to ruin my plans?"

"It appears the FBI agent, Denning, has not been able to communicate with anyone. The other FBI agent, Tavana, is wounded and has been locked up along with the traitor who helped them," he then hesitates,

"Do we proceed?"

"Of course. By the time the Americans find out what is happening it will be too late."

Sokolov asks, "So implement Phase III?"

"Yes. There's no turning back now, Viktor. Is the new currency ready for upload?"

"Yes."

"How are the Chinese reacting?"

"The Chinese Premier says China is ready to implement. They are waiting on us."

"When other currencies devalue to the point of worthlessness if anyone wants to buy or sell anything they will have to have our currency."

"It was wise, Mr. President, that you had our banks stock gold," says Sokolov.

"If needed, we shall tie the new currency to our gold reserves. China agrees."

"These are exciting times, Mr. President."

Ivan Mironovich nods this head in the affirmative while immense concern hides behind his weary eyes.

KETCHIKAN

Police Chief Robert Stone's Diary

Yura has decorated our house for Christmas and she's not even here to enjoy it.

I hate my job.

I can't wait 'til I retire.

I'm moving somewhere warmer too!

So I'm sitting in my old, ripped, cloth recliner at home watching TV. I had forgotten how funny the movie *Police Squad* was:

Frank Drebin is searching a drawer and says,
"Bingo!"
Drebin then pulls out and holds up a bingo card.[9]

"Bingo! That's funny," I say chuckling.

I look around my home and notice that nobody's ever here anymore. Everybody's working twelve-hour shifts.

I've really gotta retire.

The phone rings and I ignore it as I've just finished another twelve-hour day.

I continue watching *Police Squad* on TV but the phone just won't leave me alone.

It begins ringing again and, annoyed, I finally walk to the area of the nuisance.

I have to rifle through a tall pile of unread newspapers!

Finally, I locate the annoyance stuffed down the side of my sofa and now, really annoyed, I answer, "Hello!"

On the other end of the phone is Yura. "Where have you been? I've been trying to call you."

I check my pockets and realize my cell phone isn't on me.

"Guess I left my cell in the car," I mumble.

"Tony is at Ketchikan Aviation. A guy over there says he just flew a couple of guys out fitting our man's description," says Yura.

"Where they goin'?" I ask.

"A fishing lodge twenty miles south of town," says Yura.

"Have the pilot stall them," I exclaim, "And tell the Eskimo to fire up our plane!"

"That sounds so racist," says Yura.

"Lighten up, he's our son! Stone out."

I toss the phone onto the couch, pick up my belt and gun, and head to my gun safe.

I open the large six-foot high safe and pull out a Springfield .308 semi-auto rifle and an ammo bag before heading out the door.

Outside it's dark as I climb into this piece of crap SUV that the department owns.

Inside, I start it up as it sputters and pops. I back out of my driveway thinking: if I moved to a beach in Barbados tomorrow, I wouldn't miss this damp, musty old place.

I see this crazy Totem pole we have in our front yard that Yura has put Christmas lights on and think, it would kill Yura, a native Aleut, to move from her heritage but I'm not sure how many more cold winters I can take.

Meanwhile, Tony is on the two-way radio,

"A couple of suspicious looking guys were hanging around here on their phones."

I say, "Are they Middle Eastern looking?"

"Ya, I think so. Want me to arrest them?"

Now I'm worried saying, "On what charge?"

A long pause before Tony answers, "I dunno."

"We can't arrest people that look Middle Eastern!"

Tony answers matter of fact, "Uh, okay."

"Idiot!"

Tony yells, "I heard that!"

"Good! 'Cause you're an idiot!"

"You raised me!"

"I'm an idiot too!"

Yura now chimes in, "Boys, boys, be nice to each other."

After a really long pause Tony answers, "Okay mom."

I just shake my head as I pull up to Ketchikan Aviation.

I step out of the car, close the door and start to walk away.

Suddenly, I realize I don't have my cell phone.

Seeing it on the seat, I reach back inside, pick it up, and without looking, put it in my pocket. Then I head into the aviation building on the dock.

GULF OF ALASKA, KUIU ISLAND

A clear but cold night that would make even a Russian shiver. Commander Orlov sips some hot coffee, as his boat bobs up and down on a fairly calm Alaskan night.

The Russian GRU Special Forces team leader is twenty-one miles west of the Cape Decision lighthouse on Kuiu Island. He stands on the bridge of a 100-foot commercial fishing trawler named "King of the Crabs," sitting dead in the water.

This was the exact location where Jack Tanner was when he saw a Russian sub.

The Russians look very serious as if something important is about to happen. None are talking but rather they sit on deck, waiting. Their automatic weapons are not carried but are at their ready.

Inside the bridge, Commander Orlov, is speaking in Farsi on a Motorola SRX-2200 radio to someone. The Russian commander then says to his sonar men with very sophisticated equipment,

"Any American subs follow them?"

"Nyet," is the answer from all three Russian sonar technicians.

"Is Richag-AV active?" asks Orlov.

A sonar tech confirms by saying,

"Da, Richag is active commander."

Orlav then says into his Motorola radio in Farsi,

"Go ahead and surface."

The Richag-AV system is a DRFM (Digital Radio Frequency Memory) system that captures then blinds and confuses enemy radar and sonar so that a target seems in another location or not there at all!

All of the Russians on the bridge look port side as a submarine surfaces nearby. This is clearly not a Typhoon class sub or *TK-20*. This is a brand new *Be'sat II* submarine.

But it's not Russian.

It's Iranian!

While illegal under the Iran nuclear deal, the Iranians, flush with about $150 billion from America, have been secretly purchasing and developing all sorts of new weapons systems. One of them is the ballistic missile technology developed by North Korea.

The Russians cautiously approach the sub as movement is seen on the conning tower.

Exactly twenty-two men eventually exit the Iranian sub and stand on the front hull. The Russians throw ropes as they inch nearer to the sub. Russian Commander Orlov says, "Go get them."

"Yes, sir!" The Russian exits the bridge.

As the Iranians begin to board the boat en masse, a Russian looks to the bridge as if,

"Is this okay?"

Orlov exits the bridge and shakes his head,

Nyet!

There are to be no more Iranians on board.

Twenty-two beautiful Russian girls, now each wearing a hijab, smile and wave to the Iranians.

The Iranian men on the sub cheer as they see the girls.

Orlov walks to a tiny Iranian with large black rim glasses and speaks to him in Farsi,

"Brigadier General Bahadur?" reaches his hand out and shakes the Russian's hand.

Both have cold steely eyes as they stare down their "comrade."

Orlov asks, "You did as instructed?"

Bahadur, "The Americans think we're sitting at the bottom of the Indian Ocean. Thank you for the simulator."

The simulator to which the general is referring is actually an updated version of the Russian MG-114 Berilly self-propelled system. The American system is called MOSS (Mobile Submarine Simulator). It's a four-inch wide mobile decoy that acts and sounds like a submarine. This ingenious little device is basically a small, unarmed torpedo. In fact, depending on the submarine, it is generally deployed out of a torpedo tube.

A MOSS is designed to tool around the ocean making sounds, behaving like a normal submarine. If the water is not too deep, this mini-sub can settle on the bottom and make other sounds a real submarine might make while pretending to be hidden.

Meanwhile, the real submarine takes off undetected.

This is exactly what the Iranians were able to pull off.

It also helped that the Russians Typhoon subs had tapped all of the acoustical listening posts the United States has off its West Coast.

Orlov, suddenly becomes much more welcoming, "Come on inside!"

As they enter the galley of the commercial fishing ship it is clean and sterile. The two men sit at a table as both Russian and Iranian gunmen stand at the door.

Twenty-two large black suitcases are in the corner. Bahadur's eyes light up, "May I see?"

Orlov walks to a suitcase, picks it up and returns to Bahadur. Orlov casually slings the suitcase onto a table and opens it.

Inside is a one-kiloton nuclear device.

It has one large, silvery (Crazy Al's aluminum reference), round device in the center of the suitcase. There are two smaller silvery round chambers sitting, parallel, alongside the large rocket looking center. In fact, it more resembles a miniature Titan IIIC rocket. There are no buttons, lights, dials, or anything else but a small, sealed, polished aluminum, square box sitting in one corner.

Bahadur smiles then looks puzzled, "How do we arm this?"

Orlov, "You are not to concern yourself with such things. Did you bring your consideration?"

Bahadur motions to his men, one leaves the room and says,

"How can we trust you will stick to the plan?"

Orlov quickly answers, "How can we trust 'you' will stick to the plan?"

Both men return to their stare down. The galley door opens with forty-four Iranians carrying twenty-two very heavy suitcases. The suitcases are so heavy it takes two men for every suitcase.

The Russians do not seem to realize there are now more Iranians then there are Russians. The Iranians plunk down the suitcases and open them. Solid gold bars worth one billion U.S. dollars are revealed.

Bahadur now returns to business, "We must have a way to arm these."

Orlov, "Just follow the plan and our mutual ends shall be accomplished."

Bahadur, "I must insist that we have control over arming and disarming."

Orlav, "My orders will not allow that." Both return to their stare down.

Orlov then says, "You must have your men take your beautiful brides to America and wait for our instructions."

"Another ship, sir," says a Russian sailor.

Bahadur looks starboard side and sees another commercial fishing trawler approaching.

"That is ours."

The second commercial trawler pulls alongside Bahadur who is not happy.

"My men are taking all of the risk distributing your suitcases," says Bahadur.

Orlov replies, "And they have been compensated with one million U.S. dollars each."

"That is not enough. They must drive the nukes passed border crossings all along the Canadian border and into the U.S."

"Your men will be crossing at unmanned checkpoints. Right now, we are less than thirty miles from Canadian waters. Our people are waiting for you in Prince Rupert on the Trans-Canada highway. From there you can go anywhere in North America. You will be given passports, IDs and further instructions. We have chosen remote areas to cross into America. There will be no border agents, no cameras, and no way of identifying anyone. Your men will be newlyweds and blend in. Should be easy."

"Then why don't you send your own men?" asks Badahur.

Orlov doesn't answer.

So after another stare down, Badahur moves on to his men,

"May the peace of God be with all of you as you go fulfill His duty. Take these beautiful brides and make Jihadi warriors all. When the time comes we shall bring peace once and for all to this earth. As is written twenty-two times on our beloved national flag,"

"Allah Akbar!"

All of his men repeat, "Allah Akbar!"

As soon as twenty-two terrorists leave with their ravishingly gorgeous "wives" Bahadur pulls a Raa'd 9mm pistol to the head of Orlav.

"Have your men drop their weapons. I don't want any bloodshed."

Orlav, being outmanned, nods to his men.

The Russians slowly lay down their weapons.

"You're making a big mistake," chides Orlav.

Bahadur then marches Orlav to the bridge saying,

"This wasn't the agreement. Take us to your commander."

"I cannot do that," responds Orlav.

Bahadur, "You shall do that or you and your men will pay with their blood."

Orlav, "Then we're all dead men as my commander might detonate those suitcases unless he hears from me. And hears from me, now."

Bahadur seems unaffected by the threat saying, "Talk to him."

Orlav gives a signal to one of his men who points to a cabinet drawer.

As he starts to open the drawer, one of Bahadur's men stops him and opens the drawer himself.

Inside is a satellite phone. Bahadur's man gives the phone to Orlav.

Bahadur nods to Orlov to proceed.

Orlov calls General Victor Zelin at the Bokan Command Center.

Bahadur puts a gun to Orlov's head.

"The world shall see peace when the twelfth Imam reveals himself. Are you willing to die right now for him? I am."

Orlav looks with sarcasm at this crazy man and says, "You mean the guy who already died a thousand years ago?"

TK-20

Captain Vasili's Diary

"Y ou mean the guy who already died a thousand years ago?" I hear over *TK-20*'s speaker system.

I'm in control room of *TK-20* watching two fishing trawlers and Iranian sub from my periscope, just under the water's surface.

"Do we have solution?"

"Aye, captain," says Nikolai, my over eager 2nd in command.

TK-20 has been retrofitted to fire only four torpedoes, two of which are 650mm tubes while the other two are 533mm tubes. One '53' or '65' torpedo could easily sink one or more of these ships.

"You slimy Iranian bastards now get taste of Russia," I said.

Anything trying to escape my sub would be hit with torpedo designed to follow propeller in water and explode on impact.

None of them would stand a chance.

"Four fish in their chambers locked and loaded, sir!" an enthusiastic Nikolai reports.

I shout, "Range to targets?"

"950 yards!" calls out senior michman (warrant officer).

I then bark, "Flood tubes one and two."

"Aye, flooding tubes one and two, sir."

Over speaker system, "Conn, radio room, incoming from Moscow."

I yell back as I keep one eye buried in periscope,

"Radio room, conn, put Moscow on speaker."

"Captain Vasili, Admiral Perchinkov, stand down. I repeat, stand down."

I immediately answer, "Aye, stand down. We are standing down, sir."

In the "old days" a good sonar officer aboard the Iranian sub would be listening and could likely have heard word for word what I said over TK-20's speaker system.

However, with our new top-secret skin developed by "friends" in St. Petersburg at Roselectronics they won't hear a single word. Acoustic absorbing and reflective coatings makes us almost invisible to radar and sonar.

These Top Secret materials are so secret I don't even know their names. All I know is that several materials and coatings had been applied to my entire hull. I was told, after testing, that sonar technicians sitting next to my boat wouldn't be able to hear gunshot inside my boat!

"Follow and observe only. Await further orders."

Without hesitating I said,

"Yes, sir. Follow and observe only."

Then I thought to myself,

I don't care how silent we are, the Americans will find us sooner or later, see us as a threat and kill all my men!

Nikolai, standing nearby, seems upset that he won't get to see and hear some actual combat.

These foolish kids have no idea of what it's like to see and hear men trapped and dying inside a sinking ship.

I have to get off this thing, get back to my wife and retire. I really liked those pictures of Nebraska. I wonder what people there are doing today?

Iranians now load several "suitcases" (I had no idea what they were at this point) onto second much smaller fishing boat. This boat has several tiny rubber rafts on it.

Second boat then speeds away from *King of the Crabs* and Iranian sub.

King of the Crabs pulls away from Iranian sub.

I yell, "Radio room, conn, tell Moscow we now have three possible hostile fish. Two big fish and a little fish. Multiple packages offloaded. Little fish heading away. Advise. End Message."

After a pause, the radio room answers over ship's speaker system, "Radio room, conn, Moscow says stay with the two big fish. Let the little fish go."

"Conn, radio room, confirm with Moscow, following big fish," I say.

Soon the michman in radio room confirms,

"Radio room, conn, told Moscow. We're tracking the two big fish!"

KETCHIKAN POLICE PLANE

Diary of Police Chief Robert Stone

I'm flying in a small, floatplane, at 2,000 feet and "somewhat" fast. Onboard is my deputy son and the pilot.

Actually, this thing called an "airplane" is barely flying as it sputters and pops.

I hate flying!

Especially in this.

It's very dark in the plane.

What a way to die, I think to myself.

Jimmy Thomas, our pilot, has a large swaggering mustache. In fact, our very, very old British pilot looks like he has just flown right out of a World War I movie.

And the plane is no better.

It's probably the only plane in North America that has old World War I biplane wings, a Cessna body and lands on water (kinda)!

"This plane's really a piece of crap, isn't it?" I say.

"You're lucky you didn't see this during daylight or you would have never gotten aboard," says Jimmy. "The Eskimo's been working on this for months just to get it started."

I turn up the right side of my upper lip,

"How reassuring," I answer. Just then I realize a crucifix is sitting on our "dash." The crucifix is surrounded by green garland.

Oh! How festive, I sarcastically thought.

And Jimmy was kind of a strange one but, then again, so am I.

Jimmy's a long way from home.

He grew up in Dover, England and travelled to Alaska once when he was a boy with his parents on vacation and fell in love with Alaska. Jimmy came back as an adult and never left.

Jimmy's a pilot, like his father before him, and said he came to Alaska as he "connected with the sky here," whatever the hell that means, I thought as I sat in this death trap called our police plane.

There is something spiritual in nature here, Jimmy would always say.

"Whatever," I would always say back.

Don't get me wrong I love Alaska except for the bitter, cold winters, my old cold drafty house, my cars that don't run properly and... and come to think of it I really don't love Alaska at all. I would give anything to be sipping a cold drink on a nice warm beach!

The Ketchikan Police Department technically owns this piece of junk only because no one else wants it. This old bucket of bolts is literally flying, on one wing and a prayer!

As we fly over Annette Island, my damn phone goes off again.

At this time, I still didn't see Denning's text for help.

That's because it sits with '104' other casual texts from my wife and sons that I would routinely ignore.

I answer the phone because I can't ignore my wife any longer.

"Hi Yura."

The plane suddenly sputters and pops.

This scares the hell out of me.

The pilot and Tony don't seem upset at all.

"Oh my God! Why doesn't anything with an engine we own run properly?" I yell.

Tony pipes up, "Cause the Eskimo repairs them."

I put my phone on speaker as Yura says, "That's so racist!"

I say, "Eskimo is only racist in Canada."

Yura, "I lived in Canada."

I jokingly say, "And you can go back there any time ya want."

Yura doesn't take it as a joke. There is dead silence on the phone.

Tony says, "How can calling my bother an Eskimo be racist, mom?"

Yura, "Don't call your brother an Eskimo. Tell your son to stop talking like a racist!"

I say, "Eskimo 2, stop calling Eskimo 1, an Eskimo, you racist Eskimo, you!

Yura, "You guys all sound like racists!"

I say, "How can I be a racist? I married you!"

Yura says, "Very funny. I have a 911 call on hold."

"Okay, honey, bye," I say.

The pilot looking at me and says,

"Wow!"

In jest I say to Tony, "I'm thinking of adopting a white kid so our family can be more diverse!"

After he doesn't laugh I then ask him,

"So what did the pilot say?"

"He was taking two people all cash to Pond Bay on Duke Island," says Tony.

"I thought they were going to a fishing lodge?"

"The suspects changed their itinerary midair," says Tony.

"Well, that sounds fishy," I reply.

I look at the pilot, "What's at Pond Bay?"

"Nothing," he says.

I ask, "Did the Pond Bay pilot have IFR?"

IFR is Instrument Flight Rules. IFR allows flying by instruments in any weather conditions, day or night. Most of the floatplanes that fly around here for the cruise ships in summer don't have IFR. They only have VFR (Visual Flight Rules). VFR is for daylight, good weather conditions, not night and low ceilings (clouds) where you need instruments.

"I seriously doubt it but cash always speaks louder than words," says Tony.

"True but he could lose his pilot's license!" I answer.

Jimmy speaks up, "I could lose mine!"

"We don't have any IFR on this piece of junk?" I ask.

The pilot just stares at me as if,

Didn't you just answer your own question?

"I should arrest you right now! You can land this thing on Pond Bay, right?"

"In? Yes! On may be another story," replies Jimmy sarcastically.

I look at Jimmy long and hard, not appreciating the joke. I finally look at my phone again and see "104" text messages saying,

"I wish you guys wouldn't text me every time you think of something. I do have other things…"

I finally see Denning's text message and open it.

"Holy shit!"

"Turn this plane around. We're going to Bokan Mountain!"

"Now!"

The pilot makes a 180-degree sharp turn that would curdle the blood of a fighter pilot.

The old engine struggles to keep up with its own wings.

I hang onto the ceiling while trying to call Yura,

"I'm sending you this text now, Yura. Get it to the FBI Strategic Information Operations Center in D.C. and only speak with an HRT supervisor, okay, sweetheart?"

HRT is the FBI's Hostage Rescue Team and has an undisclosed number of Gold, Red, and Blue Teams stationed all over the United States.

But this is Alaska.

I'm thinking it could take a hostage rescue team a day or more to get up here.

And, at this time, I clearly had no idea what I was in for.

"Better call SERT and send them the same text I'm sending you now," I say, in a panic.

SERT is Alaska's Special Emergency Response Team.

They are basically the equivalent of a SWAT team.

"Okay," says Yura.

"My cell won't work much longer. You'll have ta call Jimmy on his two-way, Okay?"

Yura can sense the fear in my voice as she says,

"You guys take care."

I pretend to act tough,

"Hey, we've made it this far in this piece of junk. Nothing can hurt us!"

Yura then says, "I love you guys."

I hang up the phone and looking at the pilot I say,

"You got a gun?"

Jimmy reaches behind us where Tony is sitting and pulls up an old drab, green, army bag and unzips it.

Inside, a cadre of weapons is piled high.

"Hell, ya! This is Alaska!"

I fire off the following message:

FROM CHIEF OF POLICE
ROBERT S. STONE
KETCHIKAN, ALASKA
FBI AGENTS AMBUSHED
BOKAN MT., ALASKA
AT LEAST ONE INJURED
CONDITION UNKNOWN
TEXT WAS FROM YESTERDAY
I'M FLYING THERE NOW
SEND HOSTAGE RESCUE TEAM ASAP.
DON'T KNOW HOW MANY HOSTILES PRESENT
WILL ADVISE WHEN ON SCENE
THIS IS NOT A DRILL…
REPEAT…
NOT A DRILL!
CONTACT KETCHIKAN EMERGENCY DISPATCH
AT (907) 227-XXXX
FOR FURTHER INFORMATION

Then I made a really, really, dumb move. I text Denning's phone:

NOT TO WORRY.
FBI & SERT ON THE WAY!

I hit send.

Only then does it cross my mind, maybe that wasn't such a good idea.

BOKAN MOUNTAIN

Russian Command Center

A GRU officer stands from his monitor and walks to General Victor Zelin, interrupting him with John Denning's phone in hand.

The Special Forces team had JD's phone hooked up to their antennas on top of Bokan Mountain and had signal amplifiers monitoring every frequency in the area.

The GRU officer walks up to General Zelin and says,

"We have a problem sir. Local police and Special Forces are on their way."

"How much time?"

"Depends on where they're stationed. We probably have at least a few hours but local police..."

"I don't care about local police. Lock up the mountain."

"Yes, sir."

General Zelin looks over to another soldier at a nearby monitor.

"Where are the Iranians?"

The GRU radio specialist says, "They're here."

"And the American?"

"We've searched this entire facility multiple times. Cameras show him leaving."

General Zelin now looks at, Boris Babkin, who helped design the facility,

"Somehow he got in and somehow he got out? How?"

Babkin quickly answers, "He exploited ventilation systems in some of the old mining veins. Those are now all locked down."

"We designed this fortress to withstand a direct nuclear attack."

"No one is getting in or out now."

"Good! Keep it that way," says the general.

On the largest screen in the center of the room appears President Ivan Mironovich and he doesn't look happy. Viktor Sokolov is standing just behind the president.

General Zelin comes to attention as his president speaks.

"General Zelin, am I to understand two FBI agents are on the loose in my facility?"

General Zelin is a bit nervous. A single bead of sweat rolls down his plump, pasty white cheek as he attempts to hide his high anxiety.

"Everything is under control here Mr. President. There is only one FBI agent still on the loose. We have secured entire facility. The Americans couldn't blast their way in here if they wanted to."

The president forcefully says, "I am taking control of your operation. The suitcase codes have all been changed. Hold out as long as you can. We will attempt to make an exchange and bring you home."

"We will not let you down, Mr. President. The American will be captured," the general says.

President Mironovich doesn't want any of it, "If you come home, you will be tried for incompetence."

The president disconnects not wanting to hear any more.

General Zelin reacts to this news by staring at the blank screen, frozen in place.

POND BAY, DUKE ISLAND, AK

Two small rubber boats from *The Cod-Father* fishing trawler, with several Iranians aboard, sits silently in the waters of Pond Bay. A floatplane appears off the starboard bow and slides into the black waters of a full moonlit night.

As the plane pulls up to the fishing trawler the charter pilot kills his engine.

MAA and two "friends" are aboard the plane. MAA opens the passenger door.

Two Iranian men toss a rope as the pilot glides the plane near the boat.

MAA and his friends are all in their twenties.

The Iranians are all smiles as they welcome their friends.

Three beautiful Russian women meet MAA and his two friends. One of the women get on the plane with MAA as two of MAA's friends get into one of the rubber boats.

Each Russian woman sexily wraps her arms around her man.

The men are infatuated.

After some small talk the Iranians give MAA two suitcases.

They say goodbye.

MAA takes his two suitcases (The money and a nuke), his new bride and closes the door of his floatplane. The plane immediately accelerates and flies into the darkness.

KENDRICK BAY

The Iranian sub and the two commercial fishing trawlers, *King of The Crabs* and *The Cod-Father*, have pulled to the moonlit dock of Kendrick Bay. Inside the bridge of the trawler the Iranians are clearly in charge. Their guns are still trained on the Russians.

Russian Special Forces Commander Orlav is on a 512k encrypted satellite phone saying,

"My general wants to speak with you." Orlav hands the phone to Iranian General Bahadur.

General Victor Zelin is in no mood for these two bit terrorists trying to cross him.

"Here is what you will do. You will stick to the plan. Take your men and their brides to America and leave this area. The FBI is enroute."

"I am coming in to speak with you personally," says General Bahadur.

"That is not possible."

"Then we will kill your men one at a time."

"What do you want?"

"I want to be able to detonate these weapons."

"This was never agreed to. We must wait to see what the Americans will do."

An Iranian grabs a GRU soldier and shoots him in the head. The Russian soldier falls to the ground with the mortal wound spraying blood out the far side of his head. Another Iranian grabs a second Russian soldier and says, "Tell your general what happened."

The soldier refuses so the second Russian is shot as well.

BOKAN MOUNTAIN

Russian Command & Control Center

The command center is abuzz with GRU soldiers working at their computer terminals. Moscow automatically places on a large screen a series of 20 numbers and letters.

These are the closely guarded codes which arm and detonate the nuclear suitcases.

The digits fly by until all 20 become locked.

The largest screen turns red and a ten second countdown begins.

Even General Zelin, the tough general, who looks like he would kill his mother if ordered, looks a bit pale.

Since President Mironovich has taken total control of these nuclear codes, the general is helpless to stop this countdown.

ZAYAS ISLAND, CANADA
Iranian Fishing Boat

One of those rubber boats with a terrorist and a beautiful Russian woman, sit, while looking lovingly into each other's eyes. One of those suitcases begins beeping. She jumps into the ocean as her Iranian "husband" fires shots at the water where she jumped. He looks at the beeping suitcase and tries to open it. It's locked.

PLEASURE BOAT
Seven miles due East

A couple of Canadian teens are in their parent's pleasure boat. They are kissing on the back of the boat when a small nuclear mushroom cloud takes out the Iranian rubber boat with the nuclear suitcase.

This looks to be several miles away from them.

Spherical ripples rush across the water and an orange cloud lights up the night sky. The two lovers look at each other and simultaneously say,

"Cool!"

They go back to kissing.

BOKAN MOUNTAIN
Russian Command & Control Center

Meanwhile, back in the control room the general punches up on his large screen indicators showing that the remaining suitcases are being dispersed far away from the fishing trawlers. The remaining rubber boats with nukes are going in several different directions.

"President Mironovich, are you seeing what I am seeing?" asks General Zelin.

There is no answer from the President's office.

KETCHIKAN POLICE PLANE, KENDRICK BAY

Diary of Robert Stone

We're looking for a place in Kendrick Bay to set this "miracle of aviation" down. At this time, I was completely unaware of what we're flying into. Considering this is night and there are no proper instruments aboard this piece of junk, this is beyond stupid. We were also unaware that a nuclear device just went off just a few miles behind us.

"Let's take a look at those boats at the dock," I said.

The pilot, Jimmy Thomas, "All right, we're goin' in!"

As the plane dives, I look at Jimmy who looks to be the "Red Baron" on a low level strafing mission from World War I,

I'd laugh if I weren't probably gonna die, I think to myself.

At the last minute, just before we fly over, I now clearly see the two trawlers. The Iranian sub must've been sitting silently in front of them but, in the dark, its black hull was impossible to see.

Automatic gunfire erupts from the bridge of *King of the Crabs* and hits our prop and windshield.

Jimmy accelerates to pull up 'Kitty Hawk' over the gunfire saying,

"Aw hell!"

As the plane flies over the trawler, I open my door and with my trusty old Colt .45 revolver I empty my six-shooter in their direction.

"Shit, piss, cock suck… mother fuck! Call the Eskimo!"

"I'm the Eskimo."

The other Eskimo, your big dummy brother!"

"Oh."

I get on the two-way radio to Yura saying, "I've got unidentifieds firing full autos at us,"

"Dad! Calm down!"

I now quiet down and think before saying, "Everybody okay?"

Jimmy and Tony, both in shock, nod in the affirmative, a little.

I'm on the two-way again with the wife,

"Get everyone with everything we got over here right now! Did you get SERT on the phone?"

Yura says, "They're all in Anchorage. It would take them at least five hours to get here. They said Seattle SWAT is closer. They asked if I wanted them to call the FBI!"

"Damn! Damn!"

"Double damn, damn!"

"How 'bout the FBI? Where the hell are they?"

I'm hitting my phone on the dashboard while suddenly realizing,

"Is this dash from our '57 Chevy?"

Yura says, "What?"

"Nothing. Never mind. Is the Eskimo and our other lame-brained deputy on the way?"

Yura, disgustedly says, "Yes!"

Red lights go off on the instrument panel.

Jimmy says,

"The fuel tank was hit. Losing fuel. I have to put her down."

I then sarcastically say to Yura, "I've gotta go now Yura, we're about to die."

I drop the mic, looking for a place to land. I then point to an area out of firing range.

"How 'bout somewhere over there?" I ask.

"If she'll make it," says Jimmy.

The plane jerks and shakes as it tries to finish its 180-degree turn. We are dangerously close to the tree line.

"I can't get altitude. It's gonna be close."

Kitty Hawk 2.0 buckles and chugs and then the engine dies. We glide for a bit heading right for nothing but black.

Jimmy says, "I can't see the tree line."

Just then we hit the top of several trees.

Fortunately, we slid right past them.

Unfortunately, our plane now has a very bad angle on the water.

"Brace for impact. This will not be pretty!" Says Jimmy.

I'm too afraid to cuss, swear or even move.

I grab anything I can find as a wing hits the water first and flips the plane clean onto its back.

We slide across the black water as if the wings are the pontoons.

The hunk of junk stops fairly quickly as we sink silently into the bay.

I try to push my door open but before I can the plane sinks into the water.

Now the weight of the water makes it impossible to try and open the door.

As the freezing water quickly fills the cabin and we're about to die, all I can think about is,

I really, really want to move to someplace warmer!

CESSNA 185

MAA is piloting the Cessna 185 at about 1,000 feet and nine miles south of the Ketchikan airport. He is with his new beautiful, Russian "wife." She sits in the co-pilot's seat. The pilot is mysteriously missing. MAA's cell phone goes off and he answers.

He just listens and finds out his friends have just died in a nuke explosion set off by the Russians.

His Russian "wife" is suspicious knowing what probably is happening.

MAA gets off the phone and puts a gun to his wife's head.

She says, "You want to see peace on earth don't you? Then we must work together."

MAA says, "Your people just detonated one of those suitcases and killed my friend. Tell me why I shouldn't put a bullet in your pretty little head?"

She says, "My friend was then killed too."

This does nothing to change MAA's mind.

She then desperately says,

"I can show you how to unlock that nuke."

MAA uncocks the Glock on her head but keeps it there.

"You better, otherwise we both blow up."

She nervously reaches around behind her and grabs the suitcase, which is where a dead pilot with a bullet in his head is slouched. She opens the suitcase and says,

"Give me your phone."

MAA really doesn't trust her but decides to play along for now. He hands his phone to her.

She gets into a program on her cell phone and types a bunch of numbers.

"There. It's disarmed and there is no way anybody can rearm it."

MAA suspicious, "How do we detonate it?"

"I can show you but we need some very specialized software and hardware tools."

MAA stares at her and decides to let her live.

"Dump him while we're still over water," MAA says looking at the dead pilot.

KENDRICK BAY SHORELINE

Robert Stone's Diary

My deputy son, Tony, pulls me out of the water.

Tony says, "Did you see Jimmy?"

I say shivering and panicked,

"It was so dark. I felt him next to me. I couldn't get his belt off. I tried."

Tony says, "Dad, it's not your fault. We had no idea 'bout all this."

Tony stops talking as he realizes, I'm not listening. I am just staring at the upside down plane in the water and taking this really hard, realizing our pilot is likely still in the plane, underwater.

"That water is so deep we're never gonna recover his body," I say staring into blackness.

After eternity passes I come to my senses and pull out my satellite phone.

I look at it to see if I have a signal and start to shake it when there is nothing.

I then throw it onto the sandy beach right where we stand.

Damn! Damn! Double damn!

BOKAN MOUNTAIN MINE

A conveyor belt is taking uranium rock uphill inside a small vein and making a considerable amount of noise.

Also making noise are huge pumps sucking massive amounts of water from the bottom of this pit.

Raw uranium is dumped into a crusher that grinds the rock into a powder.

Several workers are busy and don't see me as I sneak past them to the top of the vein.

I notice workers at the top of this mining operation are all wearing masks as the powder is pushed into a covered large vat. This vat feeds into three smaller vats with horrible smelling chemicals that make the uranium now look like molasses. This is called a liquor.

The liquor is processed again and slowly poured onto a large covered table to be dried. It's now much, much lighter in color.

What used to take months with heat lamps or centrifuges are blasted with lasers in a matter of seconds.

The finished product is this yellow cakey-like substance (Yellowcake).

I'm shocked as to how all of this sophisticated and heavy equipment could be smuggled into the Unites States of America.

As I continue on, the finished uranium looks bright yellowish and powdery in texture and is 75% pure uranium. Jennifer explained to me later that this uranium 235 is now used in the nuclear reactor power plant deep in the mountain.

I feel like I'm in a dream.

But it's more like a nightmare.

This can't be happening in the United States of America! And on Christmas Day too!

The uranium 235 is then converted into weapons grade plutonium 239 after it is forced through fuel rods in the nuke reactor.

We found out later what is being created here by a new and more efficient process. It is supergrade plutonium (99% Pu-239).

The reason for the supergrade is due to the close, nearly sealed quarters in the mountain. The Russians didn't want their employees to have any more radiation exposure than absolutely necessary.

How thoughtful! I said to myself.

No one notices, as the workers all have their backs to me.

As I make my way back to The Factory walkway I have to stop and catch my breath.

The toxins in the yellowcake room alone probably just took a year off my life.

To my lungs it doesn't feel like this area is safe at all.

So I try to get out as fast as possible.

I make it past two Russian GRU guards, speaking English.

They carry on a conversation about those beautiful women they were ordered not to touch.

As I walk into The Factory room I notice a large presence of scientists all in NBC suits.

You don't wear this type of suit unless serious nuclear, biological, or chemicals are present. They are scurrying around the work floor in a big hurry.

It looks like they are trying to fill a whole bunch of suitcases with "aluminum."

They are working fast!

I head down the hall where I left Jennifer.

As I enter the warehouse room, I notice the barrels have been moved.

I panic as Jennifer is not here.

I start frantically searching through the entire warehouse thinking maybe she's hiding somewhere else in the room but Jennifer is nowhere to be found.

I call out her name, "Jennifer?"

Nothing.

Then I remember, I also left the suitcase with a million dollars right by her. Maybe she left with it to Bora Bora, I joke with myself.

Myself didn't "lol."

However, myself did shout at me saying,

LOL? I HATE THAT!

Stop it, JD. Pay attention.

The backdoor ventilation system Al showed me into this place is locked and, without a key,

I'm stumped as I stand for a minute thinking,

She better not have been caught.

I double check the ventilation grate we came into this room but, with heavy steel bars, there is no way to pry this open.

I head for the warehouse door I just came in and peer out.

Seeing no one, I exit.

As I sneak down the hall I stop, as I near The Factory room again.

Just as I'm about to cross the 2nd story walkway a gun is pushed into my shoulder blades.

I slowly raise my hands.

It's a GRU Special Forces guy with a bandage on his nose.

Uh okay, I think this was the guy I punched in the nose earlier!

I'm not asking!

"Walk," said the Russian in broken English.

So I slowly walk.

Once again, there is a buzz of activity on the reactor floor as they pack up about fifty of those large, black suitcases.

I also notice one of those beautiful Russian women in an evening gown, full makeup and hair flowing walk sexily toward me.

I've seen this routine before.

As she nears me, she stops and speaks in Russian to the soldier.

The soldier looks just for a second at what this drop dead gorgeous woman is pointing to when she clocks him in the face with the bottom of her clenched palm and grabs his gun.

Confused, I look at her saying,

"Jennifer?"

"Call me Jen. My hobbies are piano, water polo and driving submarines. Let's go!"

All that comes out of my open mouth is, "Jen?"

I've turned into a big hunk of yellowcake.

"Men! So stupid!" she says as she's already heading to the main floor by way of an elevator. She has to stop and bring me back to reality.

"C'mon!"

I come to my senses and follow her just staring at her high heels.

Jen walks back to me and finally smiles, "So you like the look?"

"I, I, I, do," was all I could form in words.

She puts her finger over my lips and looks to be in a perfume commercial so she plays it for all it's worth.

Jen, whispers, saying, "Shhh! Don't say anything."

The elevator door opens and takes us down to the main floor. We then walk a few feet into the control room.

The control room is filled with no less than 20 huge, flat, touch screen monitors.

Jen carefully looks over everything then goes to a computer terminal and begins typing.

"Good! Someone didn't log off."

No one can see us, as the room has no windows. Only many, many, flat screen monitors covering every square inch of the walls.

Jen, while typing, asks, "So did you see all of the plutonium 239?"

"What?"

"Ya, they've got enough 239 here to blow up every city in North America."

"What are you doing?"

Jennifer intently working on a computer says, "I'm forcing many radioactive nuclei of uranium atoms to each split into two fast-moving smaller nuclei in the reactor core. This is nuclear fission and it happens in picoseconds, a trillionth of a second. By overloading the fission process I'm creating a chain reaction. Bombarding the nuclei with high-energy neutrons."

I didn't understand a single word she just said. I didn't care. I'm still staring at her beauty.

"If I do this right, I will force a massive amount of energy in the radioactive uranium nuclei, releasing higher energy neutrons and gamma rays. The fission also releases kinetic energy in the smaller nuclei, about one million electron volts per nuclei! Once that first uranium nuclei is fissioned the chain reaction begins and..."

I sarcastically say, "Sorry I asked. Just hurry!"

Jen ignores me and dials up the power to overload conditions.

I become convinced this is a not a good idea,

"Are you sure this mountain will contain all the radiation?"

"It's contained the uranium radiation for millions of years. I'm trying to minimize the blast," says Jen with an intense look on her face.

I'm impressed.

She continues,

"When fuel cladding is breached with Cesium-137 and Krypton-85, it will leach into the coolant over there and that's gonna make..."

I'm not looking at her. I'm looking out the door. I finish Jen's sentence,

"One big frickin' explosion?"

"Ya!"

Jen stands up and runs out the door.

I run after her stopping her,

"Wait. I can't leave the doctor or Al. Also, I tied up Ruddy and Katrina."

"Go get the Russian doctor and Al. The others? We don't have time for."

We both stand up and walk over to where all the scientists can now see us.

Everyone, still in NBC suits, including Doctor Vladimir Peskov, freezes for a second staring at us.

I look at Jen not in any protective clothing and think, well, there goes a couple more years off our lives!

Alarm-bells begin sounding and red lights flash.

I start yelling in Russian the only word I think I know,

"Beak... Beak..."

The scientists continue standing frozen in place, staring at me, so I spray bullets into the air yelling,

"RUN!"

That, they understand! They flee toward the closest vein.
Jen grabs the machine gun and begins smashing the controls.
I ask her, "So what do we do now, soldier?"
Jen takes off her high heels then yells,
"RUN!"

RUSSIAN COMMAND CENTER

Bokan Mountain

Inside the Command Center, Russians feverously rush about as their reactor overload warning system continues to alert them about a meltdown. The general is on a computer and attempting to override the sabotage.

A Russian officer looking worried says, "We can't fix this from here, sir."

Zelin speaks to his next in command,

"Get everyone down there now and fix this or we're all dead!"

A very young and very worried young soldier walks up to Zelin who's not paying any attention to him.

"Uh, sir?"

Zelin barely acknowledges his existence and doesn't look at the kid while he continues working.

"Yes?"

"The president wants to speak with you."

Zelin stops.

"Turn off all emergency alarms. Everyone atten-tion."

All stand in the room at attention.

Zelin nods to the kid who then puts President Mironovich's image on the large screen.

The general takes a big gulp wondering how he will explain all of this.

The Russian president appears on the large screen. He is not happy.

"All of Commander Orlov's men have been murdered. Zelin, you are relieved of command."

General Zelin interrupts, "Sir, I would...

The president continues, "Destroy all evidence. If you make it out alive, I have given an order to terminate you. Do you understand?"

"Yes, sir."

The screen goes dark.

Zelin looks around at everyone.

After a very long pause, the general says,

"I don't know who will do it but do it quickly."

No one moves a muscle.

The general then says,

"Let's go. Send out the evacuation order."

Flashing green lights now turn red and on the speaker system a woman's voice says,

"Evakuirovat', Evacuate, Evakuirovat', Evacuate."

Zelin stands there a moment before talking to his right hand man again,

"The Iranian murders will be waiting for us out there. We must be prepared."

"Yes sir."

RUDDY'S ROOM

Bokan Mountain

Jen and I run down the hall to Ruddy and Katrina's room.

Jen, worried, says, "They must've captured Al and Tatiana."

I respond, "I wouldn't be so sure. They seem to know their way around."

This time I try the door instead of kicking it down. Jen nods her approval as the door easily opens.

As we search the rooms, there are no signs of Ruddy or Katrina.

There are only big trails of duct tape everywhere.

"You used duct tape on them too?" asks Jen with a bit of disgust.

I ignore her.

"Let's hope Al and Tatiana made it out alive."

We gotta go now or we'll not make it out alive," says Jen.

I agree and start to head out the door when she stops me.

"Wait. Come here."

Jen stops at the door.

"What?" I ask.

She sees an open clothes closet and starts putting on camo gear.

"We want to blend, don't we?"

I say, "Oh ya, at 6' 4", I blend!"

Jen says, "Very funny! Marissa Tomei and *My Cousin Vinny*,"[10] Then she continues, "I think she won her Oscar when the academy heard that line! There. This looks much better."

I just can't give up my trusty black parka I've been wearing for two days straight.

"I think I prefer your evening gown look," I say sarcastically as I'm looking for something more important. I'm looking through a closet of weapons. I find a large ammo bag and two AK74s.

I toss Jenn one of the AKs saying, "Cumon, let's go."

Jen follows me to the door and I open it.

As soon as we try to exit the room we're hit with gunfire from both sides of the hall. I lay down a short burst to my '3'. Jen kneels down and begins returning fire at our '9'.

"We're not getting out of this room alive," says Jen.

"Nonsense. Follow me." I say.

Looking back on this event now I think I was just plain stupid!

I run out the door to the left firing short bursts.

Jen said she just stood there petrified 'til she heard me scream,

"JEN!"

Somehow I managed to shoot two operators in front of me, who had apparently moved from their covered position at very same time I chose to go on my suicide mission.

However, two other operators behind me are still in their covered positions and shooting at Jen. She is able to fling open a door to deflect the bullets just long enough for us to get to one of the veins.

Soon more bullets fly inches from my head.

Red lights and evacuation warnings again are being broadcast.

Somehow we manage to make our way through the main vein that leads outside.

As we arrive at the huge, Cheyenne Mountain, type of steel blast door, we realize this is clearly impenetrable.

I have gotten in and out of this mine over the past two days in two separate veins but not this one.

This is obviously the main road in and out of the mine. We have ducked behind a rock just inside the giant steel blast door.

But we're trapped.

There is literally nowhere for us to run.

All the gunfire stops.

A small robot device drives toward us.

This stupid little thing is only about two feet tall and has tank treads on it.

However, it also has a huge gun mounted on it resembling an M134 Gatling gun.

I think, if this is anything like the 134, which shoots 6,000 rounds a minute, we're already dead.

As it drives up it aims it's six mean looking barrels at us.

Zelin calls out, "Face it. You're trapped. There is no way you're getting out that door unless you throw down your weapons."

Jen and I look at each other and shrug our shoulders. I say to her,

"I got nothin', you?"

Jen just stares at me with hopelessness I've never seen.

I throw out my weapon. Soon after Jen throws out her weapon and ammo bag.

Zelin and his men come walking up to us, guns trained.

With deep anger he says,

"I can't go back home now, thanks to you people."

Zelin puts his pistol to my head.

I take one last look to Jen as the gun goes off.

Zelin drops to the ground dead.

He has been shot by the GRU team leader next to him.

Zelin's gun on my forehead was grabbed and pushed into the air just a split second before the bullet flew from the chamber.

The GRU commander motions to open the door and the little robot points his massive guns toward the exit door as a Russian soldier with a joystick controller walks toward them controlling this little monster.

As this giant, round steel vault door slowly opens Jen and I stand, looking at the Russian commander in bewilderment,

"Why?"

The commander answers,

"First, the natural thorium and uranium shields anyone from knowing this is a bomb factory. Second, the close proximity to your mainland is ideal. No way we could ship thousands of nukes into your country by air or sea without getting caught. Your ports and border crossings all have nuke sensors."

"The president ordered us to make fifty nukes a week here. We were going to smuggle them onto your mainland through remote areas far away from ports and border crossings. No one is watching most of your entire northern border."

I was very interested but very confused,

"I just meant, why did you save our lives?"

The Russian, embarrassed that something was lost in translation says,

"In case we make it out of here alive, please tell your people I saved your life."

I happily answer, "Oh. That I can do."

Jen is stunned. She's even more stunned at my next request.

"Could we have our guns back?"

The Russian Special Forces operator stares into my eyes for a long, long pause before saying,

"I'll say this for you, you've got guts."

"There are thousands more just like us."

Then I boldly say, "Oh and the ammo bag, please."

We stare at each other for, what seemed like, a minute before he motions and a GRU soldier tosses the ammo bag to me. In another uncomfortable moment we pay respect to each other.

Then Jen and I quickly turn and run toward Kendrick Bay.

A siren is blasting as we run.

A crowd of scientists begins to pour out of the mountain behind us.

KENDRICK BAY

We come running down the trail to the dock at the shoreline.

Jen stops and looks back toward the mountain.

"Should'a blown by now. If they cooled the reactor, no way anyone's getting back into that mountain, anytime soon.

I say, "So what happens now?"

Jen, "If they didn't cool that thing off the next thing that will happen will be a hydrogen blast that will destroy the containment shell and then..."

A huge explosion knocks us to the ground.

We sit up in shock after a moment and look at the mountain.

I say,

"A big explosion?"

Every one of the mine entrances blows fire thousands of feet at the exact angle of that particular vein.

Jennifer says,

"Ya!"

If it wasn't so deadly, it kinda looks cool, I think before mentally slapping myself.

Just then a giant fireball with tremendous force flies out of a submarine sitting quietly by two fishing trawlers in Kendrick Bay. It shoots some sort of missile at the mountain.

We had not even seen this sub sitting there until now.

Meanwhile, on a beach nearby, I see two men standing.

Their silhouettes light up in an orange glow.

I hear one of them scream,

"What the fuck?"

Diary of Robert Stone

"Is that a sub?" I ask.

Tony, standing next to me is just as shocked. He asks me,

"Is it Russian?"

I'm just plain annoyed, even more than usual, "How the hell should I know? I can't see any markings on the damn thing."

I pull out my Iridium Extreme 9575 satellite phone and now it's working! I call my wife,

"Yura, tell the FBI to call SWAT, the Army, Navy, Air Force. Get everyone over here. Now!"

"A Russian sub just detonated a nuclear device on Bokan Mountain!"

Yura calmly says to me,

"Okay, chief, okay, calm down. I'm on hold with the FBI HRT, here listen."

"Happy Holidays and thank you for calling the FBI hostage rescue team in Washington D.C. If this is not an emergency, please hang up and call our main switchboard during normal business hours 8 a.m. to 4 p.m. Eastern Standard Time. If you know your party's extension you may enter it at any time. If you're calling about Internet related crimes, please press 1. If you're calling about…"

Yura told me she could hear me in the background cussing and swearing.

Yura says, "Not now, chief, I'm on hold you're just gonna have to be…"

Just then a phone recording says, "One moment please."

Yura says, "Sorry, chief, false alarm. Thought that was an operator."

Some pleasant elevator music ensues while Yura hears the phone recording say,

"Do you want to be one of the few, the proud, the F.B.I. may be looking for you. Call us today and find out about what exciting jobs …"

I can't take this anymore.

Finally, after an eternity passes,

"Hello, HRT. What's your emergency?"

Yura sounds absolutely calm as she says,

"This is the Ketchikan, Alaska emergency services operator. I have…"

I can hear the FBI operator rudely interrupt her in this snarky, little, monotone voice,

"What is your emergency please?"

Yura now sounds impatient, "Well, I'm trying to tell you if you would…"

FBI HRT operator says, "Ma'am you're going to have to speak slowly and calmly if you want me to…"

"Damn it, Yura put the little shit on the phone."

Yura then says,

"Okay, I'm going to let you speak directly with the Chief of Police of Ketchikan, Alaska."

"Go ahead chief."

I don't remember my exact words but they went something like:

"A NUCLEAR DEVICE HAS EXPLODED HERE."

"SEND THE MARINES, YOU DUMB LITTLE FUCK."

After a long pause on the phone, a monotone voice responds,

"Did you people call earlier?"

Yura interrupts me saying, "Yes, yes, YES!"

In a monotone voice the FBI operator calmly and slowly says,

"Why didn't you say so? I'm patching you through now. One moment please."

"Wait, what's the number? I'll have my chief call you… Hello?" says Yura to no avail.

The HRT operator is already long gone.

"Damn it! Stone, I'm on hold again," says Yura.

PETERSON AIR FORCE BASE (AFB), COLORADO (CO)

U.S. Air Force Aerospace Defense Command Center

This is the new, above ground, U.S. Air Force Aerospace Defense Command Center (NORAD) located at Peterson Air Force Base in Colorado. The old Command Center was located deep within Cheyenne Mountain but since the end of the Cold War the Pentagon, in its wisdom, wound down most operations in the mountain!

The war room looks like what you've seen in movies and a larger version of the Russia's Bokan Mountain command center that was just blown to hell.

However, there is one big difference. Christmas decorations are everywhere. Large draping red and green garland drapes around the screens that have lit up all of North America.

Small brightly lit Christmas trees adorn many of the desks.

The atmosphere looks professional but very festive.

General Norton is looking at all sorts of red lights going off in the Southeast Alaska sector of his North America map.

General Norton says, "What the hell? And on Christmas Eve too!"

"Excuse me sir, we have Ketchikan on the speaker."

"Where the hell is Ketchikan?" says the general.

A very nervous, nerdy, little airman with glasses says,

"I believe it's in Alaska, sir!"

The general really doesn't think this could possibly be something with which his valuable time should be wasted,

"Have we verified their identity?"

"Yes, sir. FBI HRT Gold team is en route and their commander is on the phone."

The general breathes a big sigh and then says, "John, what is all this?"

John A. Smith is the Gold Team leader and these guys obviously know each other. John A. Smith answers the general saying,

"I'm anxious to hear as well, general."

Stone's voice suddenly blurts out over the speakers,

"Hello? Hello? Is anybody there?"

"Send the fuckin' Navy."

"Send the fuckin' Marines."

"Send 'em all, damn it!"

"Who is this?" asks general Norton.

"Robert Frickin' Stone, Chief of Police, Ketchikan Alaska. Who the hell is this?"

"This is General Norton NORAD."

"NORAD my ass! More like Gonad!"

"How the fuck does a Russian sub detonate a nuclear weapon in my town, damn it!" retorts Stone.

The general takes him off the speaker. The general looks to his assistant,

"He has a fouler mouth than me!"

The general looks around the room,

"MWC? Can you confirm this?"

MWC is the Missile Warning Center located in the same complex.

MWC airman stands, "Satellites picked up a small light & heat signature in the area moments ago."

"Damn it! Now I'm going to start cussing and swearing."

Jerry from the FBI HRT Gold Team says,

"We'll be there in ten!"

The general adds, "We're gonna need more than a hostage rescue team if we're taking on a Russian sub. What kind of sub is it? What's Alaska Command say?"

An airman says, "Alaska Command has no assets in the area and cannot confirm any of this."

"Well that's just great," says the general.

"And Elmendorf?" asks the general.

An airman answers, "Assets are ninety-seven minutes away. Do you want me to scramble jets?"

Another airman speaks up,

"Sir, we have two F35s off the Ronald Reagan. They're 47 nautical miles away."

"Are they armed?" asks the general.

"Yes, sir, each have two - 500 pounders."

"Reroute. Send them here. ASAP. And give me an ETA!"

"Yes sir!"

"And put that foul mouth back on the speaker. This is General Norton again. Can you identify the submarine?"

"It's Russian. I'd bet my retirement on it! It has hostile intent because it just launched some sort of missile at Bokan."

The general asks, "Bokan?"

"Bokan! Bokan!" says Stone.

The general asks, "Bokan? What the hell's a Bokan?"

"It's a freaking mountain, you dumb fuck! Mother fucking...." says Stone in the background on NORAD's speakers.

The general turns off the speaker system and Stone is silenced.

The general says to an airman, "Put Bokan Mountain up there."

"Okay, Mr. Stone, I have you on the speaker again," says the general.

"There are Russians on Bokan too!" says Stone.

"So let me get this straight..."

The general continues, "You believe a Russian sub just launched a missile at themselves?"

"Do you have any evidence that Russians are involved?" asks the general.

Stone says, "All I know is somebody just blew up a mountain in the United States of America with what looks like a nuclear device. Bright orange glow above a giant mushroom core. Sound familiar? So you better get everybody over here right now, Goddamn it!"

General Norton picks up a tiny Christmas tree sitting near him saying,

"Leave it to the f'ing commies to attack us on Christmas!"

FISHING TRAWLER

King of The Crabs

Several Iranian guards with AK 47s walk the deck of *King of the Crabs* trawler.

There is an orange glow in the background on Bokan Mountain.

It's very quiet here so I have to swim slowly.

I motion to Jen who is swimming through the water, parallel to me, to board *The Cod-Father.*

We are swimming through the cold water as the two Iranian trawlers sit, moored at the end of the pitch-black dock.

I quietly climb aboard on a rope ladder near the plimsoll line that I suspect the real owner's let down as a distress signal to someone who might have noticed.

Apparently, no one noticed.

As I climb the hull I have to stop as there is an Iranian with an AK standing at the railing.

I'm hanging on to this rusty old ladder, over the water, when I realize the rust on the metal rungs have cut my hands and they are now bleeding. I have to pull one hand away and try to stop the bleeding.

This is not working very well.

If I go back, I'll likely cut my hands even worse.

Retreat is not an option.

Just when I think I'll have no other choice, I notice several scientists in white coats walking down the dock toward the boats.

As they walk to the edge of the dock, the Russian scientists, that haven't been killed from the blast, look dazed and confused.

The Iranian that was preventing me from boarding walks toward the bow of the boat to see the Russian scientists on the dock.

I'm able to board the boat and sneak up to the bridge.

I can see a man in an Iranian general's uniform talking on his satellite phone,

"Shahab 4 was a brilliant success. Praise Allah. But the nuclear EMP blast should have taken out all of the lights and electronics for fifty miles. Everything sill works on this boat. Why?"

Meanwhile, an Iranian soldier on the deck yells at the scientists who are walking in a daze, "Come closer."

As the unarmed scientists walk near the boat the Iranian soldier asks,

"Are there any others that made it?"

Doctor Vladimir Peskov stands in front of the others and says,

"Nyet. They were all killed. Could I have a glass of water?"

The Iranian then mows down all of the scientists, killing all of them.

Doctor Peskov who asked for the water, falls into the bay.

The Iranian says, "There! There's your glass of water."

The Iranians laugh at the floating body in the bay.

I stand and shoot the Iranian and it's on!

Gunfire erupts from my '3' and '9' o'clock. I lay down a burst of fire and take out the two threats on my '3'. Meanwhile on my '9' this crazy guy is charging me like a bull but not firing his weapon. I realize it's jammed. As he nears, I simply take the butt of my AK 74M and knock him into Kendrick Bay. I hit him in the temple so death was probably instantaneous.

As I look back onto the bridge the Iranian general is nowhere to be found.

I can hear gunfire on the, *The Cod-Father*, the other trawler that Jen boarded.

I run around to the other side of the boat and am met with gunfire again. I take out another Iranian who starts shooting from my '6.'

As I swing around to port side, I see an Iranian has Jen in his sights and is about to shoot her in the back. I fire a short burst knocking him into the water.

Jen wheels around and gives me a thumbs-up sign.

I can remember the last look I saw on her face before the explosion. It was one of confidence and love. At least that's how I'd like to remember it, I guess.

There is an explosion so large it knocks me backward and onto the deck.

As I jump to my feet and race down the deck, there is some splashing of debris into the water then an eerie silence.

I yell,

"Jennifer!"

There is no way anyone could have lived through this blast. It took off the entire bridge and the entire upper deck of *The Cod-Father*. I run to the front of *King of the Crabs* to see if it's possible that she lived.

"Impossible."

I thought as I looked at the utter damage of this boat. That looks like a whole lot of C4.

Then I run to the back of the boat to be sure.

I see nothing.

Nothing living in the water.

Nothing living on the boat.

Just nothing.

I find myself not caring at all about what appears to be a ballistic missile submarine sitting the furthest out on my starboard side.

I'm still running around like a chicken with my head cut off on the port side desperately trying to find Jennifer.

Finally, I realize the fact that the only person in my life that I have ever loved is gone.

This makes my legs buckle from under me much quicker than carrying her hundreds and hundreds of feet in forty-degree water!

I have to grab onto the railing or I would have dropped like a rock to the deck.

I stare at the water for an eternity before remembering that Iranian general is still on the loose.

Realizing that she's gone, I slowly walk back inside the bridge. As I do, I'm disgusted at what I see.

Russian soldiers lying, dead, in pools of blood executed by the Iranians.

Too many to count.

These monsters are barbarians from the 7th Century, I thought.

And If I find any more of them I'm sending them right, the hell, back there!

As I stand there looking at this horror, I see a little man in civilian clothing crawling slowly away from me inside the bridge. I quietly come up from behind him and when he hears me he says,

"Please, please they forced me to…"

"Who are you," I ask.

"My name is Sergei."

Russian?

"Yes."

"What are you doing here?"

The man reaches for something so I train my gun on his center mass.

"Wait! Wait I'm getting my ID."

"What is your objective?" I ask.

"We were here to…"

The man tries to go for my gun but in a very foolish manner.

He goes for the muzzle.

It's foolish as it swings the butt of the gun right toward him and I clock him with it in his left eye.

The man falls back in pain holding his eye. When he recovers again I now realize this is the little Iranian general I saw moments ago. He simply took off his uniform and put on civilian clothes.

A cell phone rings in the closet.

We both stare at each other a moment when I say,

"Maybe I'll just answer your phone and get some answers."

I walk over to the closet door and as soon as I open it the little man lunges for me again.

And again I clock him with the butt of my machine gun, only this time in his right eye.

He falls back in pain.

I pick up the phone and answer it. On the other end of the phone in Farsi a man says,

"General, we are now ready to launch all of our Shahab 4s on your command."

I recognize this is Farsi but don't really understand what was said.

The general starts screaming in Farsi,

"Launch all of your missiles at the American cities now."

An Iranian commando pops out of nowhere at my '6' and shoves a gun in my back.

"Drop your weapon."

I could fight but I'll be shot before I can wheel around.

I release my gun and the little Iranian general confidently stands, still holding his bleeding eye.

"You will now give me your gun."

A tense moment ensues as I'm frozen.

I decide I don't have any choice when I see another man walk to the door on the far side of the bridge.

"What the hell is going on here?"

It's Stone and his timing couldn't have been better or worse depending on where you are in the room.

The Iranian soldier wheels around to shoot Stone. I clock the little general again with the butt of my gun while simultaneously shooting the Iranian soldier.

A second Iranian is about to shoot Stone in his back when a bullet rings out and knocks the second Iranian soldier to the ground dead as well.

Stone and I both raise our weapons at each other not knowing from where the last bullet came.

After a tense standoff Jennifer walks into the room, soaking wet.

"The Navy didn't train me for this shit!"

I'm so relieved to see her but she doesn't look in the mood for anything.

So, again, I hold it all inside.

"Who the hell are you?" says Stone.

"We're FBI!" I say.

Stone isn't impressed.

"Got any ID?" Stone asks.

Ya, it's at the bottom of this bay"

Still suspicious Stone asks, "What's your name?"

"John Denning, Special Agent, FBI."

Where you from?"

"Portland, Oregon," I answer.

Anybody could know that," Stone says.

I throw my hands in the air as Stone looks to maybe shoot me.

"Don't make any sudden moves," says Stone.

"Why? Would it make any difference?"

I guess I was in no mood for an idiot. So I make all sorts of sudden moves.

"All right, all right, stop it!" says Stone.

Then Stone looks to Jennifer.

"And you?"

"Jennifer Tavana, Special Agent, FBI Juneau."

"I'm guessing you're the idiot Chief of Police here."

Stone still doesn't answer.

"What is it with you people?" says Stone.

Jennifer says, "Who you calling, you people?"

Stone ignores her not understanding Jen's minority status insult. Instead he picks up General Bahadur by the nap of his neck and pokes his finger in his eye.

"And who the hell is this?"

I look at Jennifer trying to figure out if this General Patton or just an idiot.

"I'm only asking one more time, then I'm poking your eye out. Who are you?"

"The general screams in pain."

"General Bahadur."

Well, now, that wasn't so hard now, was it?

"And who's sub is that?"

No answer so Stone shoves his finger a little further into the general's bleeding eye.

"Mine. It's mine."

And you're Russian?

Both stare at each other a moment. Bahadur knows what's coming so just gives up.

"Iranian."

"Why are you guys shooting at each other in my town?"

"I will not say any more." says General Bahadur.

Just then Tony, Stone's son, comes running onto the bridge.

Jennifer, Stone and I almost shoot him.

"Son, how many times do I have to tell you, never, never run into a gunfight."

I say, "Gee that's funny, that's all I've been trained to do."

"SEAL huh, well that's just crazy!" says Stone.

"You got that right," I say disgustedly.

"This is my idiot son, Tony, everybody!" says Stone.

"Thanks dad," says Tony, clearly not happy.

The general pipes up, "You can kill me but you will never get my submarine. I am Brigadier General Bahadur."

"Was anyone talking to you, Bad Odor?" says Stone.

General Bahadur confidently says, "We have ICBM's aboard that will destroy all your American cities and there is nothing you people can do to stop us, God willing."

Just then all of the remaining ballistic missile hatches open on the Iranian submarine. Fire begins shooting out of all of the hatches as the missiles prepare to launch. The fire flies into the air fifty feet above the sub's hull.

All five of us, Bahadur, Stone, Tony, Jen and myself just stand with our mouths hanging open. I can't tell you what everybody else was thinking at that moment. All I knew is that every scenario we practiced for in the FBI terrorist scenarios didn't include this!

Jen wrote in her diary:

I felt this was the end

Had not spoken to my mother in years.

At this very moment, all I really wanted to tell her was:

I'm sorry.

I love you.

A split second later, two torpedoes hit the Iranian sub in a tremendous explosion that shakes their ship.

Stone, "What the hell was that?"

TK-20
Captain Vasili's Diary

I'm on the surface looking through infrared monocular from my conn.

I shout, "DIE, IRANIAN BASTARDS, DIE!"

Next to me is a kid who I like but never remember his name. He can't be much over twenty.

I say,

"Fools! First rule of naval warfare: Never enter any waters with no escape possible."

"Yes, sir," says the blond haired, green-eyed kid.

"However, now, there's nowhere for us to run either. Better bring up my flashlight."

"Your flashlight?" the kid asks in a questioning tone.

I simply just stare at him.

"Your flashlight! Yes, sir," says the enthusiastic kid as he disappears from my conn.

Here is my chance to speak with the Americans.

If we don't get killed first.

FISHING TRAWLER

General "Bad Odor" cannot believe what he's witnessing, the sinking of his beloved boat. Stone looks on with casual confidence.

"You got some splainin' to do now, son."

I look at Jennifer dripping wet,

My first thought is, she looks pretty hot!

Thank God I didn't say that out loud. What I ask is,

"So, who just sank that sub?"

Stone confidently says, "Oh I called in SERT."

"Who?" I ask.

Jennifer, "SERT. They're kinda like Alaska's SWAT team."

"Well," I ask, "Does SERT carry torpedoes?"

"What?" Stone looks surprised.

"It's a simple question," I say. "Does SERT carry torpedoes?"

"He's right. Those were torpedoes," says Jennifer.

"What?" Stone looks out the window in a panic.

Meanwhile, I'm looking through some old binoculars and see a pattern of flashing light at the mouth of Kendrick Bay saying,

"It's Morris Code. Russian sub T-K-2-Zero. They're saying, you're B.E.L.C.O.M.E., belcome?"

Jennifer acts disgusted as she grabs the binoculars.

"Welcome. You are welcome! If that's TK-20 that's a Russian typhoon class boomer with enough firepower to take out North America."

"Shit, I almost forgot!" says Stone.

Stone takes out his phone and calls Yura.

"Hi Yura, tell NORAD that we got TK two zero a Russian sub sitting at the mouth of Kendrick Bay. Make sure… Hang on."

Stone sees General "Bad Odor" trying to crawl away so he puts his phone down and simply kicks his Alaskan cowboy boot into the Iranian's forehead.

Bahadur goes down in pain 'til Stone picks him up.

"And what the hell's a Russian sub doin' in my town?"

PETERSON AFB

Command Center

Inside the NORAD Colorado Command Center an airman walks to the general,

"General, the F35s are inbound. ETA zero two minutes 'til target acquisition, sir."

The general than says to Stone,

"Clear the area we have two fighters inbound. ETA zero two minutes. Hello?"

The general looks to an airman questioning the line.

The airman says, "The line is open sir. It sounds like there's a fight going on."

Another airman says, "Fuel is low on the F35s, sir, and there are no tankers in the air within 200 miles."

"Aw, hell!" says the general.

FISHING TRAWLER

Jen is looking through the binoculars again and reading Morse code.

"Permission ... to... come... aboard?"

Stone is angry,

"No! No! I don't want no damn Russians in Alaska!"

Jen staring at him asks,

"Does your wife wonder if you're human?"

"All the time!" says his son, Tony.

"So what are we going to do?" I say looking through binoculars.

"Aw hell, invite 'em to the party. They just saved our lives!" says Stone quickly changing his mind.

I look at Jennifer but neither of us can argue with Stone this time.

Stone pulls out a flashlight from his pocket.

"So who's talkin' to 'em?"

"Toss it," I say and Stone tosses the flashlight to me.

I begin to flash Morris code to Vasili. I then walk to a cabinet and Jenn says, "What are you doing?"

"I'm looking for something to eat. Aren't you hungry?"

Jennifer cannot believe us two Huns but she turns her attention to the Iranian,

"Can't wait to see what your little friends will do with you."

General Badakur looks up with a bleeding eye, a black eye, and a shoe imprint matching Stone's boot on his forehead.

"Not so tough without your submarine now, are ya?" says Stone.

Jen is thinking, "Isn't that a movie reference?"

"Are you for real? Were you in?" I ask.

"Nam. Vietnam. The big one! I was eighteen months in the bush and I can snap your neck in a heartbeat, sonny," says Stone.

"Really, really, you're gonna do movie lines from Tom Hanks and the '*The Burbs*'?"[11] says Jen.

"Okay, you caught me," says Stone.

"*Blazing Saddles*!"[12] Unbelievable!" I say.

Jen has been monitoring TK-20 with my binoculars,

"He's coming in," says Jen as she hands the binoculars to me and I take another look.

TK-20

Captain Vasili's Diary

This is most difficult thing I have ever done.

Easy part was torpedoing submarine full of men who helped kill our friends. A much more delicate task will be to convince my own men to surrender this boat to Americans. I have all key officers assembled on my conning tower but worried mutiny may be next.

I don't even have words to speak.

But I try,

"Gentlemen, I appreciate you hearing me out before you decide anything. I believe the Americans will not let us escape to Mother Russia. We might have gotten under the polar ice cap but it's likely the *USS Alaska* or her replacement is sitting there now waiting for us. We were able to sneak by before but I doubt we can be so lucky again. At this point, America must think we attacked the United States. I would. There will be an order from President of the United States to terminate us."

"We would all die and for what?

"Nothing."

"Absolutely nothing."

I think to myself as I'm speaking, it's hard to tell what my officers are thinking. I know most of them like family.

However, some I don't know at all.

Are they going to kill me right here?

Are they going to grab me and charge me with treason?

Like all good Russians, you play close to vest and with best poker face. I'm just putting all my cards on table now. Am I doing right thing? I continue,

"If Americans don't put me in jail, I intend to spend the rest of my natural days on this earth watching corn sway in breeze of a hot Nebraska summer. I'm choosing that over certain imprisonment or death in Russia. Any man who wants to return to Russia, I'm sure will be allowed by America. I know most of you will want to return to your families so let's get story straight. If our president and state run media don't buy your story, you will be beaten, tortured and maybe killed because you did something I ordered, which was in direct contravention of our president. I could never live with myself if any of you suffer because of me. So if you wish, you can blame me and try and return me to Russia to stand trial. The decision is yours."

"We're now in America, a democracy, so this must be put to vote."

"Majority wins."

"Do we surrender?"

"Or do we fight and die?"

"Moscow has been calling us for last five minutes so we better have our story straight, understand?"

"Questions?"

Captain Nikolai Alexi, President Mironovich's hand-picked officer, stares at me without feeling or uttering a word.

Not a single sailor, including my officers, says a word.

"All right, we stay."

"Here's what we tell Moscow…"

FISHING TRAWLER

'm flashing Morse code to *TK-20* with a can of half eaten SpaghettiOs sitting in front of me.

Jennifer disgustedly says, "What are you saying?"

"Nuclear detonation on Bokan. Area contaminated soon. Permission to come aboard?" I ask.

"Good idea," says Jen.

I look into Jen's eyes.

Weird, but I feel Jen understands my every unspoken word.

I throw away the can of, way out of expiration date, SpaghettiOs.

I feel like I've known her my entire life. Difficult to believe it's only been two days!

I stop staring at her as Stone seems to notice this.

He just smiles.

I think the idiot understands our relationship too.

Stone walks over to me,

"What'd he say?"

My mind is somewhere else, "Who?" I ask.

Stone, "The sub. Who you think I'm talking about?"

Jen tries to help out and asks Stone, "How do you know it's a he?"

Stone is so confused by this he doesn't know how to respond.

Meanwhile, I'm looking through the binoculars reading Morris code,

"Permission granted. You can have my sub. She's all yours!"

A cheer goes up from all of us. Jen, Stone and Tony and myself look at each other with a sigh of relief.

Stone sees Badahur crawling for the door again and puts his boot on Badahur's neck.

Stone looks around.

He sees an electrical cord nearby and uses it to tie Bahadur's hands behind his back.

I say, "C'mon!"

All five of us exit the bridge to the starboard side of the boat as *TK-20* pulls near.

F-35C NAVY FIGHTER JET

A pilot sits in darkness two nautical miles south of Kendrick Bay at 30,000 feet. The only thing reflecting onto his visor and face mask are multiple green heads-up displays.

The pilot's integrated night vision allows him to see for miles further than the human eye can see.

The pilot has a 360-degree view around him from multiple cameras on board, including the one on his helmet.[13]

An oxygen mask is required for all flights above 10,000 feet, as any person will start to become groggy above this altitude. In addition, if you have to pull serious Gs, a mask is necessary to feed enough oxygen to the pilot's brain.

Also, if you need to eject, a mask is clearly needed as you could easily pass out or disfigure your face.

You know what a mouthful of air feels like when you stick your head out a car window at sixty miles per hour, right?

Imagine what that air would do to you traveling at 1,000 miles per hour!

The pilot uses the radio in his oxygen mask to talk to NORAD.

"FA-146 Blue Diamond 1 to Pinnacle, FA-146 Blue Diamond 1 to Pinnacle,"

"Weapons pointed and locked. In position. Waiting your command."

PETERSON AFB

Command Center

NORAD's General Norton says to an airman, "If that really is an SSBN Boomer it could light up North America."

Another airman walks to the general, "We have a green light from the president, sir."

The general says to the pilot, "This is General Norton at Pinnacle, Blue Diamonds, you are clear to engage. I repeat, clear to engage!"

The pilot says, "Confirmed. Weapons armed and hot. I have a lock. Engaging now. Two birds in flight. Repeat, two birds in flight."

"This is Blue Diamond 2 to Pinnacle. Blue Diamond 2 to Pinnacle. Two more birds in flight. Repeat, two more birds in flight."

KENDRICK BAY

We all stand on the deck of *King of the Crabs* watching the approaching sub. I see the silhouette of a man on the shoreline. He aims what appears to be a very old hunting rifle at the Russian sub and shouts, "Die you Commie Bohunks!"

"Friend of yours?" says Jennifer to Stone as she looks through her binoculars at the black silhouette on the beach.

"Could I see those?" Stone asks Jennifer for her binoculars. She gives them to him.

Stone looks through the binoculars and says excitedly,

"It's Jimmy! He's alive! And almost deaf. I'm not sure he could hear us even if I yelled at him."

Meanwhile Stone's pilot, Jimmy, fires off another round at Vasili's sub.

"Okay, Eskimo, you're up!" says Stone to Tony.

Without a missing a beat, Tony dives into the water swimming toward Jimmy, yelling at him.

At this point I look at Jennifer thinking, what kind of weirdos live up here?

Jennifer seems to understand the silent communication and shrugs her shoulders, embarrassed.

TK-20

Vasili's Diary

'm forced to duck another bullet as it ricochets off my conning tower.
My young sailor friend helps me to my feet,
"Sure you want to go to America?"
I quickly answer, "That's what I love about this place, individuality!"
"Look at that spirit, son."
"Could you imagine some Russian shooting at an American in Moscow?"
The sailor looks bewildered, confused as he ducks from another incoming round.
I don't even flinch on this round.
I look at American on beach and say,
"Fantastic, just fantastic!"

KENDRICK BAY

'm looking through binoculars at this madness and say,

"Are all Alaskans crazy?"

Stone without missing a beat,

"No, just my employees!"

The Russian sub has now quietly pulled alongside *King of the Crabs*.

Although quite different in height, Russian sailors help Stone, Jen and me aboard *TK-20*.

Tony has now reached Jimmy on the shore and they're talking.

Vasili yells down from the conn,

"Should I be worried about him?"

Stone yells to Tony, "Is it Jimmy?"

Tony from the beach, exited, yells back,

"Ya, it's Jimmy. He's fine!"

I mumble, "I'm not sure we can definitely say that."

Then I get very serious and yell up to the captain,

"Any ballistic missiles aboard?"

Vasili says, "No. Negative."

"I have no missiles."

"No nuclear materials."

"We come in peace."

"You have nothing to fear."

Just then Vasili hears a jet fighter in the distance and asks, "Are we safe?"

Stone, "Oh sure there aren't any military assets within a thousand miles of here!"

Suddenly the ships alarms system go off and Russian sailors announce, "Radar, conn, incoming. Multiples! At least four."

"Shit!" Says Stone as he pulls out his phone and redials,

"Yura, get me that fuckin' general."

PETERSON AFB

Command Center

The young nerdy NORAD airman says to General Norton, "It's that foul mouth Alaskan again, sir."

"Put him on the speaker," says the general.

"You dumb mother fuckers. Abort! Abort! Abort! The Russians surrendered. We're on the sub. You'll kill us all!"

General, "Use EXACTO override."

Nerdy young airman, "EXACTO isn't operational sir. It's not been tested."

General, "You're testing it now!"

DARPA (Defense Advanced Research Projects Agency) had been testing a new weapon called *EXACTO* (Extreme Accuracy Tasked Ordinance). Any projectile, bomb, missile or bullet, theoretically could be adjusted by onboard computers to change course and not detonate, if done in time.

This would be a big "if."

EXACTO is the only bomb in the world right now that can actually change direction (within the bounds of gravity) after locked and released. However, the system has never been put into actual use before.

The nerdy airman is working rapidly to shut down the bombs that are seconds from crashing into the sub.

Airman, "This is gonna be close."

General Norton, "Seek shelter! Four 500-pound birds are already flying to you. Impact in three... two...

KENDRICK BAY

All I remember is crazy Stone's face as he's standing on the hull of the sub next to Jennifer and me. He throws his phone and jumps into the water yelling,

"S h i t!"

Jen, fortunately, grabs the flying phone.

All the rest of us hit the deck, literally as two bombs splash in the water right in front of us. But the good news is: No explosion! However, the impact of the bomb is so close that water splashes up and soaks all of us.

We pause and everyone quietly stands.

We're all relieved until I say the obvious,

"Didn't he say four?"

Just then another bomb splashes in the water between the sub and the beach.

"Thank God!" I mumble to myself.

Unfortunately, the fourth bomb explodes near both Jimmy and Tony.

As the smoke clears we see two bodies, face down, on the beach.

I see Stone trying to swim to them in the water yelling, "No!"

Seeing this, I think, great! If he can't make it to shore on his own, I doubt I'll be able to save him. Orca's going to pull me under.

I dive into the water and outswim the older, and much more out of shape Stone. I decide to see if I can help the wounded on the beach first.

I climb out of the water and run to the two men who are motionless on the sand.

I roll Stone's pilot over first.

After an eternity passes, Jimmy opens his eyes, sits up and says in the Queen's English,

"I believe all of my nine lives are now up!"

I then grab Tony and roll him over.

Tony opens his eyes looking at Jimmy, "He told me to duck!"

I ask them, "You guys okay?"

Both nod their heads, slowly, in the affirmative.

I now realize Stone is still in the water.

"Help! I'm drowning!" says Stone.

Tony stands up laughing saying, "Dad never could swim."

I shake my head and walk into the water toward Stone.

As I begin to swim to him I realize the water is only about four feet deep so I stand up.

Stone, seeing this, tries it and feeling embarrassed just stands up too. As soon as Stone gets closer to the beach his son runs out and hugs his dad.

On the sub I can hear General Norton screaming,

"Give me a damage report! Now!"

Jennifer and Captain Vasili are the only ones now standing on the front hull of *TK-20*.

"This is former Navy Lieutenant Commander Jennifer Tavana. Scratch one Russian nuclear facility. Scratch one Iranian sub. We have control of the Russian Typhoon, sir."

Jennifer looks a bit guilty to Vasili who nods his approval.

"Also, zero casualties from your birds, general. Repeat zero casualties from the birds."

PETERSON AFB

Command Center

Cheers have erupted from everyone in the NORAD Command Center. General Norton puts about as big of a grin on his face as you'll ever see from a general saying, "Great job, commander. Great job."

The general looks over at the nerdy little airman who stopped the bombs from exploding.

"I think we can call our *EXACTO* override test successful."

"Great job, son!"

The nerdy little airman weakly says, "Thank you, sir."

TK-20

Jennifer and Captain Vasili are on the conning tower of the sub.

Jennifer says, "I couldn't have done it without my partner, former Navy SEAL, John Denning."

"This country owes you two a great debt. Destroyer escorts will be with you from *Carrier Group 7* shortly. Sit tight."

Jennifer looks at Vasili and shrugs her shoulders, "Yes, sir. Thank you, sir."

General Norton, "In the meantime, you have a few of your friends dropping in to say hi. Norton out."

Vasili and other Russians all look confused as to what that might mean.

Jen knows exactly what he means as she looks to the sun breaking through the clouds.

She whistles to me, pointing in the air.

As the light begins to barely crack through the heavens for another day, I see the greatest sight a military man can see, the cavalry!

The FBI HRT Gold Team looks to have done a HALO (High Altitude Low Opening) jump and they're coming in fast.

The rigid hull inflatable boats (RHIBs) are dropping fast. I trained most of these guys so I thought,

Let's see how they hit the water.

It's a beautiful sight to behold.

The sun starts to peak over the snow covered Alaskan mountains which adds to the picture perfect scene.

These guys silently hit the freezing water. For a split second I actually felt a bit sorry for them.

Why am I feeling sorry for these guys? I was in that freezing water yesterday for an eternity. These guys have on proper gear and are already in their boats!

In no time, they're heading for us.

Spectacular! I'm proud to have trained them!

I hand signal to them and one of them breaks off toward me, guns drawn.

As soon as they near me they realize who I am. Their team leader is John Smith. That's right that's his real name. I did an FBI FBC (Full Background Check) on John A. Smith. Believe it or not, that really is his real name.

John's nickname is Skull.

I think, I'm probably the only guy in this bay that knows how he got the name.

As a former SEAL, on one of his first training jumps, he somehow became tangled in his own parachute.

He ended up hitting the ground headfirst.

After he came to, his first words were, "My head kinda hurts."

Back here on the beach I smile at him and say,

"Hey Skull! What took you so long?"

Skull drops his weapon and with his game face on saying,

"I was pushin' for an ROE kill order on you, Bones."

(Don't ask. I'm not telling anyone how I got the nickname Bones.)

Skull and his Gold Team partner pulls all four of us into their boat and we head for the sub.

As we pull to the sub, there looks to be a problem.

Jen yells down to me, "SEC DEF just ordered the boat searched. The captain has some conditions."

I'm worried.

"Permission to come aboard, captain?" I yell to Vasili.

He answers, "Permission granted. But just you."

I look at Skull and he says,

"Go for it, Bones."

So I hop off our small inflatable boat and onto *TK-20*'s hull.

I climb the steps built into TK-20 until I'm on top of the hull. I enter the tower door that leads me to the conn. As I pop out of the conn hatch I ask,

"So what's the problem?"

Vasili looks at me long and hard and says, "I want asylum in Nebraska."

I look at Jennifer and say, "Okay, that shouldn't be a problem."

Jennifer says, "There's more."

"Oh, okay," I say, "What else?"

Vasili says without hesitation, "I must have your word that you will give all 120 of my men asylum too. Anyone that wants can return to Russia."

I'm speechless. "Well I, you see, our military and courts will decide on a case by case..."

Vasili, "They will fight right here and right now if I don't have your word."

I'm supposed to be SEAL, FBI, and now judge and jury for 120 people? I think to myself.

But there's something about this guy that's honorable and trustworthy.

"I suppose if you vouch for all of your men, I could say, yes."

Vasili immediately salutes me. "Thank you, commander."

"But I'm not a commander and..."

"You'll always be commander to me!" says Vasili.

There's such honesty, sincerity and childlike wonder in this man that either I'm a fool or I just saved the world from nuclear war.

To this day, I still prefer to think the latter.

I look at him with wonder and curiosity. "So what will you do now, captain?"

"Retire! Retirement sounds really good."

Vasili hands me his Top Secret operational file saying, "The boat's yours, commander."

I'm not a commander but, again, all I do is shake his hand and say,

"Thank you, captain."

Stone, meanwhile, is still trying to pull his large soaked self onto *TK-20*'s steps.

"Damn it. I need some exercise!"

Tony and Jimmy are trying to help his immenseness by pushing him onto the hull.

Looking around I say, "I suggest we get inside the Typhoon as radiation from that explosion has to be falling all around us."

It appears some have forgotten about that as everyone scrambles onto the sub.

I grab the phone from Jennifer,

"John Denning to *NORAD*, general are you still there?"

General Norton says, "Go for Norton."

"General, there is radiation all around this area. Please tell your people that the boat is now yours."

General Norton says, "Thank you, Denning. Notifying now."

The sun has now gracefully ascended above Mt. Lazaro on nearby Duke Island.

Stone has managed to get on top of *TK-20*'s hull as a floatplane lands right next to the sub. Out pops a 400-pound Eskimo with another old, long, Winchester one-shot hunting rifle.

"You need me pops?"

You're a day late and a dollar short, son" says Stone.

"What?"

"Never mind. Get in the plane and go home. There's radiation everywhere."

"I fixed the radiation at work, dad!"

Everyone looks puzzled.

Stone says, "That's great son, now go home."

"Okay, popsie," says Stone's son.

The kid has already closed the door and is heading away as Stone shakes his head.

"Ever since he was little he always called a radiator, radiation."

Everyone now gets it, slowly saying, "Ahh."

The Northern sky near Mt. Lazaro is lighting up the water, trees and snow as the FBI HRT Gold Team boards *TK-20*, weapons drawn and pointing at all the threats.

"We've been given orders to search your boat. Do we have your permission, captain?" asks Skull.

Vasili, "Yes. My men will co-operate with you."

Skull says, "Thank you, captain."

While the sub is being boarded by Skull, he listens on his headpiece,

"I have just been given orders to stand down."

Skull gets back on his boat as an MH-60R comes flying in low and hot (armed).

Racing right behind is the guided missile destroyer, USS Hoon.

I say, "This is probably a SEAL platoon. I'd bet anything they just spent the last ten minutes inbound looking over the schematics of your boat to thoroughly clear it."

Vasili, "Good luck. This thing's been retrofitted for last five years. You have no schematics."

I say with confidence,

"Don't be so sure."

Vasili says, "That's what I love about you Americans. Absolute confidence."

"We Russians, we overthink everything!"

I'm standing on the conn of *TK-20* with Jen and Captain Vasili and fully expect to see SEALs repel onto the hull of *TK-20*.

This helicopter is the newest Romeo model of the series. The Romeo has one top-secret exception, there's a giant round device under the cockpit area. I was told by senior Naval Intelligence not to write anything about this device.

However, based on my current status, I have no choice but to warn you about this exotic and very deadly weapon system.

Skull shouts up to us, "I've been given an order. All of you must enter *TK-20* immediately and await further instructions below."

At the time, I didn't think anything was unusual about the order.

Captain Vasili salutes and disappears below. Jen follows him. I'm the last person off the conning tower when I remember we left our phone up there. I climb back up there and witness the most bizarre sight of my life.

These, for lack of a better word, ghosts, don't repel but literally beam from the helicopter to *TK-20*'s hull, in a sharp, tiny, blue, laser beam.

A small, bright blue cloud gathers just outside the hull and grows larger. Once the cloud reaches the size of three distinct eight-foot tall ghosts, they look to be sucked right inside *TK-20*'s hull!

The ghosts act as if the ship's hull wasn't even there!

Their vapor trail looks only to be made up of ones and zeros.

It's very difficult to describe them any further, so I'll just show you a picture taken by a Russian sailor on his phone when confronting these "things."

3D Artist: Jose Ariel Limandri

That is an actual picture of the ghosts taken by a Russian sailor on *TK-20*.

One Russian sailor said,

"I see ghosts!"

Vasili's crew already nicknamed these guys TIM!

Which stands for: The Invisible Men.

I had no idea about their weaponry or capabilities, at this time, but as every Russian sailor that confronted these things said,

"Uzhasayushchiy!" which means,"Terrifying!"

Another Russian inside said,

"I thought I was at a rock concert with lasers going in thousands of directions."

"Then I saw them."

"Terrifying!"

I am told this Top Secret system is called a Ghost Protocol Generator (GPG). Again, the U.S. Navy asked me to not talk, write or say anything.

I'm showing you this as my life is now in grave danger.

I don't have any hesitation in telling you there are thousands of great, dedicated men and women serving in the armed forces of the United States of America. However, today, I question many of the motives of the politicians giving the admirals and generals their orders.

I yell down to Jen and Vasili, "Come up here, you've gotta see this!"

So Jen and Vasili climb back up to the conn with me.

No sooner does Vasili reach the conn than I look over his shoulder and see something moving in the water. At first I think it's a reflection, as I look closer it looks like a gun and it's pointed right at us!

I yell, "Gun!" just as a shot goes off.

I shove Vasili to the deck of the conn. Jen hits the deck as well.

Automatic weapons begin firing from all directions. All three of us on the conn are unarmed. Fortunately, we are surrounded by the most reinforced steel part of the ship that is designed to punch through several meters of Arctic ice.

Vasili tries to peer over the conn but I pull him to the deck.

Good thing!

A couple of rounds go whizzing right where his head would have been.

Jen and I look at each other trying to plan our next move when the gunfire stops.

"Stay down," I say to both of them as I peer my head over the conn.

When I stand, the MH60R is flying away!

Why?

And right behind them is the USS Chung-Hoon, both in full retreat.

They should've had at least one SEAL sniper on the helicopter! I think to myself.

No one was even manning the .50 cal.

As a former SEAL, I find all of these tactics really confusing and just plain weird.

However, my primary concern is the area of the sniper threat.

I see nothing but bubbles.

That's a bad sign.

It's likely the threat has on full SCUBA gear, including air.

I'm surprised they don't have Dräger rebreathers like the SEALS. Drägers produce almost no bubbles and would have made it much more difficult to spot the shooter's location.

A couple of Vasili's men at the base of the conning tower are shooting wildly into the water. Other Russians are yelling as they exit the sub. I have no idea what is being said. All I see is Vasili, standing, yelling at them to calm down.

All of a sudden a Russian sailor is shot right in the heart and falls onto the hull.

Vasili goes nuts. He tries to head down the conn ladder but I grab Vasili's hand and stop him.

"Wait!" I firmly tell the Captain.

He insists, "I'm going down there!"

"They're targeting you. They will kill you. Stay here."

Vasili and I look each other, eye to eye. I can see he agrees.

Then I do the dumbest thing I might have ever done in my life (and I did some pretty crazy things as a teen). I jumped on top of the thick, ice breaking, top rail of the conn.

Jen yells as if I'm crazy, "What are you doing?"

I look back at them and say,

"Stay here! And close that hatch!"

With that, I jumped off the side of the conning tower. As I'm falling I figure it's only about twenty feet to a nice slick, black, gentle slope. If I hit the bottom front of the conn just right I'll miss the ICBM doors and slide right onto the side of the hull and into the water, just like a waterslide!

Well, that was the plan.

What happened was a bit different.

I hit the bottom of the sloping conning tower sideways, which took out one of Vasili's men, still firing at the water. I hit him and we both career off the hull as his weapon wildly shoots bullets in every direction. We then flew another thirty feet before hitting the water.

I instantly see powerful rifle rounds shooting at me.

They're coming from underwater!

The bubbles generated from this are tremendous, which means just one of these rounds could put a really big hole in me!

I see exactly where the threat is because of the direct line of bubbles to the firing weapon.

The threat is smart.

He's deep and out of sight.

I figure, if I can dive deeper, he won't be able to see me as the light from above is giving away my position.

I start diving when I'm hit.

I don't know how badly.

All I feel is excruciating pain in my left arm.

I pull up my arm to assess the damage when I realize it wasn't a bullet that hit me. I see a threat in full SCUBA gear at my '6' swinging again with what appears to be a seven-inch serrated knife!

We struggle as bullets continue to fly at us through the water.

I'm able to grab the arm of the threat with the knife and stop him from swinging again. However, his free hand tries to grab my throat. I have to use my other free hand to fight.

I realize that the crazy Russian kids on *TK-20* are now shooting at me too!

I have threats coming from me in at least four directions. Two human arms, and two people are shooting at me. One is underwater and at least one on the surface. That roughly translates to my '3' '6' '9' and '12' o'clock. In other words, I'm being attacked from all four directions!

A nightmare scenario.

As we fight, I try to turn my body away from the bullets and put my immediate threat in the line of fire. Then I realize my '6' is to the boat and I'm likely to be hit by one of the kids AKs on the sub.

I'm also quickly running out of air and feel the need to breathe. Again, I go back to my SEAL training. We had days and days of underwater drills and I hated almost every minute!

But, now, glad I did every minute of it as all the training comes rushing back.

I position my body so that the kids on the sub shooting are at my '9.' That way my center mass is "slightly" less likely to be hit. This means the underwater shooter is at my '3." Trouble is, it's also slightly less body mass for my knife wielding opponent to be hit. As we struggle, I open myself up again to that SPP-1, a very powerful underwater rifle.

I'm finally able to free one of my hands and punch him in the throat. This stuns him long enough for me to rip off his mask. To my surprise, he doesn't panic in the least but continues fighting. Clearly, he's well trained.

I'm looking for any dirty, cheating thing I can do to get the advantage when I, somehow, dislodge the knife in his hand. As I do, I see a beautiful gold ring with a very specific crest. As the knife slowly sinks I think: Do I go after that?

That thought was quickly banished, as I would need to turn my back on this guy and dive for it.

Impossible!

He now kicks me and I wince in pain. I'm forced to retreat.

I think he's coming for me. However, when I look around, he's swimming away! My instinct is to follow but then I suddenly realize: I need air!

So I come flying up to the surface trying to yell,

"Don't shoot!" but nothing comes out.

My lungs scream in pain for air.

My ears are ringing.

My vision looks partially black as if I'm in a tunnel.

I then experience that exhilarating feeling.

After being deprived of oxygen, there's nothing quite like the rush of it as it re-enters your body.

Four Russian sailors with AK47s pointed at me are yelling.

Vasili is now on the hull yelling,

"Ostanovit'! Nestrelyat'!

Roughly translated is also what I'm trying to say, "Stop! Don't shoot!"

Vasili is holding a young, dead, sailor in his arms as two Russians quickly put their guns down and jump in the water. Skull is racing toward me in his small boat.

Skull drags me as the Russians push, and pull me into the inflatable boat.

Exhausted I say, "They got away!"

Skull looks up to two other boats saying,

"No they didn't!"

"I need to ask Vasili something," I tell Skull.

"You take it easy right here, soldier." says Skull.

Thank God that SPP-1 round to your head missed, says Skull.

I answer, "You think it was an SPP? All I saw was a gun and pulled the captain to the deck."

"Skull says looking into the water, "You're lucky. You both could've been killed!"

I'm looking into the water and all that comes out is, "Ya."

Skull is listening to his headset as gunfire goes off in the distance.

"Gotta go," says Skull.

"Wait!" I say, trying to listen to Vasili.

"Four guys went out the hatch," Vasili yells to me. "Three got away. Nikolai Alexi is my second in command and two other officers."

I yell, "Does he have a gold ring on his little finger of a snake and cross?"

Yes!" says Vasili.

"Come on. Let's go," I say.

Skull looks at me long and hard, making a determination if I can still fight or not.

Apparently, he thought, affirmative, as he hit the gas!

I found out later Vasili ordered his soldiers to stop shooting into the water or I likely would've been killed.

Skull said his men are using a new sonar gadget to track the three fugitives in the water. He said, it's so secret that he couldn't even tell me about it. Then he proceeded to tell me about it. "It" can track any human underwater. "It" can differentiate between a dolphin and a person.

Suddenly, the FBI boat takes a couple of rounds of fire from the Russians underwater.

Although, apparently, "it" cannot defend "it"self.

By the time we get there the boat is sinking and so are the wounded guys in the boat. We're down to two boats.

A medic jumps into the damaged boat to attend to the wounded from our only other intact RHIB.

The boat with "it" on it is barely floating in the water. Apparently, no one had thought of what might happen if "it" got really wet.

The wounded are taken off the boat and head for a medical team on the USS Hoon just outside the mouth of the bay.

The last boat, besides us, breaks off searching the water for any sign of movement. Skull hands me a Dräger closed circuit oxygen rebreather and a gun.

"A...nd go!"

We both fall back into the water and head for the bubble trails.

It's hard for me to see beneath the surface as there appears to be glowing phytoplankton that light themselves, which makes it hard to see anything.

After searching the entire area and finding nothing, we give up the search.

We climb back into our small, inflatable boat empty handed.

Skull tells me,

"SEALs inbound."

"They'll take it from here."

"Our orders are to escort *TK-20* out of here ASAP."

I see four SH-60s inbound as we head back to *TK-20*.

As I'm climbing onto the hull of the sub I look back and witness another beautiful sight.

A SEAL platoon from Team 7 in full tactical gear jumping into the water from those four choppers to search for the three remaining Russians.

"If anybody can get 'em those guys can!" says Skull.

I then say, "Get me back to the sub."

Skull heads our boat back to *TK-20*.

The last FBI inflatable boat breaks off from us and flies to the front side of *TK-20* and escorts her out of Kendrick Bay.

PRINCE OF WALES ISLAND

At the southern-most part of the island a couple in rag-tag clothing is huddled along the shoreline. A small fishing boat putts up to the shoreline and the captain shouts out from his small boat,

"You guys okay?"

Ruddy and Katrina wade out to the water and are helped onto the fishing boat. Ruddy is helped on last. As the captain pulls Katrina aboard, in her other arm is one of those black nuke suitcases which Ruddy makes sure is aboard with his one good arm.

As soon as they board Ruddy looks around and suspiciously asks, "So what have you heard on the two-way?"

Captain, "Funny thing. The radio went out last night and I thought I was gonna die. So I see you guys this morning and said,

"Hey, I'm still alive!"

"I gotta pay it forward!"

Ruddy and Katrina look at each other as the boat putts away from Bokan Mountain, smoldering in the background.

TK-20

On the conn Captain Vasili, Jennifer and I chit chat when a bizarre looking helicopter with no windows, flies near us.

Vasili sees this and says, "Should I be worried?"

I say, "I've seen pictures of an MQ-8 but never in person. It's unmanned. It likely has radiation detection equipment on it."

Vasili, looking worried, "Is it armed?"

Now I'm worried, "I sure hope not." I hesitate then say, "However, some of these things have the Advanced Precision Kill Weapon System (APKWS), that system is above my pay grade to know what it does. Doesn't look like any weapons are on those sponsons."

I see I've really worried the captain. But that was nothing compared with what we saw next.

U.S. Navy's newest class of destroyers, *USS Zumwalt, (DDG-1000)* steams around the southern-most corner of Prince of Wales Island.

Our escort, Skull, in his small rubber boat puts up the "all stop" signal.

Vasili understands.

He picks up his phone and says, "Conn to engine room, all stop."

"Engine to conn, aye, captain, all stop," is heard over the speaker.

I yell down to Skull,

"You getting any radioactive readings here?"

Skull shakes his head no.

Vasili looks at the *Zumwalt* and her two 155mm guns aimed at us and says,

"I've read about the *Zumwalt*. Now I get to see her in person. I'll bet no other Russian can say that!"

I smile at this guy's excitement for all things American.

I ask, "All right, here's a question for you. How many nautical miles can those 155s shoot?

"Accurately?"

I nod affirmative.

Vasili then says, "I think it's fifty-nine nautical miles but Russian propaganda says that's just American propaganda."

I smile, "Impressive. You know your propaganda or as I'd call that: facts!"

"Here are a few other facts. Someone can control that ship from thousands of miles away. It's here to make sure we don't have hostile intent."

Vasili says, "Where's the skill in killing someone from armchair, thousands of miles away?"

I answer, "Oh the Navy kills up close and personal too. That's when they send me. At least that's the way they used to do it."

I'm now thinking about those weird ghosts I saw.

Vasili could not believe all of these strange and surreal new weapons of war.

"I think she looks beautiful," says Jen.

I am thinking the same of her. Uh oh, she seemed to catch that 'cause she smiles at me.

I quickly change the subject back to my prior thought,

"As a SEAL I killed up, very close and very personal. Personally, I'm a bit jealous of Navy kids today. More and more are out of the danger zone."

Then I thought of those ghosts again.

Are Navy SEALs like me now obsolete?

Vasili says, "Count me out of that war."

The sleek looking *USS Zumwalt* is now alongside us. A wide variety of sensors, intelligence inputs, cameras and radiation devices are focusing on *TK-20*.

Both ships are at all stop and crews are tying together.

A side door opens on the *Zumwalt* and a sailor gives me a hand signal.

I say to Vasili, "We've just been invited aboard."

Vasili climbs down the conn, "All right, then."

Jen and I follow.

The three of us pop open the side conning tower door and head for the *Zumwalt*. U.S. sailors check us for weapons.

A man in dress blues then appears at the side door on the *USS Zumwalt*. I quickly recognize the admiral bars.

"Admiral Kenneth Baker, United States Navy, welcome to The Gulf of Alaska Yacht Club."

That's funny, but no one, including me reacts.

"You must be Captain Vasili. Welcome to America. And on behalf of the President of the United States he says, thank you."

Vasili's not impressed.

However, he is impressed by the commander's opening joke.

"So that was a joke then? Yacht Club?"

The admiral smiles, "Yes, that was a joke, captain."

Vasili smiles.

The admiral teasingly then says, So, how long do you intend to visit the United States, captain?"

"Visit? I intend to stay!" says Vasili. He continues, "You think any of us can go back to Russia after giving you billion-dollar secret sub? Every Russian sub is probably on its way here, right now.

This concerns me as I know there is at least one other Typhoon lurking out there somewhere.

Admiral Baker seems totally unconcerned. "We now know what your unique caterpillar signature looks like and we know the closest Typhoon has just turned around under the Arctic and is headed back to Russia."

Vasili looks a bit sad.

Admiral Baker tries to cheer him up saying, "Looks like the three people I'm standing in front of right now single handedly avoided a nuclear war. I salute you, lady and gentlemen."

Jennifer looks to have some sense of satisfaction. She said she never, ever received that when she was in the Navy.

Suddenly there is a commotion coming from the front hatch. Armed sailors on the Zumwalt train their weapons on *TK-20*.

A Russian sailor is trying to pull Stone out of the front hatch.

"Damn it, I'm too fat to get out of this one too!"

The armed U.S. sailors still have their weapons trained on Stone as Jennifer and I laugh.

I say, "That is one large target."

Admiral Baker says to his men,

"Stand down, sailors. That, may be a threat, but not to us!"

Jen and I smile at each other again for a long time before we realize the admiral may be on to us too.

Vasili clearly didn't see or get much of that, saying,

"I'm concerned about my three missing officers, they're fighters, especially my second in command. He will fight to death."

The admiral starts to say, "I deeply regret the actions …"

Vasili interrupts, "Try to take him alive. His father and the president of Russia are close friends."

"We will do everything to take him and your other two officers alive but they have already wounded two FBI agents."

I have my wounded arm covered up with a shirt Vasili gave me.

I don't think the admiral included me in that count and I'm certainly not volunteering any more information on this.

Behind us, many of *TK-20*'s crew are being taken off the boat.

The admiral notices Vasili is seeing this and again Vasili looks very sad.

Admiral Baker tries to cheer him up again saying, "Can we not talk any more shop? I'll bet you haven't had breakfast. What would you like to eat, captain?"

"Ham and eggs?" quickly replies Vasili.

"Ham and eggs it is!" just as quickly replies the admiral.

◆ ◆ ◆

A short time later the admiral, Jen and I, along with Captain Vasili, two Russian officers, Stone and Tony sit together in one long table in the officers' mess eating breakfast.

Considering the situation, the mood seems light and airy among the Americans.

However, the two Russian officers look long faced and quiet.

The Admiral directs his fire to Jennifer,

"So commander, I'm glad you returned to commanding submarines but you did you really have to defect to a Russian sub to do it?"

The Americans laugh but the Russians don't.

Vasili translates this into Russian for them.

Now the Russians laugh.

Jennifer is still not laughing.

"Do you miss it?" asks the admiral.

After pondering the question Jennifer answers,

"I do."

She pauses thinking about this and the admiral sees he's hit a painful subject and goes back to eating. Everyone goes back to eating, following the admiral's lead.

Stone chimes in, "I'm just glad you didn't drop a bomb on my fucking head!"

All silence in the room as Admiral Baker looks at this guy up and down.

"So you're the foul mouth Pinnacle has been cussing and swearing about?"

"Damn straight!"

Admiral stands.

Everybody freaks out, standing, not knowing what will happen next.

Admiral Baker says,

"On behalf of the President of the United States, thank you for putting that foul-mouth at NORAD in his place!"

Everyone laughs!

Even the Russians laugh.

(Which still puzzles me to this day!)

Stone stands and returns the salute.

"Thank you, general."

Everyone in the room looks at the admiral realizing Stone has likely never served a day in the military, as he can't tell the difference between an admiral and a general.

Jennifer looks over at me and, after making sure no one else is looking, she smiles again.

I'm afraid all may have caught on to these romantic signals so I try to change the subject.

"So why is the 7th Fleet so nearby?" I ask.

"As you know, that information is classified, son. I will say a friend of mine, a Chief Petty Officer, tipped us off to the unique signature of these new Russian Typhoons."

Jennifer asks, "Tom Watson?"

The admiral pauses just long enough to confirm to Jennifer that this is exactly his source.

Jennifer smiles with a sense of pride in knowing her old boyfriend did his job by alerting the admiral to TK-20's unique sonar signature.

The admiral continues, "We haven't focused on anti-submarine operations lately. I guess we really shouldn't have let that skill deteriorate. Our challenges are increasing while, thanks to Congress, our funding has been decreasing."

Captain Vasili's thoughts are a million miles from talking shop as he stares at his ham and eggs.

Vasili says, "I haven't had any fresh pork since I left port."

Now everyone else is staring at Vasili who snaps back to reality.

Vasili says, "Is anyone monitoring radiation levels?"

"Yes we are captain. We have many devices actively scanning the area."

The admiral looks around the table and says, "Does anyone have a question?"

After a brief pause, I speak up,

"I have one. Captain Vasili, how was Russia able to sneak in heavy equipment, a full uranium mining operation and a nuclear power plant into the United States?"

Vasili hesitates, "First, let me just say on behalf of Russian people, neither I nor Russian people knew what was going on here. I am truly sorry and ashamed of what has been unleashed on America."

"I only found out recently there are five Typhoon class submarines like TK-20. They've all been retrofitted with special nose cone to drive equipment off our covered docks in *Severodvinsk* into a Typhoon sub. That sub travels directly under Arctic Ocean to Bokan Mountain's reinforced dock and unloads."

There is stunned silence as to the gravity of this.

The admiral then asks, "That's impossible. So how can you fit twenty ICBMs in the front half of the ship and cargo?"

Vasili then says, "We have no ICBMs on board. None of five Typhoons have any ICBMs on them. I recently found out that we were carrying parts to build something far more deadly than ICBMs."

"We were carrying parts for hundreds and hundreds of suitcase nuclear devices," Vasili hesitates before continuing, "or perhaps something larger. I just don't know. They never told me."

The stunned silence continues.

The admiral breaks the silence,

"How long has this been going on?"

Vasili, "At least five years. I'm sure your scientists will be most pleased to reverse engineer the caterpillar drive. Our water propulsion engine and screws are nearly silent."

The admiral says, "We've already found a design flaw in your new sub. While it may be true that you're nearly silent, you're not completely silent."

"We've tracked you with passive sonar by listening to the water pump for your spa."[14]

Now before you laugh, the original Typhoon class submarines actually had an onboard Jacuzzi!

That's right!

A heated spa is on all original Typhoon class submarines.

The last time I told this story, everyone laughed at me.

They laughed until they looked it up. So before you doubt my credibility, I challenge you to look it up!

Sound, any sound, however small, can travel for many miles underwater.

So back to my story. The admiral claims he is tracking the Typhoons by the signature of their Jacuzzi water pump! All the Russians, including Vasili are huddled, speaking feverishly in Russian to each other.

They look panicked until the admiral begins to laugh.

Vasili turns around hurt.

"That was joke?"

The admiral smiling, "Yes, that was joke!"

Vasili laughs, "Good joke. Very good joke. Joke had us all going!"

The admiral then asks, specifically only looking at Vasili, "Any other questions, Captain?"

Vasili turns around and says, "Just one. What's Nebraska look like this time of year?"

The admiral perks right up,

"I'm from Omaha and can assure you, captain, that it's cold there right now. Maybe not Russia cold, but it's cold."

I see Vasili smiling. This guy will make a great American, I think to myself.

The commander stands and then so does everyone else except Vasili. He's still looking at his ham.

"Was everybody finished?" asks the admiral looking at Captain Vasili.

No one will say anything even if they weren't finished. Vasili stands out of respect.

"All right Mr. Denning, your people will transfer to an undisclosed location where we shall debrief you."

"I don't think so," I say confidently.

The admiral, concerned says, "What?"

"I have a Christmas dinner date planned!"

I stand and walk down the long mess hall table to Jen.

Then I gently whisper something into her ear.

She grabs my hand, stands, whispers something back and we both walk down the mess hall and, in the doorway, I stop and look back at the admiral,

"But tomorrow we might be free."

With that Jen and I leave the room.

The admiral says, "Lucky they're ex-military or I'd say we have a UCMJ violation about to occur."

All laugh.

Stone even thinks he got the joke and laughs.

Jen and I head up to the main deck, still holding hands.

We walk to the bow of this beautiful sleek ship.

The sun shines brightly over Mt. Lazaro on Duke Island.

It's the perfect moment for a kiss.

Jen, nervously, looks around.

No one seems to be looking.

"I don't care if anybody's looking!" I say.

So I kiss her and she passionately kisses back.

My lonely life seems to have finally come to an end.

It seems my entire existence passes right past my lips to hers.

I'm so lost in her embrace that, for a moment, I forget where we are and what just happened over the past week.

After an eternity passes by Jen says,

"This could get us fired you know."

"There's no FBI policy against it," I reply.

"Well then, kiss me, sailor boy!"[15]

We both resume kissing, as the mad, mad, mad, mad world seems to float by.

And neither of us seem to care.

EPILOGUE

ABC 7 Alaska News Reporter, Stacy Macavoy, on Anchorage TV says,

"Early this morning a massive landslide sheared off an entire side of Bokan Mountain on Prince of Wales Island in Southeast Alaska. The landslide was over six and one half miles long..."

The reporter pauses and looks to her co-anchor, "Six and one half miles long?" She looks at her co-anchor again.

"It that right?"

There is no answer so she resumes,

"... making it one of the largest landslides in the world. The Alaska Earthquake Center said it was quote, unusual, unquote, for a landslide to register so high, 5.3, on their Richter scale. The U.S. military is now on scene and is keeping everyone, including pilots, at least fifteen miles from the area for their own safety. Military experts say it is likely that shifting tectonic plates actually caused the landslide. We're on the scene with our own Wayne Christian, Wayne..."

"Thank you Charlene. I'm here with Lieutenant Colonel Andrew Gibbs spokesperson for the U.S. Army."

Wayne looks at the colonel and asks, "Large flashes of light have been seen by many locals and speculation has been that there might have been some sort of nuclear explosion here?"

"I've heard that story too, Wayne."

The colonel chuckles,

"No, there was no nuclear explosion. That's just crazy talk. Experts have told me that the aurora borealis intensifies in the wintertime and can produce some spectacular colors but a bomb? Hardly. What a fertile imagination."

"Thank you, colonel. Back to you Charlene."

"Thank you Wayne," says Stacy, buying this fishy story, hook, line and sinker.

"Up next our very own meteorologist, Chuck Nature, will tell us about that ominous thunderstorm cloud that appeared this morning just south of Ketchikan in the shape of a nuclear mushroom."

A nervous Chuck Nature, part time meteorologist and full time comic stands, looking to be the only idiot on the set who suspects something.

"In other news, a large number of fisher persons in the Ketchikan area are retiring from fishing after the U.S. Fish & Wildlife Services said they will give each and every person a generous $250,000.00 stipend to stop fishing the area. Rumor is they will have to sign a very detailed non-disclosure agreement. U.S. Fish & Wildlife says it's all part of their environmental effort not to allow Southeast Alaska to become overfished."

"Finally, Ketchikan Police Chief Robert Stone retires after thirty years on the force. He says he's moving his family to a place that's more, and I quote, F'ing quiet, unquote."

NATIONAL SECURITY AGENCY (NSA)

Fred and Jerry's office is still filled with Christmas decorations but the trees look wilted. All of the Christmas lights are turned off.

Fred and Jerry are still, eating, staring at the screen of a half dismantled "Typhoon" sub.

"I'm sure that's not a real sub."

"I dunno, DNI didn't answer us. There's nothing more we can do. It has to be what's left of TK-20."

"I'm contacting POTUS!" says Fred.

Ya! 'Right!' You're calling the President of the United States?"

"That's right."

"You're crazy! Like Elsa in *Frozen*[16] you should just let it go, man!"

Meanwhile, behind them, on a huge flat screen everyone else is gathered around watching CNN.

On the TV is *TK-20* footage tooling around Alaska with the *USS Zumwalt* destroyer closely following.

The footage cuts abruptly. The Caption reads,

"RUSSIAN SUB RUNS AGROUND IN ALASKA.
U.S. NAVY, ON THE SCENE TO HELP."

Fred and Jerry are oblivious to this as they continue arguing, while both eat tuna fish sandwiches from their paper bags.

MOSCOW

Olga Kasparov's Diary

'm in studio at Russian TV-12 interviewing my crazy President, Ivan Mironovich.

"So what you're saying is that the United States of America called upon Russia to help them in Alaska?" I ask.

"Exactly, Olga. The President of the United States called me personally to ask for our specialists' assistance due to a massive landslide in Southeast Alaska."

"Can you tell us exactly how Russia will help with Typhoon class, ballistic missile submarine?"

Again, I really, really wanted to ask this question but didn't, as once again I value my life more than my phony "Tokyo Rose" job.

The president says, "Well, Olga, I'm sure our American friends don't want us to get into the details. So let's just say, we are most pleased to assist our friends in any way that we possibly can."

"Some reporters are speculating that some sort of nuclear devise accidentally went off in Alaska. Can you confirm this?"

This, I am actually allowed to ask! Don't ask me why. The president is now reading from a teleprompter,

"Olga, the U.S. government has told us that while they appreciate our assistance they do not want us to discuss this event publicly."

"So there's nothing further you can tell us regarding Alaska and Russia?" I ask as I read from my teleprompter lines.

"Well, Olga, as you know, Russians love Alaska. We once owned Alaska. We will do everything in our power to help and support all the residents of Alaska," says our coy president.

I pause knowing there is another story here and wish I could ask more but I didn't.

That was, almost, all that was written for me on teleprompter.

I know the public will not be getting any honest information from our president on this matter. I turn to camera saying my last teleprompted lines, maybe forever,

"Well, there you have it. Russia and the Russian people have always been so generous that they are willing to help any country in need."

The president beams with pride at me.

"This is Olga Kasparov reporting from Moscow. Goodnight and... sleep tight!"

GUANTANAMO BAY, CUBA

General Bahadur sits in an isolation cell in Guantanamo Bay and he doesn't look too happy. He still has two black eyes and, if you look close enough, Stone's boot print can still be seen on his forehead.

At least the floor of his cell has the direction of Mecca painted on it for him so he can pray.

However, he is busy etching into the concrete wall next to his bunk in Farsi, "Death to America."

IRANIAN TV

A middle class Iranian family sits around their large, flat screen color TV. They are watching a news report after morning prayers.

The male Iranian TV reporter, dressed in an all-black suit, says in Farsi, "And this was chanted by tens of thousands of people gathered in Tehran today after morning prayers,"

"DEATH TO AMERICA"
"DEATH TO AMERICA"
"DEATH TO AMERICA"

The middle aged male reporter continues, "In other news, the state has destroyed over 100,000 'morally damaging' satellite dishes on local residents' homes. The decadent West is poisoning our nation and its values according to a Balif militia report."

"And the Iranian military, may they be blessed by god for all eternity, have created a new submarine, The *Be'sat III*. It is expected to carry 20 ICBMs and be similar to the Russian Typhoon class Akula submarine."

The reporter reads from his teleprompter,

"Death to the Great Satan which is the United States of America."

WASHINGTON, D.C.

In the Joint Chief's Diplomatic Office sits American senior diplomat, John Anderson. Staring at him across his desk is Russian diplomat Andrei Alexeev. "In light of fact that several of our 'packages,' are missing, President Mironovich proposes we say as little as possible about Alaska incident and that we work together to retrieve them," says Alexeev.

"I will convey your proposal to our president." says Anderson.

"Good. We wouldn't want packages..." says the Russian.

"To end up in the wrong hands? Too late."

The Russian pauses long and studies his opponent like he's playing a game of chess.

"I was going to say, we wouldn't want packages reconstructed to avert our safety mechanisms."

"I will convey your proposal to our president," repeats Anderson as if he's a robot.

The Russian finally brings up the reason he is here,

"As we've said to you before, we would like our submarine back."

Anderson pauses, staring into the eyes of his opponent, ready for his next move. He smiles to himself and remembers the famous line by retired Rear Adm. John Williams. He was the former commander of the U.S. Pacific Submarine Force who once said,

'It's never good for an opponent to have your playbook.'

Anderson then confidently says,

"You can have it. We have taken out one of your caterpillar drives, some communications equipment and dissected your fabulous acoustic absorbing material on the hull but other than that, we have no use for it."

Andrei Alexeev is clearly not happy about this as the Americans now have in their possession the quietist submersible motor in the world and hardware that communicates with the entire Russian Armed Forces. Russia will now have to spend, in U.S. dollars, hundreds of billions upgrading every piece of communication and quiet hull technology or risk eavesdropping by the Americans.

The American then says,

"Captain Vasile just wants his wife back."

The Russian diplomat is puzzled,

"A billion dollar Akula sub for wife?"

"I'm told he's a real romantic!" says Anderson sarcastically.

Alexeev, now, is really not happy.

"Then we're in agreement." Says Anderson cheerfully, "You will say privately to the Iranians that the Americans destroyed their sub and we shall privately confirm this. That way you can retain your relations with Iran.

After a very long pause Alexeev begrudgingly says,

"Agreed."

"And we agree upon the exact location?" says Anderson.

Alexeev, now seething in anger wants something else, "Only if it's directly above Russian flag!"

Anderson, after a long pause,

"Always with the symbolism, eh Andrei?"

Andrei Alexeev, ignores the slight and continues, "And Admiral Perchinkov wants to see captain face to face."

Anderson again a little too cheerful, "I'm sure Captain Vasili wouldn't want it any other way!"

GEOGRAPHIC NORTH POLE

Seven months later.

It's a quiet, beautiful, perfectly clear day for an arms transfer at the North Pole.

And when I say, at, the Russians insisted at!

82.7° N 114.4° W to be more precise.

The ice is pure white, almost bluish in some thinner spots. The air temperature was exactly that of Moscow in the dead of winter – 0 C but this is July!

The deal almost didn't happen as the Americans insisted on some symbolism of their own.

The exchange must take place only on the 4th of July and the Russians finally agreed.

Geo North, or G. North, as it's sometimes referred, was laid claim by the Russians in 2007 when they were the first country in the world to plant their flag on the seabed 13,980 feet below this very spot.

That's almost three miles underwater!

Quite a feat!

No one had ever travelled to the bottom of the pole and done that before.

After they planted their flag the Russians then proceeded to brag to everyone in the world about what they'd done.

"You might have planted a flag on the moon first but we Russians planted our flag on the seabed at the North Pole first," exclaimed Olga Kasparov, Russia *TV-12* anchor reading from her teleprompter.

It was the line that the state had ordered her to say.

The Russian expert Olga interviewed said,

"The estimated value of just the minerals in the Arctic is worth up to two trillion dollars."

"And this doesn't include ninety billion barrels of oil or 1,669 trillion cubic feet of natural gas, about one quarter of the world's known gas reserves."

"All of these rich resources are the reason Russia had gone ahead with their promise and have begun building ten airfields in the Arctic. Russia's Federal Agency for Special Construction (Spetsstroy) had promised some time ago to build military facilities on six Arctic islands."

G. North sometimes has ice thick as ten feet! No sub in the world could punch through that much ice.

This year, however, the ice is only about six feet thick (two meters) which is about the maximum a sub can penetrate.

Suddenly, the quiet of nothing is interrupted by the massive nose cone of *TK-20.*

I'm the first person to climb out of the front hatch. Message traffic from the admiral said I could wear my Navy dress whites for the occasion.

I help Captain Vasili onto his hull for one last look.

Then I help Admiral Baker onto the hull.

We are all in our Navy dress.

I'm standing next to Captain Vasili.

All three of us stand in amazement at the beauty of this pristine place.

"May I ask you a question, captain?"

Captain Vasili quickly replies trying to act American, "Shoot!"

"Why do you always stand so close when you speak to me?"

The captain smiles, "A Nebraskan asked me this at feed store. All older Russians do this. Habit I guess. When we were ruled by dictators you wouldn't want a Soviet agent overhearing your complaints about the government.

The captain takes a step back.

I quickly smile and say, "No, no. I don't mind. You have a fascinating culture, captain."

Vasili thinks then says, "I'll always be Russian but my heart is now in America."

It seems like an eternity passes as we stare across hundreds and hundreds of miles of nothing but Arctic ice.

"Are you gonna miss her?" I finally ask.

"I've been missing her since I left St. Petersburg."

Vasili is obviously referring to his wife.

He looks like he could care less about this old bucket of rusting bolts.

Admiral Baker, "It's none of my business, Agent Denning, but what did you say to Agent Tavana on my ship at breakfast that made her grab your hand. You guys made every man in that room jealous."

I'm actually embarrassed and that's pretty hard to do.

"I just said, Jen, what are you doing for dinner?"

The admiral sees there is definitely something going on here beyond his pay grade, so he smiles and wisely shuts up.

Russia's newest SSBN, the Borei class sub, Knyaz Vladimir, recklessly crashes through the ice immediately next to us, making all of us, Vasili, the admiral and myself have to catch ourselves.

A Russian sailor immediately pops the front access hatch and steps onto her hull.

The sailor then helps out a much older and slower Admiral Perchinkov who, according to Captain Vasili, looks to have aged 20 years.

He doesn't look happy but if you lived in temperatures like this, you likely wouldn't be happy either!

More sailors emerge and toss a plank across so Perchinkov can walk directly onto *TK-20*.

Admiral Perchinkov then proudly walks to us on *TK-20*.

After he is aboard he makes eye contact only with Captain Vasili and he doesn't look happy.

Perchinkov says, "You know, Vasili, we have five submarines watching you."

Without a missing a beat Vasili replies, "Five? The Americans said it was six, not counting us. And 'we' want you to know we have nine watching you."

A new Cold War standoff has begun.

Right here!

Right now!

As the two, old steely Russians stare down each other with contempt, Admiral Baker opens his mouth but before he can speak, I look at him as if, "I wouldn't!"

The admiral wisely takes my silent advice and decides against stepping into this private war between these two Russian titans.

Vasili then says,

"I don't want to see water any more. I found the people of Nebraska to be quite lovely."

Admiral Perchinkov shows Captain Vasili a picture of the Russian flag planted three miles beneath them on the seabed.

"See Vasili," (as a slight I notice Perchinkov refuses to use his title as captain) "You've made one huge mistake. Where we're standing and, as for as far as you can see, in any direction is a Russian gold mine."

Vasili responds,

"Your president is very good at weaponizing information but he's not so good with truth. Just because you plant a flag somewhere doesn't make it yours. The Arctic belongs to all of us. Ever see corn and wheat waving in a Nebraska summer breeze? I have. Come visit me sometime, comrade!"

Everyone watches this stout Russian admiral, as his neck slowly turns red. His blood rises somewhere above eye level. If his blood pressure gets any higher it just might blow his head clean off!

Further, if Perchinkov had a weapon it looks like he would kill Vasili! Right here and right now.

Vasili gives him a stoic Russian salute then motions for his wife to walk to him. Perchinkov does not return the salute.

We all feel the weight of a thousand years of Russian history transpire as Vasili's wife walks to him. Vasili won't ever again look at Perchinkov. Vasili grabs his wife and hugs her.

After eternity passes of Perchinkov staring at this horrid sight, he turns and walks to his front hatch and enters "his" sub.

A twenty-one-year-old, hulky sailor leans over to me and asks, "What just happened?"

I say, "It would take a thousand years to explain, son, at least a thousand!"

Russian sailors look around confused as to what is happening next.

I worriedly ask, "Ya think Perchinkov just might leave us out here while he submerges?"

Vasili ignores my worry and instead says to me, "So what will you do now commander?

I smile at the commander line again and then answer,

"I don't know. Maybe I'll start my own local chapter of the ASPCA."

Vasili asks, "ASPCA. What is that?

I sarcastically answer,

"The American Society for the Prevention of Cruelty to Acronyms!"

Vasili looks at me sincerely as he studies my game face then says,

"Was that good American joke?"

I sincerely ask, "I don't know, was that good American joke?"

The captain is sincerely confused and does not know how to answer.

Admiral Baker steps in laughing and says,

"Hell ya!"

"That's great American joke."

The admiral then mumbles under his breath, "ASPCA! Now that's funny."

The admiral hands me a Motorola SRX 2400 and says, "Why don't you do the honors?"

I reply, "I'd be happy to, admiral." I speak into the Motorola, "Okay, we're gonna need a lift home." I hand the admiral his phone. He looks a bit put off by my casual behavior.

I respond sincerely, "Sorry sir. This is what you get when you ask a civilian to do a military job."

The admiral smiles as the *USS Alaska* elegantly emerges from the ice on our port side. As she gracefully ascends, I can tell exactly who has given those commands.

As the front hatch opens, former Lieutenant Commander Jennifer Tavana is the first person to appear. She is allowed to wear her Navy dress whites for the transfer too.

She looks a lot better than I.

That image of her standing proudly on the front of the ship she once commanded is etched into my memory forever.

I know she was grateful to the Navy and Admiral Baker for allowing her this one last honorary command.

Sailors help us transfer to the *USS Alaska*. The Lieutenant Commander holds out her hand for Captain Vasili.

"Welcome aboard captain."

She holds out her hand for me in a very "different" manner.

I grab it and step aboard. "Welcome aboard commander," she says teasingly.

"Thank you but…"

Jen salutes me and I think,

What the hell!

I salute back saying,

"Thank you, Lieutenant Commander."

Jen starts to say, "Former…" but the word doesn't make it out as she looks to think, what the hell, as well!

No sooner did we say that, then it seemed we quickly disappeared beneath the ice.

ANTIGUA, CARIBBEAN

A waiter delivers drinks to a man and woman sunning themselves at the luxurious Rosewood Resort in Jumby Bay.

A man, in designer sunglasses, pulls up a briefcase and pulls out a hundred-dollar bill and casually gives it to the waiter.

"Gracias, senior."

It's crazy Al and Tatiana, his Russian doctor girlfriend!

Crazy Al is unrecognizable without his Santa beard.

They are sitting by a sparkling blue pool near a beach sipping cold drinks.

Tatiana, in a bright red bikini, is unrecognizable as well. She looks much more relaxed and happy. This looks much more to be her calling than her job as a Russian military doctor.

Tatiana, sunning herself, says,

"I've been meaning to ask, where did you find that suitcase?"

"Funny thing, I was hiding from some of your people in the warehouse and I found this just sitting there behind some fifty-five gallons drums that contained…"

"Uh huh," comments the doctor, as her designer sunglasses point directly at the sun and not Al.

Al pauses, realizing she's not paying attention. He then says, "By the way, you look fabulous."

"Thank you darlink, thank you," says Tatiana.

Washington D.C.

It's January 20, 2017 and tens of thousands of people are gathered in Washington, D.C. to see the presidential inauguration of Donald J. Trump. The ceremony is taking place on the west front steps of the U.S. Capitol Building. This gathering on the National Mall stretches for as far as the eye can see.

Donald Trump's beautiful wife, Melania Trump, looks on lovingly at his side. She has gorgeous brown hair. Two beautiful models, looking like Russian agents, stand next to Melania.

In the crowd creeps MAA, with his nuclear suitcase, politely, trying to get closer to the new president.

Tens of thousands of people are totally unaware of what is about to unfold.

Kauai, Hawaii

There are now an alarming number of terrorists running around North America with nuclear suitcases. Mohammed Al-Aqsa (MAA), his Russian bride, Ruddy, Katrina, Kapitan Nikolai Alexi, his two TK-20 Officers and who knows how many other terrorists are lurking about with nukes.

However, I'm not worrying about any of this at the moment. I need a vacation. Normally, I would go to Alaska and wonder around a wilderness for days at a time. I don't think I'll be doing that for a while.

When I was freezing in those Alaskan waters I decided I wanted to visit Hawaii again. So, I fly in to a perfectly clear Lihui airport this morning on the beautiful island of Kauai, Hawaii. The lush green countryside in some ways looks a whole lot like Oregon, except for one noteworthy exception: it's about twenty degrees warmer.

I had rented a car and couldn't wait to get on the world famous Mt. Waialeale trail. As I walk to the trailhead I stop to read a sign:

WELCOME TO
MT. WAIALEALE TRAIL
THE WETTEST SPOT ON EARTH

TOTAL RAINFALL PER YEAR:

OVER 38 FEET!

"Perfect!"

READ
JOHN DENNING
BOOK TWO

PROYEKT 252:
CALIFORNIUM

Christmas 2017

APPENDIX

Interesting Sites and Videos

1. Navy SEAL Special Warfare Center (SWCC)
   Click: DOWNLOADS for hi-res pictures
   http://www.sealswcc.com

2. U.S. Virginia Class Submarine Drill
   https://youtu.be/pepf956oLvU

3. Russian Typhoon Submarine2.
   https://www.youtube.com/watch?v=oo-qGfW6KAE

4. Russian Typhoon Submarine3.
   https://www.youtube.com/watch?v=OiUSsFGkfaw

5. 3d images of Bokan Mountain above and below ground: https://www.youtube.com/watch?v=po9ZcdFMzWw

Interesting Facts and Pictures

1. Russian Submarine Dismantling
   http://www.businessinsider.com/how-russia-dismantles-its-old-nuclear-subs-2014-10?utm_source=feedburner&utm_medium=feed&utm_campaign=Feed%3A+businessinsider+%28Business+Insider%29

2. Typhoon Submarine Blog
   https://www.reddit.com/r/WarshipPorn/comments/2dchpf/everything_you_ever_wanted_to_know_and_more_about/

FOOTNOTES

1. *A Mad Russian's Christmas* by the Trans-Siberian Orchestra (1996) Lava records, Producer Paul O'Neill and Robert Kinkel

2. *Surise* by Duran, Duran (2004) Sony Music, Simon Le Bon, John Taylor, Roger Taylor, Andy Taylor, James Bates

3. *Pirates of the Caribbean*: *The Curse of The Black Pear*l (2003) Walt Disney Pictures, Composer Hans Zimmer, Buena Vista Music Group, Walt Disney Records

4. *Dust in the Wind* by Kansas (1978) Kirshner Music, Writer: Kerry Livgren

5. *So Very Hard to Go* by Tower of Power, (1973) Warner Bros., Writers: Emilio Castillo and Stephen Kupka

6. Norman Polmar, Unites States Naval Institute, usni.org

7. *Fantasy* Words and Music by Maurice White, Verdine White and Eddie Del Barrio. Copyright (c) (1977) EMI April Music Inc. and Criga Music. Copyright Renewed. All Rights Administered by Sony/ATV Music Publishing LLC, 424 Church Street, Suite 1200, Nashville, TN 37219 International Copyright Secured. All Rights Reserved. Reprinted by Permission of Hal Leonard LLC https://www.youtube.com/watch?v=r58GQYFZeLE
   [AUTHOR'S NOTE: Listen to the four octave, "otherworldly falsetto" voice of Philip Bailey live at 24:00-25:00] https://www.youtube.com/watch?v=-qehsJRbwZ0

8. *Funeral for a Friend* by Elton John (1973) UMG

9. *The Naked Gun: From the Files of Police Squad!* (1988) Paramount Pictures

10. *My Cousin Vinny* (1992) Twentieth Century Fox

11. *The 'Burbs* (1989) Universal Pictures

12. *Blazing Saddles* (1974) Warner Brothers, Mel Brooks

13. F35 Heads-up display: https://www.youtube.com/watch?v=Ay6g66FbkmQ

14. Norman Polmar, http://www.usni.org/author/norman-polmar

15. *Fantasy* by Earth, Wind & Fire, (1978) Sony/ATV Music, Writers: Maurice White, Verdine White, Eddie del Barrio https://www.youtube.com/watch?v=r58GQYFZeLE

16. *Frozen* (2013) Walt Disney Animation Studios, Walt Disney Pictures, Fair Use / Parody